Myra Duffy divides her time between Glasgow and the Isle of Bute where her cosy crime novels are set and has family connections to the island stretching back several generations.

Myra says the Isle of Bute provides inspiration because it offers a 'contained' setting and the history and the geography of the island are important in providing a background to the action.

For more information visit:
www.myraduffywriter.com
or contact her on duffyma308@googlemail.com
@duffy_myra (Twitter) or on Facebook.

THE ISLE OF BUTE MYSTERY SERIES

The House at Ettrick Bay
Long-buried secrets lead to murder.

Last Ferry to Bute
Mysterious deaths at a nursing home and a shady antiques dealer.

Last Dance at the Rothesay Pavilion
Past events cast a shadow over the present as the Pavilion is renovated.

Endgame at Port Bannatyne
The world of film-making hides a deadly secret.

Grave Matters at St Blane's
A proposal to build a theme park is the catalyst for violent events.

Death at the Kyles of Bute
The Kyles of Bute Hydro Hotel is again open for business, but someone has murder in mind.

Bad Blood at Rothesay Castle
A party of American tourists is on Bute, but a killer is stalking one of them.

Deadly Secrets at the Standing Stones.
A family wedding is not what it appears to be.

When Old Ghosts Meet
Dangerous events are sparked off by a chance sighting on the Edinburgh to Glasgow train. (Prequel to the series).

*

The Motley Crew and the Mystery of the Queen of the Inch
(A mystery story for children). Who has stolen the Bronze Age necklace from the Bute Museum?

The Lunch Club at George Square (Contemporary)
Love is Another Country (Romantic Suspense)

THE BRYDESHILL AFFAIR

MYRA DUFFY

Adams and Straiton

First Edition

British Library C.I.P.

A CIP catalogue record for this title is available from the British Library.

ISBN 978-1-913461-09-6

Characters in this novel bear no relation to any persons living or dead. Any such resemblance is co-incidental. While some real locations are used, these may have been adapted for purposes of the plot.

For Judith

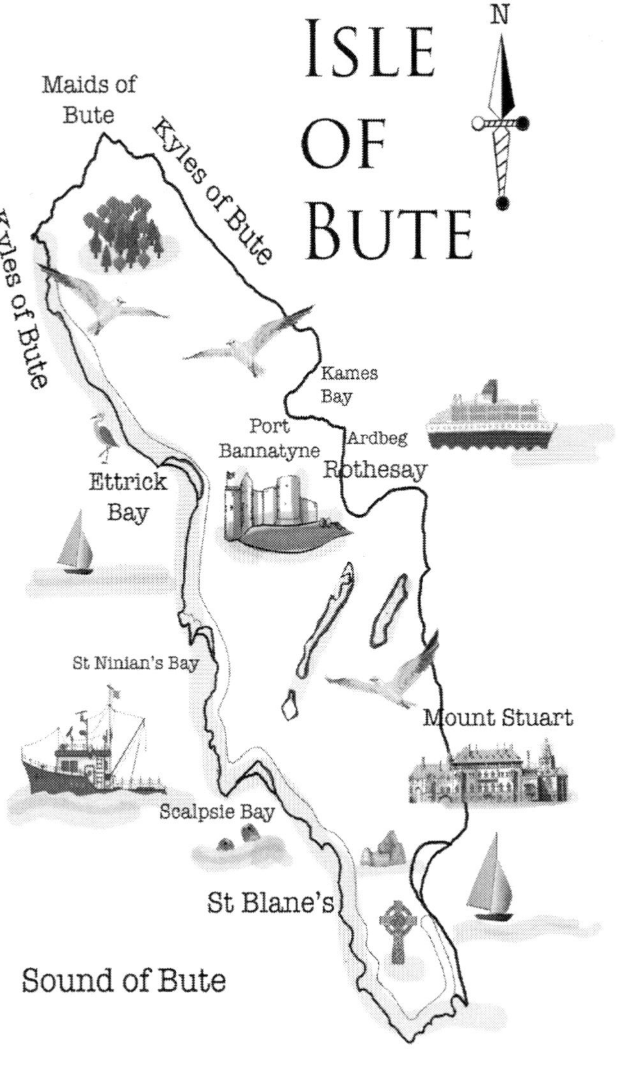

ISLE OF BUTE
N
Maids of Bute
Kyles of Bute
Kyles of Bute
Kames Bay
Port Bannatyne
Ardbeg
Rothesay
Ettrick Bay
St Ninian's Bay
Mount Stuart
Scalpsie Bay
St Blane's
Sound of Bute

The Isle of Bute

The Isle of Bute lies in the Firth of Clyde, off the west coast of Scotland, a short journey from the city of Glasgow.

The island has been occupied for over five thousand years but rose to prominence in Victorian days when its proximity to a major city made it a favoured spot for the wealthy to build grand villas away from the smoke and the grime of the city.

As statutory holidays became more usual, the working classes also began to enjoy the delights of the seaside in the many rooms available for rent during the holiday season.

Bute is the ancestral home of the Stuart kings of Scotland and the 800-year-old Rothesay castle (now ruined) was built by a hereditary High Steward of Scotland.

Today the island is a haven from the hustle and bustle of city life with quiet beaches, woodland walks and an abundance of wildlife.

PROLOGUE

The moonlight glimmered on the stable yard, casting long shadows across the silent fields. Deep in the undergrowth a rabbit hesitated, nose twitching, before scuttling away, leaving no impression on the long grass.

In the end stable beside the summer pasture, one of the horses began neighing loudly, stomping its hooves and banging against the stable door. Thump, thump, thump. The farm dogs began to bark, louder and louder.

Kath wakened with a start. Her first thought was that she'd been dreaming. Then that she'd overslept. But why was there no light filtering through the skimpy curtains? Of course. It was not yet dawn. The rapid beating of her heart began to subside. But something had disturbed her and now fully awake, she became aware of noises from the stable block.

She scrambled out of bed, shivering as her feet hit the cold linoleum and she reached for the old coat hanging on the door peg. There had been emergencies before in the livery yard, but it was unusual for the animals to be so restless during the night. She listened intently as she ran downstairs. It sounded like Topper, one of the oldest horses in the stables. That was strange. If it had been one of the younger horses she would have understood. Or Marvel. But he was fitting in well after a successful career as a racehorse, but it took time for a horse to adapt to new surroundings.

She hurried through the hallway, blinking at the sudden brightness as she switched on the overhead light before going through to the kitchen to pull on the ancient boots sitting by the back door. After the heavy overnight rain the yard would muddy.

There was no way she'd be able to go back to sleep if she didn't check the stables. It would take no more than a few minutes, she told herself, leaving the back door on the latch. She fumbled in her pocket for a torch. At this time of year an unexpected frost could make the rain puddles dangerously icy.

It must be that dratted fox again, she thought as she picked her way across the yard, almost losing her balance as she slipped on a patch of mud. Thank goodness the chickens were securely shut in for the night. Oh, for the days when there were no foxes on the island.

The dogs, Nyx and Baron, came running up, tails wagging, and Kath bent to calm them. Topper's loud neighing had set off the other horses. If only she'd been quicker. Now it would take ages to settle them and she might have to waken Gemma and ask her for help. Calling softly, shivering in the cold morning air, she picked her way towards the stable block, making sure she was sidestepping the worst of the slicks of water in the ruts in the yard.

She stopped suddenly, flashing the torch around in every direction. Quickening her pace, she made her way to the end stable, ignoring the whickering from Caffrey's stable. Oh, no. There was Dusty wandering about near the old barn.

'Not again,' she said, catching up with Dusty and edging her back into her stable. 'We're going to have to find a stronger bolt for your stable door.'

Dusty tossed her head as if in disdain. Kath felt a sense of relief. It was as simple as that. Dusty had escaped again and disturbed the other horses. But as she persuaded the horse back inside, lured with a top-up of the hay net, she caught sight of the end stable. There was something wrong with the door. That was odd – the bolt had been pulled back. Surely Topper hadn't also learned to open his door. At least he'd stayed put, not gone wandering around the yard.

'Shh…it's okay,' she murmured as she approached the frightened horse, reaching out to stroke him. A sheen of sweat glistened on Topper's jet-black coat. He was wild-eyed, snorting in fear, shaking his head. What had spooked him?

As she continued speaking softly, trying to calm him, her foot caught on something lying in the deep bed of straw covering the floor. She swung the torch down to see what looked like a pile of wet clothes. Then she thought, why on earth would anyone have left them here.

She shone the torch directly onto the bundle, before jumping back in horror. A face stared back at her, his eyes wide open, his mouth agape.

She knelt down, lifting the man's wrist to feel for a pulse. No sign of life. He was beyond help.

She sat back and examined the dead man's face. Whoever he was, she didn't recognise him. Why was he in Topper's stable? And what had happened to him?

ONE

Life as a freelance writer is never dull. But pitching a new idea is worrying no matter how experienced you are.

This time the editor of a book on Victorian seaside resorts was looking for contributions and to my delight (and relief, as I'd no other work in prospect) accepted my proposal to contribute a chapter about the Isle of Bute as a popular holiday destination.

This suited me in lots of ways. My younger daughter, Deborah, had taken up a temporary job at a livery yard and stables on the island and I could combine a research trip with an opportunity to catch up with her. Though I was curious to know why she'd decided on this choice of occupation. A degree from Art College was an unlikely preparation for looking after horses, as I'd said in my last telephone call to her. A conversation that hadn't been quite as I'd anticipated.

'But you know nothing about horses. How did you manage to secure this job?'

There was a pause. Then, 'Oh, it's fine. And I have had SOME experience,' she said.

'You mean a donkey ride at the seaside when you were a toddler? As I remember it, the donkey bolted.'

Deborah chuckled. 'You must recall the time I went on a riding holiday in Spain with a couple of friends. Remember? When I was at Art College. We had several lessons, including stable management, before we were allowed to take part.'

A vague recollection stirred that the holiday hadn't

been a great success, but I wasn't about to say so. 'Mmm,' I said, 'but why would you choose to do this? And why now?'

Another hesitation. I could picture her standing there, twisting a strand of hair round her finger. 'Do you remember Freddie Lawson – we were at Art College at the same time. Gemma works at the stables – she's Freddie's cousin. Well, Owen, who also works there, has broken his leg and won't be back for some time. Usually her friend, Pam, would step in, but she's gone off to Inverness to look after an aunt who's just out of hospital…'

'Stop, stop, I understand.' I said, confused by these arrangements. 'And this is a temporary job?' I didn't add, 'Again,' given the variety of jobs my daughter has tried. Somehow Deborah never seems to find a full-time permanent job, but whether through choice or bad luck I often wonder.

'Of course.' She sounded glum as she said, 'And there are no jobs in my field right now. This seemed better than waiting round.' Then she brightened. 'I am enjoying it, Mum,' she said. 'So different from anything I've done before.'

About to move on to other family matters, I was brought up short by her next words. 'I'm glad you're coming over, but I have to tell you there's been a further problem…' Her voice trailed away.

'I can't help in the horses, 'I said in horror, worried she might think I could be useful, no matter how short-staffed the livery yard was. 'Last time I saw horses close up was several years ago, when Dad and I went on that holiday to York and he persuaded me to spend a day at the races.'

And we lost money on every race, I added under my breath.

‘No, no. You don’t understand. It’s not about the horses.’

Thank goodness. ‘This visit to Bute isn’t a holiday. I’ve lots of research to do, and there won’t be much spare time.’ But then again, I hadn’t seen Deborah for some months. And I was looking forward to exploring the countryside around Brydeshill, where she was working, a part of the island I didn’t know.

Aware how abrupt this sounded, I said, ‘But I’m looking forward to seeing you, Deborah. I’m staying at The Ferry Rest in Rothesay, so I won’t be too far away.’

‘Yes, it seems ages since we had time together. And you’re right. Problems at Brydeshill aren’t your concern.’

But now she’d sparked my interest, I had to ask, ‘What do you mean? Are there other “problems”?’ Her silence spoke more eloquently than words and with a rising feeling of alarm I said quietly, ‘Tell me what’s wrong.’

She gulped before she spoke. ‘No, no. It’s nothing to do with the horses.’ She stopped. ‘Not directly.’

Wondering what was coming next I said, ‘And?’

Her words came out in a rush. ‘I didn’t mean to tell you till we met, but someone has been found dead in one of the stables.’

This was the last thing I’d expected. ‘What! You should leave right away. You don’t want to be mixed up in this. What happened?’

She went on, ‘It’s being called a “suspicious” death, of course, and the police are involved, but we think it was an accident, that Topper kicked him in the head, and that was what killed him.’

I interrupted. ‘You don’t have to stay on. It sounds too dangerous. Come back to Glasgow with me.’

‘But I can’t leave, Mum. Not now. As you can imagine, it’s awful…awful for everyone. And the horse, Topper, is usually so well-behaved. He must have had a bad fright to make him lash out like that.’

‘You shouldn’t be worrying,’ I heard myself say. ‘I’m sure the police will get to the bottom of it.’ Then, ‘So who was it – the man who died? One of the stable hands?

‘No, that’s the trouble. No one knows who he is. He was a stranger, and he had no reason to be in Topper’s stable…or in any of the stables.’

‘Surely he must have had some identification?’

‘There was nothing except a scrap of paper with the name of the Brydeshill in his pocket. The police are trying to find out who he was…and what he was doing at Brydeshill.’

‘Don’t worry. We can talk about it when I come over,’ I said. ‘You can decide what to do then.’

‘Sorry, Mum. I promised myself I’d wait till you arrived before I told you all of this. It’s not your concern.’ Deborah was right. This incident was nothing to do with me. I had more than enough to keep me occupied while I was on Bute.

TWO

I was beginning to feel like one of the world's jet-setters, between my recent trip to Los Angeles to holiday with Susie, my long-time friend, followed by a stopover in Washington to see my husband, Simon, and now this visit to Bute.

Simon has been living and working in Washington for the past few years on a contract that wasn't quite what either of us hoped. He'd be coming home soon, but that might create a whole new set of challenges. In one of my regular phone calls to him, I'd told him of my plans and of Deborah's latest job. 'A livery yard and stables?' he'd said in astonishment. 'Why would she decide to go and work there?'

'It's a place called Brydeshill, not somewhere I know. One of the stable hands, Owen, had an accident and Deborah was asked to help out.'

'It still sounds odd.' He sounded concerned.

I tried to explain. 'I'm going to Bute to finish research for my latest commission and it's a chance to see Deborah. This job of hers is temporary so I expect she'll have other possibilities in mind. But she seems to be enjoying doing something completely different.'

He started to say, 'Not another….' But instead he said, 'Yes, if you have to go to Bute, Deborah will be delighted to see you.'

'It's not a holiday, Simon,' I reminded him. 'I will be working.'

He grunted. 'Even so. Given what you've told me about Brydeshill being short-staffed, I hope you won't be roped in to help.'

‘Of course not. I did suggest Deborah come back to Glasgow with me, but she doesn’t want to walk away when Owen will be unable to work for some time yet.’ I didn’t mention the man found dead in one of the stables. Best not to alarm him and by now the police would surely have found out who he was and why he was at Brydeshill.

Simon said, ‘Yes, I suppose it will be an opportunity. I can’t tell you how much I’m looking forward to seeing the family once this contract finishes and I’m back home for good.’

‘Don’t worry, Simon. I’ve no intention of spending time at Brydeshill. I’ve booked a room in The Ferry Rest in Rothesay. But I’ll have plenty of time to meet with Deborah.’

A couple of weeks on Bute was as much as I could manage. Having given up the lease on the flat Simon and I had been renting, I’d managed to secure a short-term rental of a (very) small flat in Partick. It was no more than a stop-gap, fine for a few months to give me a chance to sort out a longer-term option when Simon returned home. We’d be in Glasgow for a while, but after that anything was possible. If he kept to his decision to retire, that is.

The trip to Washington had certainly cleared the air: my worries about our marriage, about Simon’s job, about whether he would return home, had been resolved. Or most of them. I was still uncertain about this job of his, what it was, but these thoughts I dismissed. Sufficient that we were back on track as a couple. Better to concentrate on the big picture. Anything else we could sort out once we were together again.

And this trip to Bute wasn’t merely a whim. I had to spend time on a section of the article I was finding difficult – being on the island, seeing the locations which had been so important during Bute's Victorian heyday, would give me a fresh perspective. Besides, this was likely to be my last trip to Bute for some time. Once Simon retired, I suspected trips to more exotic locations might be planned.

The early April morning was bright as I set off a few days later, the road down from Glasgow to the ferry terminal at Wemyss Bay almost deserted. Except that is for the broken-down lorry blocking the road at the traffic lights near Branchton, forcing drivers to crawl along in a single lane.

I pulled into the ferry queue of three cars, behind a large estate car with a family setting off on holiday, judging by the brightly coloured buckets and spades on the parcel shelf. On the back seat a couple of children bounced up and down excitedly and I hoped the weather would stay fine for them to enjoy one of the many beaches on the island.

Of course I was curious about the death at the yard where Deborah was working, but a quick check online while waiting for the ferry produced little in the way of information. Apart from a brief few lines about the "Man found dead at Brydeshill stables" there were no further details.

My thoughts drifted to other matters. I was looking forward to telling Deborah about her dad's plans to come home for good once his current contract in Washington ended. Something I was very much looking forward to. Simon and I had been apart long enough.

As I thought about Simon's homecoming, I felt happier than I had for some time and I watched the ferry glide into the harbour, anticipating a couple of weeks of combining work with pleasure. The Ferry

Rest was somewhere I'd stayed on previous occasions and it was such a perfect location, right on the seafront with views over Rothesay Bay.

A knock on the car window startled me out of my daydream.

'Tickets, please,' the CalMac ticket collector said and I scrabbled in the glove compartment to find them.

There was little time on the short journey across the Firth of Clyde to Rothesay to fret about Deborah's problems. There were several people I knew on the ferry and the trip passed quickly as I caught up on the island news. In a small community, everyone knows what's happening and I enjoyed listening to the stories of new babies (true), clandestine relationships (possibly) and plans to build anti-terrorist barriers at the Rothesay ferry terminal (most unlikely).

As the MV Bute swung round to berth at the pier, a message came through on my mobile. It was Hettie, the owner of The Ferry Rest. 'Call me as soon as you get this,' the text said.

Ignoring the robotic voice on the loudspeaker urging passengers to return to their cars, I phoned her, wondering what could be so urgent.

'Alison, I'm really sorry. We've had a disaster here…a burst pipe… and we're flooded out. I've had to cancel all our bookings.'

As she continued to apologise, I said, 'Please, don't worry. I'm sorry this has happened, but I'm sure I'll be able to find somewhere to stay.'

'How kind of you to be so understanding,' she said. 'I'll…' She broke off suddenly. 'There's the plumber. I'll have to go.'

I sat staring at the phone, then sprang to my feet to make my way downstairs to the car deck. What was I going to do now? I'd arranged to meet Deborah in town for lunch, but my first stop had to be the Discovery Centre Tourist office to find alternative accommodation. I rang Deborah's mobile. 'Hopefully, I'll find something quickly,' I said, 'so we could meet a bit later.'

'Wait. There might be another option,' Deborah said. 'There's plenty of spare accommodation here at Brydeshill. I'm sure Kath would be happy to let you have one of the rooms.'

I hesitated before replying. A comfortable hotel was my preference, and I wasn't sure how I'd feel about living at the stables, even though my stay would be short.

But Deborah was insistent. 'Wait for me at Guildford Square,' she said. 'I'll go and ask Kath now. If she says no, we can go along to the Tourist Office. It would be good to have you here at Brydeshill – and give us plenty of opportunities to catch up.'

Unable to think of a good reason for refusing, I agreed to her suggestion and as the cars rolled off the ferry I made my way over to Guildford Square, luckily securing a parking space. I went into Toffoletti's for a newspaper and a bottle of water, prepared for a long wait, but fifteen minutes later there was a knock on the window and Deborah came round to climb into the passenger seat.

'That's fine. All sorted,' she said with a smile.

'That was quick.'

'Gemma gave me a lift – she had to come into town. Kath's happy to have you stay at Brydeshill,' she said. 'But be careful. Don't say anything about the dead man unless Kath raises the subject.'

'Of course not.' Though I wasn't sure I could

pretend I didn't know.

'The police are remaining tight-lipped about the death. We assumed they'd quickly confirm it was an accident. That was bad enough but now…'.

Suddenly aware the parking area was becoming busy, 'We'd better move,' I said, starting up the car. 'You'll have to give me directions.'

Once clear of the town traffic, Deborah directed me along Marine Road to turn left at the mini roundabout.

'Isn't this the way to the main Co-op supermarket?' I said.

'We bypass that and go straight ahead to turn right at St Andrew's church, then follow the road up to Chapelhill. It's quite easy.'

On the drive to Brydeshill, Deborah filled me in on the details about the death at the stables.

'Kath found him – she's the owner. She heard a disturbance, heard Topper, one of the horses, neighing loudly in the middle of the night and went down to investigate. She can recognise each horse. She knows them so well.' Then, going back to her story, she said, 'There he was, lying on the stable floor.' She shuddered. 'Kath said it was awful to see him like that.' She glanced sideways at me. 'There was nothing she could do. He was already dead.'

'She believes the horse trampled him?' I didn't think you could accuse a horse of murder but that seemed the most probable explanation for the death.

Deborah shook her head. 'No, it wasn't like that. Dusty's stable door was open. She's an old horse and has learned a lot in her years, including how to lift the latch on her stable door. She doesn't go far, just wanders around the yard. She's really sweet and gentle – just cunning.'

‘But Dusty was responsible for this man’s death?’

‘No, no. He was found in Topper’s stable.’

Deborah would have to explain again once we stopped. I was having enough trouble concentrating on the road as it wound its way up into the hills above the town.

As we drove through what appeared to be a housing estate I was finding it hard to imagine where this riding establishment might be. ‘This area is more built-up than I expected,’ I said.

She grinned. ‘It wasn’t always so. We’re about to pass the site of the old chapel dedicated to St Bride. There were lots of churches in Scotland dedicated to her. That’s where the name Brydeshill comes from.’

I risked a glance out of the side window. ‘I can’t see any ruins.’

‘Long since gone. There’s a house on the right-hand side with a turret – that was the site of the original chapel and then of the first Bute Museum.’

I caught a glimpse of the house before turning back to concentrate on the road. I’d had many trips to the island, but I wasn’t familiar with this part of Bute. Gradually the houses became fewer and as we passed a derelict flat-roofed building of concrete and glass with a spectacular view of the bay Deborah said, ‘That’s the old Rothesay Academy, built in the late 1950s after a serious fire in the original school.’

‘I think I’d better concentrate on the road,’ I said, a decision justified as I had to slow to a crawl behind a lumbering tractor until it suddenly veered off on a road leading to one of the farms.

As I rounded the next bend, a car came towards us and I had to wrest the steering wheel over to come to a stop in a passing place. The driver waved to me, as though there was nothing unusual about his behaviour.

Deborah shook her head. 'Yeah, that's the trouble with roads like this on the island. Some of the locals know them so well, they forget others don't.'

Which was small consolation and I started up the engine again, proceeding with caution and slowing down to a crawl as we approached the next curve in the road.

Then we were past the Westlands Recycling Point and out in open country, high above the town with a view over the bay and the hills beyond. I resisted the temptation to look, as the twists and turns in the road demanded all my concentration, but I did spot a marker for part of the West Island Way. A reminder of how often Simon and I had promised we'd walk this route. One day, perhaps. Something to put on the bucket list for when he retired.

'Just another mile,' Deborah said, before adding, 'Be careful…there's a left turn almost immediately. It's difficult to see because of the trees.'

Following her advice, I drove at a snail's pace, careful not to miss the turning. It was clearly signposted Brydeshill but as we started up the long driveway, there was no point in speeding up. The road was badly potholed, in need of repair, and I feared for my car's suspension. Here and there an attempt had been made with limited success to fill in the worst of the potholes with rough stones and we bumped the last few yards to draw up in front of a large farmhouse building, narrowly missing a chicken strutting across our path.

At the far end of the yard I caught sight of a long stable block, which looked new compared to the other buildings on the property, but there was no sign of any horses. In the field opposite, where I'd expected them to be, a herd of llamas grazed peacefully, the nearest one lifting its head to regard us thoughtfully while continuing to chew as though reluctant to interrupt his meal. This was something Deborah hadn't mentioned. They looked peaceful enough, but I remembered reading somewhere that they could be dangerous if they took a dislike to you. Not that it mattered. I'd no intention of going near them.

'Quite a set up,' I said. 'But where are the horses? I thought this was a livery yard and stables.' Though for a moment I wondered if the llamas might be part of the riding school. Nothing would surprise me.

'Oh, they're in the winter field on the far side. You can't see it from here. We bring them into the summer field next to the llamas in late Spring.' She frowned. 'Now, Mum, you will be careful, won't you? It's all perfectly safe, but there are a lot of animals about.'

As though to confirm what she said, a couple of dogs came bounding up as we stepped out of the car, barking loudly.

I stopped mid-stride, then stepped back, taken by surprise.

'It's okay, they're friendly really though they sound fierce – exactly what you need in guard dogs. Down Nyx, down Baron,' she said, and they moved back, wagging their tails as they recognised Deborah.

'I'll keep well away from the animals,' I said, not quite trusting the dogs.

Deborah scuffed her feet, making little clouds of dust rise from the path. 'There's something else. It's all become a bit more complicated…'her voice tailed off, as she avoided my gaze.

I said. 'I'm not going in to meet Kath until I hear the full story.'

‘I suppose that’s only fair.’ She took a deep breath. ‘I told you the man who was found in Topper’s stable was a stranger. Kath had never seen him before, nor had anyone else who works here.’

If the man was unidentified, this was a task for the police. ‘Fine,’ I said. ‘This isn’t a problem for me, Deborah, or for you.’

She gazed into the distance, as though riveted by the sight of the largest llama which had now come over to the fence and was regarding us with an imperious stare.

‘It’s not quite like that,’ she said turning to me. ‘We don’t know yet who the dead man is, but there’s another difficulty.’

‘Oh, yes?’ What was coming next?

She turned away, avoiding my gaze. ‘You remember I told you we initially thought he’d been kicked by the horse…though that still didn’t explain what he was doing in the stables.’

‘Yes…’

‘No one here can say for sure, but the police are refusing to confirm that his death was an accident.’

‘So what else could have happened?’

‘There’s a possibility Topper did kick him, but by then he was already dead.’

THREE

‘Let’s go into the farmhouse. Kath’s looking forward to meeting you,’ Deborah said.

The farmhouse was rather grander than some of the others I’d seen on visits to Bute, more like a country house, though close up it was clear the building had seen better days. A cursory glance showed the window frames were ill-fitting and the front door in need of a coat of paint, the roof missing tiles here and there.

The hallway was surprisingly narrow, made narrower by a wall of pegs holding an assortment of old coats and hats. Shoes and boots took up a large part of the floor and Deborah kicked aside a stray wellington saying, ‘It’s not always like this, but everything has been a bit haphazard since the incident in the stables.’

She led me through to the back of the house and opened a door leading into an enormous kitchen. On the far wall a range cooker sent out waves of heat where two cats, one ginger, one black and white, were lying asleep on the shelf nearby and had clearly claimed this spot as their own. As we came in, the black and white cat opened an eye, stretched and then, deciding we were of no real interest, settled down again to sleep.

A woman stood at the range cooker, concentrating on stirring something in a large pot, the volume of the radio playing beside her muffling the sound of our approach.

‘Hi, Kath,’ said Deborah in a loud voice, making

the woman jump. 'What a fright you gave me,' she said, almost dropping the spoon into the pot as she turned around.

She wasn't as I'd imagined her. When Deborah first told me about Kath, I'd imagined someone tall and sturdy, well-used to the outdoor life, to heaving bales of hay and mucking out stables. From the back, her tumble of fair hair and slim figure gave the impression of youth, but her face had the lined look of a heavy smoker. And she was smaller than I'd expected from Deborah's description. But contrary to appearances, I learned over the next few days she was very capable, more than able to cope with the demands of running Brydeshill.

Kath held out her hand, 'So you're Deborah's mother? I've heard a lot about you.'

'All good I hope,' I said, wondering what Deborah had told her.

She didn't reply and her grip was like steel, my fingers tingling as she released my hand.

Hesitant, uncertain how much Deborah had said about the reason for my visit to the island, I added, 'And thank you so much for agreeing to put me up at short notice.'

Kath nodded in acknowledgement. 'Not a problem. There's plenty of space here, though you'll find us a bit rough and ready.'

I thought about The Ferry Rest with its comfortable room and ensuite, no longer a possibility. I'd have to make the best of my accommodation at Brydeshill. 'I'm looking forward to time on the island,' I said, injecting a note of gaiety into my voice. 'I'll be busy with research of course, but it's always a pleasure to be back. And the weather forecast looks promising. It will be good to be here as the days get longer, as I can explore this…’I stopped, aware I was wittering on to no purpose.

‘Mmm. You know Bute well then.’ A statement rather than a question.

‘Yes, I’ve been here a few times…’

Kath interrupted. ‘Yes, I’ve heard of you,’ she said, glancing over at Deborah as I went on, ‘I’ve not visited this part of the island before. Most of my work has…’

Deborah jumped in this time, probably afraid I’d say too much. Guess she didn’t want to remind Kath about my previous exploits on my visits to Bute.

But I wasn’t to be let off so lightly.

‘You’ll have heard about our spot of bother here,’ Kath said gruffly.

I’d have thought what had happened would have been described as more than “a spot of bother” but I merely mumbled something in reply before she went on, ‘Bloody inconvenient. This is one of the busiest times of year, with the annual Horse Show next month. All we need is the police tramping all over the place. We’ve a couple of new horses here and it takes a lot of work to settle them in.’

She sounded more concerned about the horse show than the dead man.

Aware Deborah was frowning at me, but I feeling I had to reply, I blundered on, ‘Yes, I was sorry to hear about that death on the premises,’ I said, deliberately avoiding the use of the word “suspicious”. ‘That must be causing some disruption.’

But Kath had no such qualms. ‘And how. Let’s hope the police will soon be able to find out who he was. And why he was in Topper’s stable. No one here has any idea.’ She frowned. ‘Whoever he was, he’d no business here. He was trespassing. And it’s the effect on the business I'm worried about.' There was no mention that the police might be dealing with more than an accident and she turned away, trying to control a spasm of coughing.

'Are you okay?' Deborah said, lightly touching her on the arm.

Kath shrugged her off. 'Smoker's cough. I'm trying to give up, but none too successfully.' She took a deep breath. 'Best to get on. I'll see you later, Mrs Cameron.' She turned back to the stove, effectively dismissing us.

'I'll show Mum around,' Deborah said hastily, propelling me out by the arm.

'That went well,' I said to Deborah, but she didn't pick up on my sarcasm.

'I guess so,' Deborah said, chewing her lip. 'You can understand what this death means for Kath, can't you? Money's tight and this latest blow is going to be hard to recover from. Lots of youngsters have riding lessons here and their parents will be wary after what's happened.'

'Is it not strange they haven't yet identified the man who died?'

Deborah shook her head. 'Mmm. Or if they have they're not telling us.'

'There was no driver's licence, passport or anything?'

'No, pretty odd that. All there was in his pocket was a piece of paper with the name and the address of the stables on it. You can see how worried Kath is ... not only is there the problem of the police investigation, but it's going to take some time till the area is clear again and we can restart the riding lessons and the other activities.'

'And I can understand why it's going to make

people think twice about coming along here to ride.'

'Absolutely. No matter what the truth, the rumours are that he was kicked to death by one of the horses. No one will take into consideration that he shouldn't have been here in the first place.'

What a difficult situation. 'And you believe you should stay on to help?'

'Yes, that's why I don't want to leave. I'd be letting Kath down.'

Realisation dawned. If the death of the stranger could be proved an accident, it would allow the business to pick up more quickly. But if it was murder, if he had been killed beforehand, that would be a completely different matter.

FOUR

The tour of Brydeshill didn't take long. There was plenty of open ground and several fields, but apart from the farmhouse, other buildings were few. There was an ancient barn which Deborah identified as, 'The temporary riding arena. The new one is being built on the far side of the stable block.'

I followed the direction of her gaze. The stable block appeared to have been constructed recently and from where we were standing I could see the foundations for a new arena were being dug. There was no sign of any workmen: the digger sat in the middle of a sea of mud.

As she noticed my frown, Deborah added, 'If Kath has the money of course. It's so expensive building an indoor arena. I guess the old barn will be in use for some time.'

There were several other outbuildings, but most seemed to be in a state of disrepair. Clearly the business wasn't making much money. What a setback this death would be to Kath's plans.

I said nothing. This was to be my home for the next two weeks and I'd do my best to fit in.

As we made our way across the yard, a tall figure emerged from one of the stables.

'Hi, Deborah. Tell Kath I'm off.' His grin made him look almost boyish. 'I've left instructions about Sparky with Gemma. Her cough is just an allergic reaction, so with dust free bedding and with her hay well-soaked she'll be fine.'

With a wave of his hand he walked across to the

field where the llamas were grazing peacefully. 'One more check to do,' he called.

'That's Duncan Bradstone,' Deborah said. 'He's the vet Kath uses…partly because he doesn't expect his bills to be paid quickly.'

'Will this horse…Sparky…not be able to work then?'

Deborah shrugged. 'She's a new horse. Let's hope Duncan will sort out the problem.' She smiled. 'Come on, time to meet the chickens.'

'What do you mean, meet the chickens?'

She grinned. 'If you're going to be living here you have to earn your keep.'

'Excuse me,' I said in astonishment. 'You said I wouldn't have to help. I know nothing about chickens.'

Deborah laughed. 'Don't worry, Mum. It's only a suggestion. You won't have to feed the chickens if you're afraid of them.'

'I'm not afraid, it's only that…' I blustered.

She stopped, a pleading look on her face. 'Seriously, there's so much work to do round here that if you could take on the job of feeding them it would be a great help. It's not difficult and I'm sure you'd manage fine.'

What could I say? But I didn't feel any more confident I'd cope as she chatted me through the routine after collecting the bucket sitting at the entrance to the coop.

'I'll give it a try,' I said doubtfully. 'But if I can't manage…'

'You'll be fine,' Deborah said. 'You're used to small animals.'

'I've only ever had a cat as a pet and a cat isn't quite the same as chickens. Besides...'

She cut me off with a wave as a tall young woman dressed in riding gear came over saying, 'I'm taking Felix out for a ride. He's such a sweetie, I really enjoy riding him. I won't be long.'

Deborah introduced us. 'This is Gemma,' she said. 'What she doesn't know about horses isn't worth knowing.'

Gemma smiled, 'Good to meet you,' she said, tucking her long, dark hair under her riding hat.

As Gemma headed off to the field to collect her horse, Deborah said, 'Come into the farmhouse and see where you'll be sleeping,' and I trotted behind her as she walked briskly away.

The attic room in the farmhouse wasn't as basic as I'd expected. The steep stairs up from the first floor might prove a challenge, but the room itself was light and airy, a relic of the times when building on a large scale had not presented problems in terms of cost or finding labour.

Judging by the fading wallpaper with its frieze of circus animals, this room had been used as a nursery and I wondered who had once lived here. The windows were small, but the view out over the fields and down to the distant Firth of Clyde was impressive.

I'd be comfortable enough, I thought, testing out the single bed by bouncing up and down though I'd have to be careful not to bang my head on the sloping ceiling. It might not be as luxurious as The Ferry Rest, but it would be fine.

'I'll let you settle in,' Deborah said. 'Come downstairs when you're ready.'

I organised my few belongings, deciding against stowing my clothes in the chest of drawers in the corner of the room. A musty smell of damp made me think it hadn't been used in a long time. I could live out of my suitcase. Apart from the chest of drawers and the single bed, a chair, a small bookcase, and a wardrobe of sorts, converted from a shallow cupboard by the addition of a few coat hangers, were all that furnished the room.

Although there wasn't much furniture, there had been some attempt to make the room cosy. A large striped rug covered the wooden floorboards, the way it was folded over at the far wall a sign of a previous existence in a much bigger room.

I stood up and went over to open one of the windows, tugging at the latch to open it fully and gazed down at the yard below.

There was a bustle about the place, signs that there was an attempt to return to normal. Kath was leading a large bay horse across to the field on the far side of the farmhouse. This must be the winter field Deborah had mentioned and I guessed the other horses had already been turned out there.

Outside the old barn that served as the riding arena, I spied the vet, Duncan Bradstone, deep in animated conversation with a man whose close-cropped hair, faded green jacket and muddy boots marked him out as one of the stable hands. Their voices drifted up to me, but although I was unable to make out any of their conversation from where I was standing, I didn't want to appear to be snooping and I closed the window quickly.

The attic area had a tiny toilet but no shower. Something else to be investigated.

I picked my way carefully down the steep steps, holding on to the banister. I'd have to check where the stair light was for night time. One accident at Brydeshill was enough.

The kitchen was deserted, quiet except for the faint purring of one of the cats which jumped down from an old rocking chair beside the window to greet me.

There was a lingering smell of coffee and a scatter of breakfast dishes lay on the huge, scrubbed pine table which dominated the room, chairs carelessly pushed back a sign of a hasty departure. Packets of cereal stood in a row on the middle shelf of an old-fashioned dresser and I suddenly realised I hadn't eaten since yesterday evening and was now ravenously hungry.

Unconcerned about choice, I lifted the nearest box and had to check several of the cupboards before I found a clean bowl.

The next task was to find milk: there was no sign of a fridge in the kitchen, but there was an ancient SMEG in the scullery adjacent, so old-fashioned to be antique, but still in working order judging by the coldness of the milk. After a quick sniff of the milk bottle, just to make sure, I had a meagre breakfast.

As Kath had rejected my offer to pay for accommodation at Brydeshill, I guessed I'd have to do as Deborah suggested and take on the task of feeding the chickens. Kath had waved away my suggestion of money, saying, 'Of course you don't have to pay. Glad to have you here.'

Even so, I could help by making a start on clearing the messy kitchen. There was no sign of a dishwasher and I steeled myself to tackle the stack of dishes by hand.

I'd almost finished washing up in the large, cracked sink (at least there was a plentiful supply of hot water), when the back door was flung open and Kath came rushing in, closely followed by a man I recognised as the vet. She stopped abruptly when she saw me.

'Oh, Alison,' she said, laughing. 'There's no need to do that. We usually leave everything until there are no clean dishes, then we all pitch in.'

This explained the dirty dishes occupying every surface, but all I said was, 'Thought I might as well make myself useful.'

She lifted the coffee pot from the stove, feeling it carefully. 'Thank goodness. Still warm,' she said. She turned to the vet. 'Do you want some?'

He shook his head. 'Thanks, but I have to get over to one of the farms at Ettrick Bay. They have a cow in trouble.'

He moved forward and extended his hand to me. 'I'm Duncan Bradstone, a local vet.'

As I shook his hand, Kath said, 'Sorry. I forgot you don't know anyone here, Alison.'

Duncan grinned, making him look almost boyish. 'I'm off.'

'I'll see you out,' Kath said.

When Kath came back in she sat down on one of the kitchen chairs with a sigh. 'Lovely as Duncan is, he seems to be here more often than is good for my bank balance. No wonder he can afford to live well if he's as busy at other places as he is here.' Then she chuckled. 'Though there may be other attractions of course. Gemma, for instance.'

'Yes, I met Gemma earlier,' I said.

She fell silent and all I could think of saying as I stood watching her sip her coffee, was, 'I suppose it costs a lot to look after the horses. The death in the stables must be such a worry when you have a business to run.'

'Mmm.' She turned away from me, concentrating on pouring more coffee into her large mug, so it was impossible to see the expression on her face. 'Especially when I'm trying to build it up. The place was a mess when I took it over.'

I made no comment: perhaps my standards were different, but judging by the state of the farmhouse, there was still plenty of work to be done. Perhaps she'd spent what money she had on upgrading the stables.

'And there's no word yet about who this dead man is,' she said. 'Strange that none of us recognises him.'

The merest hesitation, as though she was weighing up how she should continue.

'I'm sure the police will discover what happened. Deborah said there was a note found with him with the address of Brydeshill. That might give them a clue.' I'd no idea what might happen but there was no harm in trying to sound positive.

Kath shrugged, then she seemed to come to a decision. 'I've remembered how I know about you. You've been involved before in several mysterious events on the island.'

I couldn't deny this, so I mumbled, 'True. But not recently.'

Kath ignored my last comment. 'I've no idea why that man was found dead in Topper's stable. Nor why he would be prowling around the place at night. Oh, I know the police are working on it but if we don't get this sorted soon, I'll be ruined.'

'But it wasn't your fault, surely?'

She frowned as though I'd said something odd. 'No, of course it wasn't. But the police have said little and I must get this busines back to normal as soon as possible. You do understand, don't you, Alison.'

'Why, yes,' I said wondering what was coming next.

She clenched her hands into fists. 'The problem is, did Topper kick him hard enough to kill him, was he killed earlier or was there an accident? I rather hope it was the latter. I can't believe Topper trampled him and I certainly don't think he was murdered. And,' she added, her voice rising in anger, 'there was no reason for him to be there.'

'Was he trying to steal one of the horses?' I said, thinking this might absolve the stables of blame.

Kath laughed, then was seized by a fit of coughing, and moved to sit down at the table. 'If he wanted to steal a horse, there would be no point in choosing Topper. He's the oldest horse here, and unlikely to be of much value.' She paused, then said, her voice rising, 'But a rogue horse would spell disaster. Word would get about – if there's one horse like that, are the others also not to be trusted? We run classes for children on Saturdays and Topper is a favourite because he's so gentle. Already the numbers are dropping.' She turned away, but I noticed she was now rigid with anger.

Uncertain about how to comment on this, I mumbled a non-committal reply.

Then to my surprise she said, 'If you're going to be here for a couple of weeks, perhaps you could try to find out what happened. Someone at Brydeshill has the answer. Of that I'm sure. No one here knows you, so you're ideally placed to find out.'

'I don't think so,' I said quickly, having no desire to be involved.

'I'm pleading with you,' she said. 'Just try. If I can get to the truth quickly I can rescue the business. If not, Brydeshill will go under.' She appeared on the brink of tears.

Before we could continue, the door was flung open

again and the man I'd spotted talking to Duncan Bradstone burst into the room.

'Hello,' Kath said, turning away to wipe her eyes.

The man didn't return her greeting but merely grunted in reply as he lifted the coffee pot from the stove and shook it. A look of annoyance creased his face as he realised it was empty.

'I'm afraid you'll have to make a fresh pot,' Kath said. 'There's a new packet in the pantry.

He grumbled as he went off in search of coffee, clutching the coffee pot as though worried someone might try to steal it. Kath said to me. 'Don't mind him. That's Fritz Hofferman. He's the manager. He isn't one for chat, isn't exactly sociable,' she said, 'though he seems to get on well with Duncan. But he's great with the horses. And right now I need all the help I can get.'

Fritz came back into the room and I smiled at him, but his response was a sullen look.

He busied himself with the coffee, tearing open the new packet with his teeth and tipping the coffee into the pot rather than taking the time to measure it out.

All the while Kath watched him, but she didn't say another word.

Fritz might be great with the horses, but I'd the distinct impression he was far from friendly.

And what was I going to do about Kath's appeal for help?

FIVE

Despite the basic nature of the attic accommodation, I was tired and slept well, wakening early to lie staring at the ceiling, trying to gather my thoughts as the light gradually filtered through the dusty windows, bare of curtains. Perhaps I could ask Kath if she had any spare. It was becoming light so much earlier now. This was one of my favourite times on Bute, as winter gives way to Spring with the promise of soft summer days to come.

Was it foolish for Kath to think I might be able to find the answer to the mystery of the death in the stables? Much would depend on the result of the post-mortem. And while it was true I'd been involved in previous suspicious events on the island, on every occasion there had been a direct connection to my reason for being on Bute. Or so I told myself.

But then, even ignoring Kath's request, I knew how concerned Deborah was, given the detrimental effect on the business. Until the mystery of the stranger was solved, the riding establishment wouldn't be able to return to normal.

I felt I couldn't refuse her request. I'd tell Kath I'd ask around, gather what information I could, but I wasn't promising I'd be able to solve the mystery. Then again, despite the denials, someone must know who the dead man was. Someone at the Brydeshill? If not, what was the stranger doing here. Even from a brief tour of the yard, there appeared to be nothing of worth.

If Kath was right, there would have been no point in

stealing one of the horses. She gave me the impression none of these horses was particularly valuable, not even Marvel whose racing days were over.

This was impossible. There was no sense lying here brooding.

I swung my legs out of bed and scrambled into my clothes. A shower would have to wait till later.

Down in the kitchen Deborah was sitting alone at the table.

'Any news this morning from the police about the man who died?' Kath wanted me to make enquiries about the death of the man in the stable, but I wasn't sure my daughter would be happy if she found out I was involved.

Deborah frowned. 'Not as far as we know. Though they might well have a name and be keeping quiet about it for some reason.' She made a face. 'And we wouldn't be first on the list to be told.'

I let the subject drop. There would be lots of gossip on the island though, plenty of speculation. Everyone would have an opinion on what had happened, but concrete evidence was scarce.

Then I decided this was a chance to find out what her long-term plans were – if she had any.

'I don't know, Mum,' she'd said. 'This was meant to be a stopgap, but I've nothing else in view and Kath is so short-handed.'

I didn't want to point out it might be better if she focussed on a proper career. As though anticipating my thoughts, she held up her hand, saying, 'And don't mention Maura and how diligent she is.'

Now that her eldest, Connor, and the twins, Noah, and Iona, are growing up, my other daughter Maura has gone back to work a couple of days a week.

What I didn't tell Deborah was that she'd said it was nothing to do with getting back on the career ladder, but "to preserve my sanity, make me feel like an adult again".

But Deborah wasn't in the mood for further discussion of her options. 'Must get on.' She stood up quickly from her seat at the kitchen table. 'Do you want to come with me?'

'Think I'll wait, have another cup of coffee,' I replied. It was clear she'd plenty to do without her mother tagging along. Besides, I wasn't too sure how well I'd cope with being around horses. I wasn't exaggerating when I said I'd no experience and some of them looked intimidating. One in particular Deborah had pointed out, 'That's Topper, the one whose stable was where the man was found dead,' looked large enough to cause some serious damage if you got too close. As though aware of what I was thinking, she added, 'He's 17.2 hands. Pretty big. But he's very good-natured.'

Far better to have a slow walk round the rest of the yard, find someone to chat to, before venturing near the stable where the unfortunate victim had been found.

A second cup of coffee later, I was ready to explore my new surroundings. As I came out of the kitchen door, I almost bumped into Fritz carrying a large bale of hay.

'Hey, watch out,' he said in a gruff voice. 'I almost knocked you off your feet.'

'Sorry, sorry,' I said, backing away.

He put the bale down on a large pallet nearby. 'Can I help you?'

Close up, now I could see him properly, I was struck by his weather-beaten and pockmarked face which looked as if he might have had a serious illness at one time. Perhaps I was misjudging him.

'I'm Deborah's mum,' I said, holding out my hand to shake his.

But he ignored my outstretched hand saying, 'Yes, I saw you in the kitchen earlier. There was no one else you could be.' As he turned away, he said, 'You have to take care around the yard, watch out for the unexpected. It can be a dangerous place.'

For a moment I wondered if he was referring to the dead man, then dismissed this idea as fanciful. He was doing no more than warning me to be cautious. There was junk everywhere: piles of old tyres, wooden pallets piled up precariously, empty boxes and feed bags carelessly discarded. You'd have thought Kath would have put more effort into keeping the place tidy.

'Yes, I certainly will,' I stammered, anxious now to be away from him. He didn't look any more friendly than earlier.

He merely grunted in reply and walked off towards the wagon in the far corner where so many bales of hay were piled up they appeared to be about to topple over. I watched him go, noticing his slight limp. Maybe it was especially difficult for him, working in a place like this with such a disability.

No matter. It was unlikely I'd have much to do with him while I was here. I'd other things on my mind. Though now, I'd no idea where to start.

And I wasn't equipped for the yard, I thought ruefully, looking at the increasingly muddy town shoes I'd thought would be perfectly adequate for this trip. I'd have to go into town and purchase boots, or at the very least a sturdy pair of wellingtons. Sooner rather than later.

And I could combine that with making a start on the research that was my main reason for being on the island. I'd visit the Bute Museum to look at their display of holidays 'doon the watter' as the trip to Rothesay from Glasgow was dubbed in earlier days.

I began to wander around, this time taking great care not to disturb anything…or anyone. There was an air of activity about the yard though the stable where the dead man had been found was still cordoned off. The tattered blue tape fluttered in the breeze, but the stable hands were mucking out the other stables while the horses were out in the field.

I spied Kath, sitting on a low wall at the front of the stable block, smoking a cigarette. By way of conversation, I said, 'I'm probably displaying my ignorance about horses, but I would have thought they would be out in the fields all the time, given it's Spring. That's why I was surprised to hear the dead man was found in one of the stables.'

She coughed and struck her chest, before discarding the cigarette and grinding it under her heel.

'This is Scotland, Alison. Yes, usually the horses are out, though rugged up, but the last few nights have been very cold and wet. In an enterprise like this you can't afford to have your fields churned up by the horses' hooves. We were taking precautions. And now with all that's happened, we decided to bring them in every night.'

She gestured towards the stable hands busily mucking out, filling the wheelbarrows to take them over to what looked like a steaming midden in the far corner. The smell drifted across, making me wrinkle my nose, then pinch it in the hope she wouldn't notice. She was clearly used to this odour.

'Means a lot more work for everyone, but

sometimes you have to make a judgement, no matter how unpopular that might be.'

'I guess so,' I mumbled.

She looked me straight in the eye. 'You've thought about what I said? You'll help then?'

'I'll try,' I said, 'but I can't promise I'll be able to make much progress. The police…'

'Oh, the police,' she said scornfully. 'If we wait till they come up with an answer, we'll be broke.'

She coughed again, then stood up as Fritz came towards us. 'This is Deborah's mum,' she said, nodding to him as he came up beside us.

'I know,' he grunted. 'We've met.'

'Sorry,' said Kath. 'Of course you have.'

Fritz grunted again. 'Another problem. Minty is lame again. Looks like she's been kicked by one of the other horses.'

'Damn,' said Kath. 'That's all we need. More vet's fees.' She sighed. 'Well, nothing else for it. Give Duncan a ring.'

Fritz nodded and limped off, saying, 'That vet does nothing but make money.'

Kath stood looking after him, then turned to me. 'You mustn't mind Fritz. He had a bad accident a few years ago. The horse he was riding got spooked by a car coming too close and bolted. He's a great horseman but even he couldn't cope. He fell off and broke his leg in so many places, it's held together now by a series of metal pins. Some days his limp is more pronounced than others. He says it depends on the weather.' She shook her head. 'He's in great pain most of the time. I took him on when I bought Brydeshill – he worked for the previous owners.'

Kath's story explained a lot about his surly behaviour. 'Anyway, Deborah says you'll be willing to help?'

'Yes, I'll do my best,' I said, concerned that Kath had discussed her request with my daughter.

She must have registered the look on my face as she grinned, 'She mentioned something about the chickens.'

'I'm not sure…' I began, but Kath went on, 'Have a try. They haven't been fed yet. Come with me. We like to let them roam around, free range, you know. But sometimes if we're busy we shut them in the coop. Less trouble that way.'

What could I say? I followed her back into the farmhouse kitchen and through to the scullery, where she pointed to a large zinc bucket. 'That's where we put the scraps of vegetables like cabbages and cauliflower to mix in with the chicken feed. Aren't too fussy, chickens, though recent legislation means we must be careful about the proportions. And we give them corn pellets in the late afternoon. Means we get a good supply of eggs for little outlay. Unlike the horses, which cost a fortune to keep.'

'When will you be able to re-open?' I said, lifting the heavy bucket awkwardly, taking shallow breaths as the smell of chicken feed caught at my throat.

'The police say on Monday. But that's not the issue.' She bit her lip and I waited for her next words. 'The problem is will riders return, especially if there's no decision about what happened? Oh, there are a few horses in full livery here and their owners are desperate to have everything back to normal, but we rely on the classes we run, especially at the weekends.'

I nodded in sympathy. I could understand why some people might be reluctant to return.

Together we walked back out into the yard. 'And,'

she went on, 'you can see how much it takes to maintain this place.' She waved her hand vaguely in the direction of the makeshift riding arena. Even a cursory look had shown it to be in serious need of repair: the walls made of ramshackle wooden boards, daylight coming in through the gaps in the corrugated sheets that made up the roof. According to Deborah it was one of the barns of the original farm, but years of neglect had left it in a sorry state. 'I've had to halt work on the new arena,' she said.

'Because of the accident?'

She gave a hollow laugh. 'Because I've run out of money,' she said, then added, 'Anyway, anything you can find out will help, Alison.'

'I'll do what I can, Kath. But I'm not sure I'll be able to discover anything the police can't.'

'Thank you, Alison. I need this resolved as soon as possible. Call me if you need help with the chickens.'

With that she walked off, leaving me to cope as best I could.

Grasping the bucket firmly, I made my way over to the chicken coop where around a dozen chickens strutted about, pecking at the soil. I tried not to show my nervousness as I filled up the various bowls lying around, scattering the last remnants on the ground as instructed, feeling rather pleased I'd managed this on my own. Maybe I could get used to this responsibility after all, but I wasn't so certain of the other task I'd taken on.

Deborah appeared from the side of the stable block, leading a white horse that had the merit of being small.

'What's this lovely white horse's name, 'I said gingerly approaching it, trying not to show how fearful I felt.

‘Pixie,’ she said. ‘And she’s a pony, not a horse and not white, she’s grey.’

‘Looks white to me,’ I muttered in a low voice, but she heard me. ‘The colours of horses aren’t as you might think. I’ll give you a lesson sometime.’

‘And is this one of the Brydeshill horses?’ Pixie eyed me suspiciously as though aware I was an amateur as far as horses were concerned, shaking her head to show her scorn.

‘She belongs to Tuesday, but she hasn’t been able to come to the stables since that incident.’

‘But Kath says the stables will be open again in a couple of days.’

Deborah’s words echoed Kath’s. ‘Yes, but there’s a worry some of the owners will take their horses elsewhere.’

‘I thought this was the only riding stables on the island?’

‘No there’s another livery yard further out past Craigmore and there are plenty of farms willing to offer accommodation and,’ waving her hand around, ‘as you can see the so-called riding arena here isn’t in the best of condition. And that’s one of the things riders like – somewhere to work the horses when the weather is bad.’

Small wonder everyone was depressed. I’d no idea what the other riding stables was like but this one didn’t appear to offer much in the way of competition. Rather than continue this conversation, I was about to say, ‘I’m going into Rothesay to buy a pair of decent wellingtons, when Deborah said suddenly, ‘I saw you talking to Kath. How is she?’

‘I’ve just arrived,’ I protested. ‘I don’t know her well enough to comment.’

‘Sorry, sorry,’ she replied. ‘Of course not. It’s only

that I'm worried about her, about what's to happen if the dead man isn't identified soon.'

'Yes, it would be a help if the police could put a name to the victim. That would be a start.'

Unless they already know, but for some reason are keeping quiet, I thought, but I didn't say. And I'd no intention of telling my daughter I'd be making enquiries at Kath's request.

Deborah didn't comment. Instead she said, 'I'd better get on. I'm helping Kath with the horses. When they're out during the day, you check from time to time. One or two of them are prone to mischief.'

'As with Minty?'

'Exactly.' She began to lead Pixie away, calling over her shoulder, 'If you do go into town, bring me back a couple of doughnuts from the Electric Bakery.'

Deborah's suggestion of doughnuts made me think I should check with Kath if she needed anything from town. And I'd tell her my first encounter with the chickens had given me confidence. I felt pleased about how I'd coped. Uncertain about where she might be, I began to walk towards the stable block, but she was nowhere in sight. The arena – I could try that.

I went in through the large opening at the front – the building didn't boast the luxury of a door – and looked all around. Kath wasn't there, but Fritz was. I stood still, watching him as he moved back and forth, levelling the sand where it had been churned up by the horses' hooves. Daylight filtered in through the skylights in the corrugated iron roof on to the arena and the walls had clearly been patched with mismatched wooden boards. Apart from the far corner where striped poles for jumping sat in front of several mounting blocks the only other items were a couple of large cupboards against the far wall. A makeshift table held some mugs, a jar of coffee and a kettle, but I wouldn't trust the electrics in here.

I stood quietly, unwilling to disturb Fritz, continuing to watch. There was something different about him and I couldn't immediately think what it might be. Then I realised what was nagging at me. As he moved in a steady rhythm across the arena floor, there was no sign of a limp.

SIX

Once again my plans changed. After a sunny morning, clouds built up, the wind swung round to the west and it started to rain heavily. Better to leave the trip to town and sort out a work space in the bedroom. Deborah found a small table in one of the downstairs rooms and together we wrestled it up the steep stair to the attic.

It was the next morning before I'd the opportunity to go into Rothesay. I was already beginning to feel part of life at the yard, having now been designated as the person in charge of the chickens. I'd almost lost my fear of them and might become fond of one in particular, a large white one which ran to greet me as soon as I appeared.

After the previous day's rain, early morning mist had turned to sunshine and being here, so high up among the hills, the few wisps of clouds seemed so close you could almost touch them. I paused from scattering the feed to look down over the fields to the Firth of Clyde. The ferry was making its way towards the harbour at Rothesay but from this distance it looked tiny, like a toy boat. Daffodils filled every corner of the verges, their yellow heads nodding as though in conversation. But although it was sunny, it was still early Spring, and the breeze was chilly.

Lingering around the yard wasn't an inviting prospect. I might be called upon to do more than look after the chickens, so with a quick word to Deborah to tell her I was going into town, I hurried over to where my car was parked and set off to Rothesay.

I drove carefully, mindful of how narrow the road was and the possibility of an encounter with a lumbering tractor on its way to a local farm, or with one of the locals… as had happened on my first journey to Brydeshill.

Although I was being cautious, as I rounded a bend about half-way down, an ancient black car came hurtling towards me belching smoke and I had to brake sharply to avoid a crash, almost landing in the ditch at the side of the road.

Either the driver didn't notice me, or else he wasn't aware he might have collided with me. I watched him roar on up the hill without stopping. Two encounters in such a short time left me anxious and it was several minutes before I felt confident enough to set off again. But I couldn't stay here on the verge for long. I was in the way of any other careless motorist who might come tearing round this blind bend, driving too fast.

Moving off slowly, I began to pick up speed as I approached the signpost for Rothesay, glad to be back on a major road. Once I was in town, I'd make the most of my few hours of freedom, as I was beginning to think of them.

Rothesay was busy, but I finally found somewhere to park, almost half-way up the High Street, across from the Police Station.

The pleasant weather had encouraged tourists to take advantage of Bute being so easy to access from Glasgow and in the café at the Electric Bakery there wasn't a free table. As I passed the Bute Tool Company shop an assistant was busy arranging summer stock in one of the large windows. A hope that summer would soon be here, judging by the array of buckets and spades and brightly coloured fishing nets. Soon the clocks would change, the days would lengthen, a prospect to be enjoyed.

With a supply of cash from the bank ATM safely tucked in my purse, I walked further along to the end of Montague Street. From what I remembered, last time I'd been here one of the local shops had had a good choice of shoes suitable for walking on the island. But as I came nearer, I saw to my dismay that the shop was closed. I shaded my eyes as I peered in through the window, but all I could see were boxes haphazardly piled up in the corner and a couple of chairs upended in the middle of the room.

What to do now? I was annoyed with myself for not thinking of this problem before I left Glasgow. Although I'd originally planned to stay at The Ferry Rest, I should have realised I might be paying several visits to Brydeshill and my current footwear was entirely unsuitable.

As I stood pondering my next move, a voice said, 'Why, if it's not Alison Cameron. What are you doing back on the island?' I turned to come face to face with Tyler, the owner of *Speedy Computer Repairs*, the business on the far side of Rothesay between a Zavaroni's ice cream shop and a charity shop.

He grinned. 'I'd have thought you'd be glad to stay at home for a while.'

I wasn't about to begin a long explanation of the reason for my return, so all I said in reply was, 'I'm visiting my daughter.'

He blinked in surprise. 'I didn't know you'd a daughter living on the island. I thought I knew most people here.'

'No, no, she's working here in a temporary job – at Brydeshill.'

A shadow crossed his face. 'I heard about that.

About the man who was found dead there.' He paused. 'There's no clue yet about his identity?'

'Not as far as I'm aware,' I replied, wondering if Tyler might have heard something. I'd have to be careful, though. There would be enough gossip and speculation on the island and anything I said might be misquoted. 'I'm sure the police have it in hand.'

He stroked his chin. 'Even so, even so… someone must know who he is...or was. We don't have a big population here.'

'But he might be from off-island…' I said then stopped. Exactly what I'd promised not to do – speculate. 'But you haven't…' before I could finish a car drew up alongside us and a voice said, 'Hi, Tyler. Skulking off|? I've a computer needing urgent attention.'

Tyler laughed as we turned towards the speaker. 'Just nipped out to get myself some breakfast. Must keep up the energy levels to deal with the mess some people make of their machines. I'm on my way back now.' Did I detect a note of relief in Tyler's voice that our conversation had been cut short?

I stared in fascination at the car. The driver had wound down the window and I glimpsed a shock of red hair. But that wasn't what caught my attention. As I watched the smoke billowing from the exhaust, I realised this was the car I'd seen earlier on the road from Brydeshill.

SEVEN

It was clear the driver had no idea who I was – there was no reason he should. I was tempted to complain about his motoring skills, then thought better of it. The police would catch up with him soon enough if he continued driving around the island with that dodgy exhaust.

Tyler and I watched as he drove off in a cloud of smoke and I couldn't resist asking, 'Who was that?'

Tyler shook his head. 'You don't want to know him. He's nothing but trouble. Steer well clear of him. Anyway, I'd better be getting along. Time is money,' he said, moving away.

As he left, Tyler turned to me and said, as though it was an afterthought, 'His name is Edwin Michel. His family owned Brydeshill at one time. Fritz worked for him.'

'Yes, Kath told me.' I hesitated. Here was an opportunity. 'He seems to have problems.'

Tyler laughed. 'He's not the kind of guy you'd want to have a pint with. Though I've seen him in The Black Bull with that vet, Duncan.'

His tone of voice made it clear he wasn't willing to say more and he hurried off, mumbling, 'Can't keep the customers waiting.'

But his words made me curious. There was a story there, some reason the family had sold up and I wondered what it might be. From what I'd seen so far, the stables, the farmhouse and probably the land were in poor condition, run down.

I wished Tyler hadn't told me about the Michel

family. I'd have to quash my natural inclination to ask Kath. There was enough to take up my time, without becoming involved in this story.

In the meantime I was left with the problem of finding footwear suitable for tramping about the yard. My only hope was one of the charity shops, but even there I drew a blank. Resigning myself to a trip over to the mainland, I decided that wasn't for today and after purchasing a supply of doughnuts from the Electric Bakery, I walked briskly up the High Street towards the museum. One of the main reasons I'd come to Bute was to do research, and now I was in town, this was an opportunity to start by paying a visit to the Bute Museum.

As I walked along Stuart Street, I saw Edwin's car parked in the last bay. Or rather mostly in the last bay as it spilled over the edge almost to the end of the road. He was no better at parking than driving then. Of Edwin there was no sign.

My trip to the Museum was more successful than expected. There was a new display of items associated with Bute as a holiday destination in the Victorian era: models of famous steamers, a cup and saucer from the time when you could sit back and enjoy a meal as you sailed down the River Clyde to Bute, postcards and posters advertising the benefits of a holiday on the island.

One of the museum volunteers came over. 'Those were the days,' he sighed. 'I remember my granny telling me about it.'

'I expect as Glasgow became more and more industrialised people were eager to be released from the grimy city during the annual Glasgow Fair week.'

'Yes. And Bute soon became a favourite destination. Tiny villages, perhaps with a stone jetty, became resorts with wooden piers and villas, hotels and public houses.'

'It's amazing to think how busy the island was.'

He chuckled. 'Everyone tried to benefit. Locals would let out rooms, and the number of boarding houses grew. But even here there was a divide: the wealthy built sandstone villas to which they could commute daily, or weekly, during the summer.'

'Many of which are still here today,' I said.

Just then the phone rang, and he hurried off, leaving me to continue exploring the exhibition.

An hour later, my notebook crammed with information about the various steamers…the Lucy Ashton, the Talisman, the Jeanie Deans, and the Waverley…I said goodbye to the member of staff on duty. This visit had given me hope I might now manage to complete my assignment before the deadline.

I made it to Brydeshill with no mishaps, slowing down more than necessary for the bends, though that meant I had to take care not to be distracted by the views.

Deborah greeted me as though I'd been gone for a month. 'Where were you?' she said. 'I was beginning to worry.'

Ignoring this comment, I held up the bag of doughnuts.

'You went all the way down to Rothesay for some doughnuts? I thought you were looking for boots.'

'No luck, I'm afraid. And I need better footwear if I'm going to be around here for a couple of weeks. Anyway, my main purpose is to finish the research. Perhaps you'd forgotten that's the principal reason I came over.'

Ignoring my remark about research, she said, 'Why

didn't you remind me? I thought you were looking for something smart. If it's boots for round the yard, there are plenty of spare boots here – riding boots and wellingtons. Kath keeps a supply in the cupboard in the riding arena. Some of the people who come here do so on a trial basis and of course don't want to buy boots or riding hats till they decide if they like it. Come on, I'll show you.'

With that she strode off across the yard as I scurried behind her, trying to keep up, avoiding a large piebald horse that was a little too frisky for my liking. Nyx and Baron trotted at our heels, anticipating excitement.

She went straight to the two large cupboards set against the far wall before stopping at the first and standing on tiptoe to retrieve a key from the top. As she opened it, I recoiled from the smell of stale sweat mingled with leather. Did my daughter really expect me to wear a pair of boots from here?

Blissfully unaware of my misgivings about using any footwear that might be in this cupboard, Deborah said, 'What size are you, Mum?' and when I replied, 'Size five,' she scrabbled about for a few minutes before triumphantly hauling out a pair of stout wellingtons from the back of the bottom shelf. Holding them out for my inspection, she said, 'These should do meantime. Try them on.'

To my relief this pair looked reasonably new and sitting down on a wooden bench, I slipped off my town shoes and struggled into full-length wellingtons. They were uncomfortable, but they'd keep my feet dry if it rained. The yard was muddy enough as it was: any more rain and boots like these would be essential.

As I tested them out, Fritz came into the arena,

stopping abruptly when he saw us.

'What are you doing, Deborah?' He sounded angry, but Deborah was more than a match for him.

'Getting suitable footwear for my mum. Why?'

'These cupboards are supposed to be kept locked at all times. Where did you get the key?'

Deborah crossed her arms and drew herself up to face him. 'Everyone knows where the key is. And I don't think there's any harm in making use of the equipment in this cupboard.'

Fritz stared for a moment. 'I suppose so. Just make sure you lock up properly when you're finished,' he said grudgingly

'As if I wouldn't.' Deborah made a face.

'Make sure,' he repeated, turning on his heel and striding off, calling out to one of the riders in the arena, 'No, no. Not like that. Don't hold the reins so tightly. Stop jabbing his mouth. Do you want to hurt the poor horse?'

'He's in a bit of a mood today,' I said, staring after him and noticing his limp had returned.

Deborah frowned. 'No idea what's got into him. Not that he's usually very sociable. I think Kath only keeps him on because he's so good with horses.'

'Are he and Kath a couple?'

'Don't think so. There's no sign of a relationship other than a working one. No romance as far as I can see.' She raised her eyebrows. 'Unlike Duncan and Gemma. Duncan always seems to be here.'

She locked the cupboard and waved the key in the direction of Fritz, before replacing it on top of the cupboard. But he was too busy to notice, adjusting the horse's tack and scolding the rider, who looked close to tears.

'Let's go.' Deborah grabbed my arm. She grinned.

‘Have you done your daily chores yet? Fed the chickens? Kath said there were more eggs today. They must like you.’

‘Don’t make light of it,’ I replied. ‘I’m still not sure of them.’

As we left the arena I looked back. Fritz had moved away from the rider and was standing beside the cupboard, tugging fiercely at the door, no doubt to make sure it was securely locked.

I looked down at my feet. None of the boots I’d seen, including the ones I was wearing, appeared to be expensive. Why was Fritz so insistent the cupboard was secure? Then I realised that as Deborah opened the boot cupboard, I’d been standing beside the cupboard next to it. I’d already learned Fritz was grumpy by nature but, even so, what could be in that cupboard to make him react so angrily?

EIGHT

Fritz's strange behaviour nagged away at me. Why make such a fuss about old cupboards holding no more than a variety of ancient footwear and riding gear?

I'd no time to ponder this as it was time for the chickens again and I went into the farmhouse to make up their next feed. I was beginning to develop a routine and mused how quickly you could get used to anything, though there was a lot more to looking after them than throwing a few scraps. The daily routine of collecting the eggs and providing fresh water and food was easy, but I needed help shutting them in at night. And I'd avoided the job of cleaning the chicken house. I was willing to help, but there is a limit.

As I came up they cluttered and clustered together, pecking each other in their scramble for food. I tried to do as instructed and scatter it as widely as possible, but I hadn't quite got the hang of it yet.

Duty done, I was at a loss and wandered round the yard, but everyone was busy, occupied mostly with the horses. It seemed that the concern over the body found on the premises had assumed lesser importance as the belief was it had been an accident, though the police hadn't confirmed it. And though Topper's stable was still out of bounds, the rest of the yard was back in business.

Unable to settle, I decided to risk walking past the llamas grazing in the far corner of the large field. There was a footpath alongside the field, and given the weather was pleasant and I'd nothing else in mind, a stroll seemed a good option. Luckily, apart from one young one, the llamas showed no interest. A walk would give me the opportunity to mull over the material I'd collected from the museum and now properly shod, I set off in good spirits.

The path disappeared in a tangle of high grass and brambles, leading to what looked like a small wood. Buoyed up by the opportunity for some proper exercise, I quickened my pace.

Summer was on its way. The trees were in leaf and some had already begun to come into full bloom. The sunlight was scarcely able to penetrate this part of the wood and once or twice I almost stumbled, glad of the sturdy boots Deborah had found for me.

But despite my plan to use this walk as time to reflect on my article, my mind kept drifting back to the problems of the stables and the man found dead there. Why did Kath think I'd be able to find out anything?

Suddenly realising I was hungry, I glanced at my watch. Time to be getting back. I'd been out longer than intended. One thing I would say, the meals provided at Brydeshill were both plentiful and tasty. Good, plain fare but I suppose for people out in the open air who worked so hard, this was a necessity.

Within half an hour of brisk walking, I was back on familiar ground, out of the trees and on the rough path leading to the yard. Skirting round the llamas, who were far too busy eating to pay attention to me, I hurried the last few yards.

The livery yard was busy as I came in: several horses were being tacked up ready for a ride. Deborah was helping a youngster to saddle up one of the ponies and I heard her call over to one of the stable hands, 'Make sure J-Bear and Caffrey are tacked up and ready for the hack.'

Then she spotted me. 'Hi, Mum,' she called. 'I'll be in in a couple of minutes. One of the stable hands is leading the hack.' Surely this activity was another good sign business was beginning to pick up.

Tyler's story about Edwin Michel's family having owned Brydeshill intrigued me and after a substantial lunch (a very much help yourself affair) I went to look for Kath. There might be a story here, one I could use for an article. So many of the properties on Bute have a story, been passed down through many generations and if the Michel family had fallen on hard times I'd be interested in their story.

After ten minutes of fruitless searching in the farmhouse and the livery yard, I eventually found her at the back of the stable block, cleaning tack.

She looked up as I said, 'Hello, Kath. I can see you're busy.'

She grimaced. 'Not too busy to have a chat to relieve the tedium of doing this.'

'Isn't this something one of the others could manage?'

'You'd think so, wouldn't you. But we're so short-handed and I can't afford to hire anyone else until the place begins to make some money. Gemma and the other stable hands are fully occupied.'

This was an ideal opening for my questions. 'Oh, haven't you always owned Brydeshill?' I wasn't going to mention my meeting with Tyler until I heard what she had to say.

'No. I only bought it a couple of years ago when it suddenly came on the market, and it's been a struggle made worse now that man has been found dead. Not the best advert for what we do, especially as we have so many youngsters riding here.'

‘It’s always been a livery yard and stables, though?’

She turned away to stifle a cough. ‘No, it was a working farm, a family business owned by the Michels. But as had happened with so many such farms, the market declined, and the farm went bankrupt. I paid Edwin Michel a decent price for it.’ She waved her hand around. ‘But you can see the place isn’t in a good state. There’s even more to be done than I guessed.’ She stopped. ‘I should have paid more attention to the survey for sure.’ She sounded bitter.

This was strange. ‘But it looks set up like a livery yard and stables, especially with the riding arena.’

Kath gave a hollow laugh. ‘That’s one of the old barns that we’re using temporarily. The stable block is new, as you can see. That was a necessity – fortunately the bank was willing to lend extra for that.’ She made a face. ‘Keeping up the payments will be the problem.’

‘But Deborah says you’re building a new riding arena. You’ve already made a start.’

She stopped cleaning the saddle and stared down at her hands. ‘That was the plan, but as you’ll have noticed the digger has been sitting idle. Goodness knows when we’ll be able to start up again.’

I felt a pang of sympathy. Probably running an establishment like this had been her dream and this latest upset must be hard.

‘I’m sorry…’ I began but before I could complete my sentence, her phone rang, and she scrabbled in her jacket pocket only to find it as the ringing stopped.

She gazed at the screen, a frown crossing her face. ‘That’s the police. I’d better see what they want.’

With a curt nod, she walked quickly towards the farmhouse, leaving me gazing after her, hoping this might be good news.

I turned to go back to my room, thinking it was time I made a start on the article rather than merely thinking about it. Fritz and Deborah came over from the stable block.

'Where's Kath off to in such a hurry?'

'A phone call from the police. She went into the farmhouse to take it.'

We stood in silence for a few moments, Fritz awkwardly kicking aside a stray piece of wood with the toe of his boot. Conversation seemed pointless.

When Kath returned, her face was grim.

'What did the police…' Fritz began, but she cut him off with a wave of her hand.

'Get everyone together,' she said and as Fritz looked as if he was about to speak again, 'I said get everyone together. We'll meet in the farmhouse in ten minutes.'

I followed Kath to the front door. 'We're going into the sitting room. It's the biggest room in the house,' she said.

This was a room I hadn't been in and the size surprised me…not to mention how tidy it was. The carpet was well-worn, but the old-fashioned furniture, gleaming with polish, spoke of loving attention.

Fritz arrived next, followed by Gemma, while the other stable hands straggled in behind her. This meeting was for the employed staff only: the volunteers were left outside to carry on with the work.

'This must be important,' I heard Gemma whisper. 'We're not usually allowed in here.'

Kath paced up and down as we all settled in the chairs scattered around the room, eager to hear what she had to say. There was a feeling of tension in the air. Fritz cleared his throat, possibly to catch Kath's attention, remind her we were here, waiting.

At last she turned from the fireplace where she'd been gazing into the empty grate as though seeking inspiration. 'Where's Deborah?' she frowned as my daughter came flying in just at that moment saying, 'Sorry, sorry, I had to finish sorting out the hay nets,' and sat down with a thump on the stool beside Gemma's chair.

Kath took a deep breath. 'I called you all together because I don't understand what is happening and one of you might be able to help.'

Out of the corner of my eye I caught sight of Fritz. His face was red, and he was clasping and unclasping his hands.

Kath continued, 'I've had a phone call from the police. They've identified the victim at last. When they told me, I can't say I was surprised it has taken so long. She pulled a piece of paper from her pocket. 'I wrote his name down so I wouldn't make a mistake. He's…' another deep breath '…Jose Molina Lopez but the police have as yet no idea why he was found here, in one of the stables.' She stopped as though waiting for a comment, but no one spoke. 'I'm sure it was an accident, pure and simple.'

'The police have confirmed that?' Gemma said.

Kath frowned. 'I'm certain the police will tell us it was an accident.'

'But it still doesn't explain why he was here.' Gemma was persistent.

Kath ignored this last remark. 'That's why I called you all together. The police are on their way to interview everyone again. But I'd rather know the truth before they arrive. If someone here does recognise him better to say now.' She fixed us with a steady gaze. 'And I can't help because I haven't a clue.'

Kath hadn't answered the important question – had the police confirmed the death was no more than an accident?

Fritz stood up. 'I should be going. I've work to do,' he said. 'Of course it was an accident.' But he stopped at the door, looking back.

'Yes, we all hope that,' Kath snapped. 'But we have to have proof.'

Was that comment directed at me? I certainly hadn't made any progress with finding out about the dead man.

I could only hope Fritz was right. The young man's death had been no more than an unfortunate accident.

NINE

There was silence in the room after Kath finished speaking. She gazed from one to another, but no one wanted to be first to say anything. Fritz was still standing at the door and eventually he said, 'That's ridiculous. I've never heard of the man. Why would someone like that turn up here?' He spun round, then appeared to be about to topple. Gemma put out a hand to steady him, but he shrugged her off.

'Has anyone else? Any of you heard his name?'

'It's a most unusual name,' Gemma ventured.

'Not if you're Spanish,' I muttered.

'What? What did you say?' Fritz glared at me. 'Speak up.'

But I shook my head regretting I'd mentioned this.

Deborah came in, saying, 'The police have a name, so they must know something about him. What else did they say, Kath?'

'Nothing. All they did was give me a name, ask if I recognised it, if I knew why he would be here at Brydeshill.'

This was a ridiculous conversation. If anyone did know this man, there would have been no point in keeping quiet. It would be too easy these days to find out if there was a connection between the dead man and someone at Brydeshill.

'What was his name again?' Deborah said.

'Jose Molina Lopez,' Kath replied fluently.

'Do you speak Spanish?' I said.

Kath didn't reply, merely shook her head and turned away, saying, 'I hope the police can sort this out…and soon.'

'Yes,' Fritz growled. 'Don't want to sound unfeeling, but this isn't good for business.'

The conversation petered out. There seemed no more to say and eventually Kath sighed, 'Let's get back to work. The police will be here to interview us again. In the meantime there's plenty to do. Best way to keep our minds occupied. If anyone has any bright ideas, please let me know.'

There were murmurs of agreement and the stable hands drifted off. There would be only one topic of conversation tonight.

Gemma sat down on one of the armchairs beside the window, curling her legs up under her. 'Perhaps the police will be able to solve this quickly, let you get back to running the business.'

'That's not going to happen any time soon, is it?' Kath snapped, then sat back and closed her eyes. 'It's all such a mess. What's more, if we can't organise more classes soon, I'll have to start dismissing some of the stable hands. I can't pay them for more than another couple of weeks.'

'Oh, hopefully it won't come to that,' I said sounding resolutely cheerful, with visions of having to stay on to help with more than the chickens.

Kath stood up suddenly. 'We'll see.'

She made it clear she wasn't going to speculate further, and I followed her out into the stable yard.

Dusk was beginning to fall, and there was a chill in the air. The valley beyond the field where the llamas grazed was already in darkness and the lights in the stable block suddenly sprang into life. As the purple light of the gloaming drifted into nightfall I stood gazing over the fields. The last ferry of the day was making its way into Rothesay, its lights glittering.

Here and there other farmhouse lights came on and over the copse of trees beyond the fields the rooks were gathering, preparing to roost, wheeling and surging high in the air, their noisy chatter piercing the quiet of the evening.

Deborah came up beside me. 'What do you make of that?'

'I've no idea,' I sighed. 'I'm sure the police will give Kath more information when they come to interview everyone. Though there's certainly nothing I can tell them.' My feeling was one of relief. In spite of agreeing to help, I no longer felt under pressure to find out who he was, confident the police had made a breakthrough.

'But a Spaniard? Do you think he might have been here on holiday, come up to the stables intending to ride?' She was beginning to concoct a story based on nothing more than the dead man's nationality.

'Let's wait.' I didn't say that no matter how desperate he'd been to have a riding lesson, it was extremely unlikely he'd trudge up to Brydeshill in the middle of the night. Then I had an idea. 'Are you busy tonight? Have you finished all your chores?'

She shrugged. 'Yes, that's me pretty much done.'

'Then let's go into Rothesay for a meal. It would do us both good to get away from here for a while.'

'What a great suggestion.' She glanced at her watch. 'Give me fifteen minutes to have a shower and change.'

Without waiting for my reply, she dashed off, humming to herself. I'd better change as well, I thought, though I'd have to wait till Deborah was finished to use the shower. I didn't want to appear in town smelling of chickens. I thought longingly of The Ferry Rest with its ensuite and luxury rain shower, rather than the trickle of hot water available here.

It would do both of us good to be away for a while from this febrile atmosphere. The only talk at Brydeshill this evening would be about the dead man. And to no purpose.

I wandered over towards the farmhouse, pondering what to wear. There was someone at the side of the building, lurking in the shadows. I could hear the murmur of voices, one sounding urgent, anxious. Now curious, I edged closer, trying to appear as if I was doing no more than going slowly into the farmhouse.

As I came nearer I recognised a voice. It could only be Fritz, with that distinct guttural undertone to his English, a reminder of his German roots, no matter how long he'd been in Scotland.

I stopped and listened, but it was difficult to make out what he was saying. All I could hear was the tone of voice, now sounding angrier and angrier. Probably nothing. A spat over whose turn it was to check the yard, make sure the horses were safely locked in their stables given what had happened recently.

There was no point in loitering about here. Deborah would be ready soon and I was still in my working clothes. But as I moved away, quickening my pace, Fritz dropped his voice. I was almost right beside him and I could make out one or two words, but they didn't make sense.

'...your fault...warned you...expect...'

The other voice was one I'd heard somewhere recently, but I couldn't for the life of me place it.

Now, curious to find out who Fritz was talking to, I'd a sudden brainwave. They were right outside the kitchen window. If I hurried inside and up to my bedroom, I could look out while pretending to draw the curtains. But I was too late and was left wondering who it could possibly be, meeting with Fritz like this?

The voice nagged at me. I recognised it from somewhere. Then a few minutes later as I sat down at the mirror to comb my hair, it came to me. It was Duncan Bradstone.

Ah well, whatever their disagreement, it was no concern of mine. Time to get ready to go to dinner with Deborah.

TEN

An opportunity to have a break from the troubles at Brydeshill came in a phone call.

'Heard you were back on the island. Why didn't you get in touch?' Tara McKenna, a friend from years before, scolded me.

'I thought I'd only be here for a couple of weeks and I am supposed to be working, researching.' I paused. 'I'm staying at Brydeshill, and it's rather complicated,' I said by way of an excuse. Guiltily thinking of how seldom I'd been in touch with her, I added, 'I thought you might have moved to the mainland.'

'Mmm. Really?' She sounded amused rather than cross. 'You'll surely be allowed to escape for a couple of hours to have coffee with me.'

Tara and I had worked together on writing a history of the Rothesay Pavilion while it was being refurbished several years ago. The last time I'd met up with her was during the Bute Noir Crime Writers' festival, but Christmas cards had been the only contact since then.

'Yes, that would be good,' I said. 'Where are you living?'

'We've bought an old farmhouse out near St Ninian's Bay…the Straad road. Watch out for the bend in the road…it's about half a mile on.'

I must have sounded hesitant as I said, 'Oh, right,' because she chuckled as she said, 'The name of the house Meikle Straad is on the gate.'

Much as I'd like to see Tara and even if I stopped

only for a quick cup of tea, it would take at least an hour and a half there and back.

Tara interrupted my deliberations. 'Do come over, Alison. I'd love you to see where we're living now.'

How could I refuse? 'Of course. Tomorrow afternoon about two?'

'Perfect. I'll see you then.' She rang off and almost immediately I wondered if I'd been too hasty. While it would be good to see Tara again, I was almost midway through my stay and had no information that might help solve the mystery of the dead man, far less made progress with my research.

My notes lay reproachfully in the folder on the desk where I'd left them on my return from the museum and I hadn't yet found time to go to the Rothesay library to check through the back copies of the local paper. So much for the idea of having time to write in the peace and quiet of Bute. The days were sliding past in a slow routine and I was finding it more and more difficult to concentrate.

Then I thought – if Tara was living on the island, she might well have heard something. Right now any crumb of news would be useful, even if it later proved to be no more than gossip.

In the meantime I wanted to ask Deborah more about Fritz.

As always happens when you're in a hurry, it took longer to feed the chickens. The bucket used for the scraps wasn't in the usual place, there was no one around to ask, and when I did manage to find it, located in the cupboard at the back of the scullery for some reason, the chickens were squabbling among themselves.

I'd almost got over my fear of them, but not when they were behaving like this, peck, pecking away. It might have been no more than hunger because I was late, and I threw the last scraps into the far corner, trying to distract them from coming too close.

I didn't have to look for Deborah. She came up beside me as I finished.

'You're looking a bit flustered,' she grinned. 'Everything okay?'

'Of course,' I said, somewhat abruptly, but she only grinned again. 'All it takes is practice.'

'I won't be here long enough to become any kind of expert,' I reminded her.

'Oh, I'm sure you're managing just fine,' she said, about to walk away.

I grabbed her arm. 'I have to talk to you,' I said.

'I'm supposed to be mucking out. Can't it wait till later?'

'This won't take long, but there's something I have to ask you.' I glanced around. Kath was talking to a couple of youngsters and one or two of the horse owners were leading their horses across to the riding arena.

'Come with me to the stable block, then. I'm doing Marvel's box – it's the one next to the empty stable and we shouldn't be overheard.'

I began to follow her, trying to keep up as she quickened her pace.

Once inside the stable she fussed over Marvel, before one of the stable hands came to lead him out to the field, then said, 'What's so urgent?'

Briefly I explained about seeing Fritz the night before. She didn't seem to think there was anything strange about this.

'But people wander about here at all hours,' she said, stopping and leaning on the pitchfork. 'This isn't a nine to five job. Or maybe he was on his way back from town?'

'I don't think that's likely, do you? Even if he went into Rothesay, it's hardly likely there would have been anywhere open till that time of the morning.'

Deborah looked puzzled. 'You surely don't think Fritz had anything to do with the death of that Spaniard? Why on earth would he? He said he didn't know him. None of us had seen him before.'

That was interesting. Did everyone now assume the dead man was Spanish? I said, 'That may be so. But is it the truth? What do you know about Fritz?'

She shrugged. 'Not much. But surely if he was under suspicion Kath would have acted. She wouldn't have let a killer roam loose on the premises if she'd any doubts.'

This was a fruitless line of enquiry. Deborah evidently thought I was making a fuss about nothing. 'There could be all sorts of reasons why people here are about late at night. Don't get involved. Leave this to the police.'

She hesitated. 'Don't tell me you're trying to find out what happened. Not after the other times you've got into difficulties when working on Bute.'

She sounded upset. She meant "trouble".

'No, no, of course not.' I dismissed her concerns. And there was some truth in this – there was little I could do.

Deborah was right. In spite of my promise to Kath, it wasn't my business, and now planning to abandon any pretence of investigating, I opened the stable door, saying, 'I'll see you later.'

But as I backed out, I almost bumped into Fritz, standing at the door. As we came face to face he turned on his heel and hurried off.

I stared after him, my first thought being that he

was spying on us. And if so, how much of our conversation had he heard?

ELEVEN

Tara's house was spacious, a successful conversion from what had once been a dilapidated farmhouse out on the road to Straad. The original low stone building formed the central area, but on each side an extension had been built of mellow stone in a way that successfully blended the new with the old.

There had been so many farms on the island at one time, thriving enterprises that had been there for generations. But times had changed, and many had become family homes. Or even, as Brydeshill had, become a business of a different kind.

A pretty garden, dotted with large plant pots, took up the space previously devoted to machinery and inside the transformation was as surprising. I'd been in several buildings like this during my visits to Bute and all shared similar features. They were sturdy enough, but the thick walls, small windows and low ceilings weren't necessarily suitable for modern tastes. Yet many of them were being updated and sold on, or leased out, as the number of working farms declined. Tara's appeared to have been one of the smaller ones: there was no gigantic barn and outbuildings as there was at Brydeshill and although there had been additions to the original building, the property was more self-contained.

'This is lovely,' I said gazing around. Somehow, while the original features remained, the front room had been brightened by a judicious use of colour.

'We decided on having blinds on the windows instead of curtains as a way of letting in as much light as possible,' she said.

'You've made it so comfortable.'

Tara laughed as she motioned me to sit down on one of the two squashy sofas on either side of the wood burning stove. 'Oh, I'm afraid we didn't do any of the work. It was like this when we bought it and all we had to do was move in our furniture. Neither Warren nor I have time for renovations.'

'Lucky you,' I said, thinking of all the houses I'd lived in where we'd had to make do with someone else's dubious taste, or had to do much of the work ourselves.

'It's so good to see you, Alison,' she said. 'Why don't you relax while I fetch the tea. Or would you rather have coffee?'

'Tea is fine,' I said, wondering if it would be rude to ask what kind of tea she was offering. I seemed to remember when we'd worked together some years before she'd preferred exotic blends. Not something I was partial to.

But it was as though she read my mind. As she came through from the kitchen, bearing a tray laden with a teapot, cups, and an array of biscuits, she said, 'You'll be glad to know it's breakfast tea.'

'Ah, you've abandoned your herbal brews ?'

'Not entirely,' she said beginning to pour the tea. 'But Warren can't stand herbal teas, so I've developed a taste for the real thing.'

We settled back, sipping our tea in companionable silence. Now I was here, where to begin? I gazed around the room, thinking how quiet it was.

'Are the children not at home?'

She smiled. 'One at school now and one at nursery. They've grown up a bit since we last met, during that Crime Writers' festival.'

Ah, yes, Bute Noir. A guilty pang as I thought of all my good intentions about keeping in touch. But her next words made me feel less embarrassed. 'I did mean to keep in contact with you, but you know how it is. And life seems to be so hectic with small children.'

'I understand. What's more we've moved around frequently since then.'

That awkwardness out of the way, we settled back to catch up on what had been happening since we last met and as we chatted, I remembered what good company Tara was.

'And you're happy here?'

'As long as Warren has his job at Mount Stuart House. He loves it there…plenty of opportunities to be out in the open air. He did have a desk job once, but he hated it. This, and living on the island, suits him much better.'

She stopped, then looked over at me. 'Would you not think about moving to the island permanently? After all you know it so well. It would be lovely if you and Simon decided to move here.'

'Mmm.' I considered my next words carefully, but she pre-empted me by saying, 'Didn't you tell me in your last Christmas card your husband will be retiring soon? This would be an ideal place. I mean, not right out here in the country, but somewhere nearer Rothesay. You're a writer, you can work anywhere.'

'I'm not sure how Simon would view that suggestion,' I said. 'He is due home soon, once he's tied up the loose ends of his contract in Washington, but there's a lot to discuss, decisions to make.'

She laughed. 'Even so, I guess you've become quite the country person now that you're working up at Brydeshill?'

‘That’s an exaggeration,’ I hastened to disabuse her of any notion I might be inclined to take up a more permanent position at the yard. ‘I’m only here for a short time to combine work with pleasure – to see Deborah.’

But I didn’t have to explain. ‘It was pretty awful what happened there. And I guess they’re no nearer to finding out what happened?’

‘No, no one seems to know anything about the dead man except his name.’

‘Odd in a small community like this. Especially as his name suggests he might be Spanish. We don’t have many Spanish people on the island.’ She stopped, frowning in concentration. ‘In fact I don’t know of any, not people living here permanently.’

‘I’m sure the police have it in hand,’ I said. ‘And he may have been a visitor to the island and become lost.’ Even as I spoke I thought how rash it was to suggest this. I waited, thinking Tara might have heard some island gossip. But all she said was, ‘No one I’ve spoken to has any idea where he came from or why he was here.’

To move on quickly, I said, ‘What gave you the idea I was working at Brydeshill?’

She looked surprised at the question. ‘One of my friends has a daughter who rides up there. She saw you a couple of days ago. That’s how I knew you were on the island.’

This didn’t explain why she thought I was working there.

‘…and,’ Tara continued, trying to hide a smile, ‘she said you seemed to be in charge of the chickens. A bit of a change of career.’

‘Of all the jobs I might choose, looking after chickens isn’t one of them,’ I said. But Tara’s comment reminded me how the rumour factory on the island worked. And she might be a useful ally in making progress with the mystery of the dead man. Although she'd no news right now, the island would be abuzz with gossip. Someone must know who he was and why he'd come to Bute. It was only a matter of time, surely, before the mystery was solved.

There was no more to be learned from Tara – at least not yet – and I'd no intention of telling her Kath had asked me to investigate. Perhaps now the dead man had a name someone would come forward.

Suddenly she jumped to her feet, glancing at the large wall clock and saying, 'Sorry, Alison, I have to collect the children.'

'How quickly time passes,' I said. 'I should be going anyway. It'll soon be time to feed the chickens again.'

'You could come with me,' she said. 'I'm sure the children would be delighted to see you.'

'Perhaps next time,' I said, thinking this would be a good way to make sure we'd meet up again. And to emphasise the point, I added, 'Perhaps I could come over again soon?'

'What a good idea,' she said. 'Warren would also like to meet you again.'

'Yes, I only met him briefly at the end of Bute Noir.'

We left together with Tara promising to get in touch about another visit.

I walked back to my car, which I'd parked a little distance away, uncertain as to the exact location of Tara's house. It was still only just after three o'clock and, despite what I'd said, I didn't have to be back at Brydeshill for some time yet.

As one the main reasons for being on the island was

to research holidays on Bute in Victorian times, I decided to go over to Kilchattan Bay for a walk, telling myself I could soak up the atmosphere. I'd taken copious notes from my main reference book, 'One Island, Many Voices,' and this would give me the opportunity to add to my material. The afternoon had turned out fine, with no more than a hint of coolness in the air. A perfect day for a brisk walk along the shore at Kilchattan in the afternoon sunshine.

I drove slowly past Kerrycroy, noticing that the houses in this little enclave had recently been painted. Even the disused maypole in the centre of the village green had been restored and there were a few people on the beach, while others were strolling on the pier jutting out over the water. The road up to Mount Stuart house was quiet: most of the visitors arriving on Bute would be in town.

Suddenly the sun disappeared behind a bank of threatening clouds and I considered abandoning my visit to Kilchattan Bay, to opt instead for a visit to the tearoom at Mount Stuart house. But remembering how few opportunities I'd had for walking since arriving on Bute this time, I carried on determinedly along the twisty road past the War Memorial. A few minutes later Kilchattan came into view, nestling snugly in the crook of the bay.

Good decision, I thought, as the clouds broke, the late afternoon sun shone down on the waters, glinting steel grey.

I parked the car at the end of the village street and began to walk slowly past the houses. It was a tight-knit little community, far enough away from the main centre of Rothesay to be independent yet served well by the local bus service. Behind the hotchpotch of houses consisting of the original fishermen's cottages and stout Victorian redbrick terraces the gardens rose steeply towards a ridge of hills. Pity the poor gardeners here.

Once past the cluster of cottages, now very upmarket holiday homes, I paused and looked back. I'd happy memories of renting one of these while working on the history of the Pavilion.

Remembering this brought Tara to mind again. She had proved herself an excellent researcher, but could I trust her to find out about the man found dead in the stables at Brydeshill? Rely on her to be discreet? Yet how else was I going to be able to make progress? I was at a loss.

Perhaps a stroll along the beach, watching the tide come in, would clear my head, give me some inspiration. I picked my way across the grass and scrambled down on to the beach. A few dog walkers were enjoying the late sunshine and I went as far as the water's edge, gazing out over the bay. Strange to think this had once been a bustling port, unloading cargo, a thoroughfare for commerce. Now the village is quiet, except when visitors arrive in the peak holiday season.

Engrossed in my thoughts, I didn't hear the man come up beside me and was startled as he said, 'You seem to keep popping up everywhere, Mrs Cameron.'

It was Tyler.

'The same could be said of you,' I said when I'd recovered from my surprise. 'What are you doing round here?' And not working again, I could have added.

'I live here, over in that house where the yellow dayboat is parked.'

I followed the direction of his pointing finger. A

solid house of red sandstone, in the middle of a terrace, looked as if it was the building he was indicating.

'How are you getting on at Brydeshill?'

Now was my chance. 'I'm fine, but unfortunately there's been no word on the man found dead in the stables.'

Tyler sniffed. 'They say he's an illegal immigrant.' He waited, an eager expression on his face.

'I haven't heard any such story,' I said.

'And he's Spanish.' Tyler wasn't to be deterred. 'From the south of Spain.' He grinned. 'Probably came to Bute for the weather. Couldn't stand all that sunshine.'

'Where did you hear that?' I said, but he merely shook his head. 'Dunno. Someone must have mentioned it.' He stepped back. 'Must go.' And with that he walked quickly away towards his house.

Where did the information about the south of Spain come from? Perhaps there was someone on the island who knew more than the police did … or were telling us.

TWELVE

Energised by my walk at Kilchattan Bay, I drove back down Mount Stuart Road to go back to Brydeshill ready to tackle anything.

My calm frame of mind didn't last long. As I reached the entrance to the yard, there was a frantic air about the place, an almost tangible feeling of agitation.

'What's happened?' I said, winding down the car window as I caught sight of Gemma, striding across the yard clutching a large bale of hay.

'Better ask Kath,' she said, nodding towards the farmhouse. Without another word she hurried away.

I slid the car into a space near the house and jumped out without bothering to lock up. Kath was standing outside the front door, deep in conversation with Duncan Bradstone, the vet.

She broke off as she spotted me coming towards them.

'Oh, there you are, Alison,' she said, laying a hand on Duncan's arm as though to stop him speaking.

The only word I can use to describe the expression on Duncan's face was wary as though I'd interrupted something. 'Has there been a development?'

Kath looked at Duncan before replying as if seeking reassurance, or perhaps permission.

'It's Fritz,' she said hesitantly. 'He's disappeared.'

'What do you mean "disappeared"? Surely not? Might he not have gone to the mainland?'

'He does go over to the mainland about once a month, but he always tells me. He said nothing this time and he wouldn't go off unexpectedly with so much to do here.'

'When did you last see him?' I asked.

Duncan spoke before Kath could reply. 'I'm sure it's a fuss about nothing.'

'Was he okay when you saw him last?' I said. Duncan might know.

Duncan shrugged. 'I haven't seen him for a couple of days, but he was fine then.'

Kath said, 'There's been no sign of him since yesterday. We've searched everywhere.'

Should I mention I'd seen him lurking around the riding arena in the middle of last night? Remembering Deborah's reaction, I thought better not to say. Time enough if he didn't return.

'Perhaps you're worrying unnecessarily,' Duncan said.

'I guess so. If he doesn't turn up by tonight, I'll have to call the police.' Kath looked miserable. 'There's so much work to be done here and we need all the help we can get.'

Duncan patted her shoulder awkwardly. 'It will work out, Kath. Wait and see. I'm sure he'll be back with some good reason. I know you need extra help, so I can recommend a couple of vet students who are looking for a placement. They'll be available as soon as they complete their current module.'

Kath looked doubtful. 'I haven't time to be training up newbies,' she said. 'I really need people with experience…and now.'

'I'm sure they could manage the chickens,' I said. 'Remember I'll be leaving at the end of next week.'

A look of surprise crossed Kath's face, as though she hadn't been expecting this. 'I thought Deborah said you'd be staying on for a while.'

‘No. My intention is to leave at the end of next week. I’ve a list of things to do back in Glasgow.’ I thought guiltily of how I’d have to cram the rest of my research into such a short time on the island.

Kath shrugged as Duncan said, ‘I’ll be off then, Kath. Pixie seems fine. A false alarm to be honest. That girl worries too much about her horse. Call me if you need me.’

‘I’d better have a word with Deborah,’ I said and strode off, trying to conceal my frustration. What had my daughter involved me in now?

Deborah was in the stable block, in J’s stable, topping up the hay net. She looked up and as I came in.

‘Hi, Mum. Did Kath tell you about Fritz? There’s probably a simple explanation, but it’s hugely inconvenient.’

I didn’t reply to her question, saying instead, ‘Why did you tell Kath I’d be staying on?’

She opened her eyes wide as if she hadn’t expected this, though I guessed it was an act. ‘I thought you were enjoying it here, a complete change for you. And,’ a look of uncertainty crossed her face, ‘your help with the chickens is much appreciated. One thing less for Kath to worry over.’

About to say, ‘All I wanted to do was take the opportunity to see you while I was on the island finishing my research,’ I thought the better of it. She might ask me how much research I’d done.

Instead I said, trying to sound determined, ‘I have to go back to Glasgow. And I’ve a list of research questions about Victorian Bute to answer before I leave. That will take up much of what’s left of the time.’

She sat down on the nearest bale of hay. ‘Why?

Dad's not due back home for a while yet.'

'Yes, but I have to complete this article and then pitch for another couple of projects. Part of the idea of coming here, apart from finishing this one, was to give me a break, sort out my thoughts about what to do next. Though I'll be lucky to finish my article on Victorian holidays by the deadline.'

She narrowed her eyes. 'And have you managed to get on with your article as you planned?'

'No, not yet,' I admitted reluctantly. 'I'm finding it difficult.'

'Well, then you should stay on here until you get over your writer's block. No point in rushing back to Glasgow.'

All of this was true, but although everyone (or almost everyone) had made me welcome, this wasn't a way of life I wanted to continue for much longer. Not to mention that what started out as helping with the chickens had morphed into my being the expert on their care. I didn't particularly like chickens, though I'd come to a kind of agreement with them. What's more, I was dreading I might soon be asked to dispatch one for the pot.

'I appreciate that, Deborah, and you're right…but this was only meant to be a short stay, an opportunity for us to catch up. It would be better to go back to Glasgow but…'

She didn't let me finish the sentence. 'You can surely do some of the writing here in the peace and quiet?' She didn't wait for my reply. 'You'll stay on then? Please, please. Kath says you're becoming quite knowledgeable.' She scarcely paused for breath, hoping to talk me into agreeing.

Exactly what I feared. How was I to get out of this? Unless I came up with a good reason I'd be here for some time.

I held up my hand as she looked as if she was about to speak again.

'Fine. I will consider staying on, but not for an indefinite time. I want to put a limit on it. I'll consider being here till the end of the month and then we'll see how things are.'

Deborah stood up and did a little jig. 'Great. I'll go and tell Kath. She said she was sure I'd be able to persuade you.'

'No, don't say to her just yet. I said I'll think about it.'

Much as I might protest, I knew I'd end up agreeing to stay on. Fritz's disappearance was a further complication for Kath, but there was nothing I could do to help with that problem.

As I watched her hurry across the yard, I noticed Duncan was still there. He was standing with his arm round Gemma and from the expression on her face she was close to tears. It was true then – they were in a relationship.

THIRTEEN

There was still no word of Fritz and the police were becoming almost a permanent fixture at Brydeshill. Though they didn't say as much we had the impression they thought the death of Jose and Fritz's disappearance were somehow linked. Everyone was questioned, even me, despite my protestations that Jose's death had occurred before my arrival.

'But you were here when Fritz Hofferman disappeared?' Constable Brevin seemed intent on putting me on the spot. The way he looked at me made my heart pound, made me feel guilty.

Half-way through it dawned on me why he was questioning me so closely. I suddenly remembered I'd met him before. Some time ago, certainly, when I was a guest speaker at the rebuilt Hydro Hotel out behind Port Bannatyne. Did he recognise me? If so, he didn't mention it and I sighed with relief when he said, 'That's all for now, thank you, Mrs Cameron. Please stay on the island meantime.' He hesitated as he turned to leave. 'Or if you do have to go off island, leave us details of where we can get in touch…quickly.'

Perhaps it was as well I'd now decided to stay on a little longer, though I didn't see how I could be of help. Once again I considered telling the police about seeing Fritz the night before he disappeared, but then decided not to. It could all have been quite innocent.

The atmosphere round the yard was tense once the police left with everyone ready to snap at the slightest thing. Even Gemma, normally placid, had taken to giving a sharp reply if asked to do anything extra, anything over and above her usual duties and Kath was fretting about every minor incident. Although Brydeshill was open again for lessons, few people had returned. Those with horses stabled there, like Tuesday, were regulars, but the children who came for riding lessons could be counted in single figures.

'You can't blame them,' I said to Deborah as we watched Gemma take a class in the riding area. A class that consisted of three children, where typically there would be at least eight.

'Why? The death has nothing to do with the riding establishment. It's not likely there's a killer roaming around.'

I didn't comment. Her loyalty to Kath was commendable, but I was sure if it was my choice I'd be extremely cautious about letting my child return.

'Besides,' Deborah said, 'There must be a good reason for Jose being found dead in the stable. Something the police haven't yet found out. Topper must have been spooked. He's usually such a placid horse.'

Somehow, now the dead man had a name, it made the task of finding out what had happened more urgent. Unless the truth about Jose's death was discovered soon, life could only become more difficult for Kath.

Just then, Kath came out of the farmhouse, slamming the door behind her before striding over to us and cutting short our discussion. This case was quite different from any I'd been involved in on previous occasions, but I was concerned about my daughter and knew she wouldn't leave Brydeshill while there was so much uncertainty. Now there was the complication of Fritz's disappearance.

‘The police have been on the phone again,’ Kath said. She looked agitated, wisps of hair escaping from the way she’d piled it up on top of her head. Her face was ashen, and she kept biting her lip. Over the past few days her cough had become worse.

‘Any news of Fritz?’

Kath shook her head, and more bits of hair escaped. ‘No, they seem to think we know something, that we’re hiding information from them.’ She gave a hollow laugh. ‘As if. If I knew where Fritz was, I’d go looking for him myself. We’re so short of helpers and it’s impossible to get extra staff right now. The vet students Duncan suggested won’t be available till next month. By which time we may not need them.’

I smiled sympathetically. ‘I guess no one wants to come and work here while there are still doubts about Jose.’

Kath looked puzzled. ‘I’m not talking about that. I don’t think that would put people off working here. But we can’t afford it. With so few people coming for riding lessons our income is way down.’ She jerked her head towards the stables. ‘And that’s Dusty’s owner just phoned to say she wants to move Dusty to one of the farms that can offer her livery at a better price.’

‘And this isn’t the only riding establishment on the island?’ Deborah had mentioned this briefly, but I was curious to hear what Kath would say.

Kath shook her head. ‘There is one other on the far side of the island. Tuesday has said she might move her horse there, or perhaps over to one near Colintraive. Not as convenient, but she probably feels it’s a lot safer.’

I snuck a glance at Deborah, but she was gazing intently at a couple of riders setting out on a hack.

Perhaps she couldn't think of anything to say that might comfort Kath.

'And if one goes…' Kath continued.

She didn't finish. She didn't have to. If the other horses in livery left, there would be no income and Brydeshill would have to close.

There was a shout from the farmhouse and Gemma came rushing over. 'That's the feed suppliers on the phone, Kath. They want to know when the last bill is going to be paid.'

Kath made a face. 'Tell them…' She stopped. 'No, I'll tell them myself.' She turned on her heel and strode quickly away.

Gemma looked at us and shrugged. 'It's not the only account that's overdue. I don't know what Kath is going to do.'

Without waiting for a comment, she sprinted off to catch up with Kath.

'Oh, this is impossible for them,' said Deborah, running her hands through her hair. 'And there's nothing I can suggest. It's not the kind of place that can run on a shoestring. Apart from the feed and the hay, there's the cost of regular shoeing. And that's before you factor in the loans on the place and all the other expenses.'

She sounded close to tears and I put my arm round her shoulder. 'I know you're fond of Kath, keen to help. But honestly, there's not a lot you can do. Except perhaps continue to work here.' I thought for a moment, then added, 'As I'll do.'

'I know this isn't where you'd rather be, but if you don't have to rush back to Glasgow, your help will be appreciated. Especially by me.' She clapped her hands, and then leaned forward to hug me. 'Oh, thanks, Mum. I knew I could rely on you.'

‘No matter what, I can’t extend my stay beyond the end of the month,’ I reminded her. I’d the feeling my protests about a time limit were falling on deaf ears.

A little niggle of worry beset me as I watched her go. Not about the murder. Who had killed Jose and why was a matter for the police, and they must by now have some idea about what had happened. I could take a step back, now they knew his identity.

Nowadays it’s hard to keep anything secret and the police would now be able to track down his family.

No, what was bothering me most was what Kath would do about allocating tasks, given there was so much work to cover. The chickens I could just about cope with, but I was worried I might be expected to take on a chore that wasn’t as easy as feeding the chickens. Looking after the llamas, for example.

FOURTEEN

Another day passed and Fritz was still missing. Kath wandered round as though in a daze and it was left to everyone else to pick up the slack. Fritz's disappearance had only added to her problems. Not that anyone found it easy. Rumours were plentiful. He'd gone into town, got drunk and was lying injured somewhere. He'd decided he was being overworked and left. He knew what had happened to the dead Spaniard and had fled before the police found out he was involved.

When examined logically, none of these seemed likely. And despite several other horses having been removed by their owners, it took Deborah, Gemma, and the stable hands all their time, working long hours, to keep the animals fed and clean.

The horses seemed to sense something was wrong: they were restless, edgy. Not that I went too near them, but as I passed the stable Topper had been reallocated, Gemma was there, trying hard to settle him, before bringing him out. But he was leading Gemma a merry dance, tossing his head, rolling his eyes so the whites showed – an alarming sight to someone like me who had little experience of horses.

Gemma didn't appear to be too worried though and she grinned as she saw me back away quickly.

'Don't worry, Alison, he's not as fierce as he looks. If he did kick Jose he must have been badly spooked.' She called to me over her shoulder as she walked him out, 'We'll be as pleased as the horses when it's time to let them into the summer fields. A couple of the horses that are out all year have been moved there already: Felix and Breeze. They are a lot less work than the stabled horses.'

I was prepared to take her word for it and hastened over to help Deborah with the feed for the llamas. 'I told Kath that I'd do this today,' she said. And, yes, ignoring, or trying to ignore, my worries I'd been roped into helping, but only helping. The way the leader of the pack eyed me up sent a shiver down my spine.

I contented myself with standing by the gate while she ventured into the field. For some reason the llamas had chosen to congregate at the far side, over where the field led into the small wood.

'Drat,' Deborah said crossly as she unlatched the gate, 'they would decide to move over there today of all days.'

I passed the buckets over to her once the gate was securely locked again. There was no way I was risking going in among the herd.

She seemed to have read my thoughts and she grinned as she set out across the field. 'Don't worry, I wasn't going to ask you to do this with me. I know how you feel about them.'

I nodded in reply, thinking how amazing it was that Deborah, whom I'd always thought of as a city girl, had appeared to take to country living with such ease.

As I leaned on the gate and watched her she strode confidently across to the first of the herd. But even the sight of the buckets of food failed to make an impression on these creatures. They stood stock-still, regarding her with haughty disdain, though one of the young ones made tentative steps towards her.

She rattled the buckets, and I could just about make out what she was saying. 'Come on, you silly creatures. This is food I'm bringing you.'

She rattled the buckets again, then as there was still no response, she started to scatter the feed around. This appeared to tempt one or two of them, but most of the others continued to stand quietly.

Having finished scattering the food, she came walking over to the gate, casting a look back at the llamas.

'I can't understand it,' she said, shaking her head. 'They're usually eager to get at the food, especially as it's a treat for them. In fact they're a greedy lot and you have to be careful to keep clear of them, so they don't knock you over in the rush.'

I could offer no explanation of this odd behaviour, except to say, 'Perhaps they're not hungry? The grass is certainly growing well. Maybe that's what they prefer?'

'No, something's not right. I'm going to have to speak to Kath. There's a lot of money invested in that herd and with all the troubles she's been having lately…'

She didn't finish the sentence. She didn't have to. I knew exactly what she meant. If sickness had broken out among the llamas, that would be another terrible blow, given the cost of vets' fees.

'I'll come with you,' I said. 'A bit of moral support.'

Deborah acknowledged my offer with a smile, and we set off in silence to the farmhouse, hoping Kath would be there. And on her own. It was important not to say anything in front of the others, not until we'd discovered what the problem might be. More rumours were the last thing needed.

Kath was in the farmhouse, sitting alone at the big table in the kitchen. Spread out in front of her was what looked like a ledger and piles of receipts.

She looked up as we came in and pushed the paperwork to one side. 'Glad to see you,' she said. 'I need a break from all this nonsense. Why the government thinks we want to spend all our time filling in forms I've no idea.'

She smiled. 'Sorry about the rant. Fritz does these. It's part of his job as manager. I'm not sure I'll manage. I can't make head nor tail of them. He clearly had his own system.' She stood up and went over to the kettle. 'Fancy a cuppa?'

Deborah shot a glance at me as Kath turned away to fill the kettle. I shook my head. Best to wait.

Kath stretched up into one of the cupboards. 'I think we may still have a biscuit or two somewhere. Ah, yes, here we are.' She took down a large, battered tin which looked as if it had been there for some time and rattled it. Not a good idea for the biscuits I thought but said nothing.

Deborah and I exchanged another look as Kath said, 'All well with the llamas, Deborah? I'm grateful you took them on today. I've no idea how I'm going to deal with all this paperwork.'

'That's what we wanted to tell you,' Deborah said, all in a rush. 'When I went to feed them, they seemed to be strangely unsettled. I can't really explain it, but they were in the far corner by the wood, seemingly uninterested in the food.'

Kath put her cup down with a bang, causing little drops to spill onto the table. She wiped them away with her hand, saying, 'That is odd. They usually prefer to keep to this side of the field and I've never known them be other than greedy with their food.'

She stood up, sighing, 'I suppose I'd better go and look. Let's hope there's not a problem with the herd, though it's unlikely they would all be sick at the same time.'

'I'll come with you,' said Deborah, rising to her feet.

'No, no, sit where you are and finish your tea. You've earned it. To tell the truth I'm not sure why I bought those llamas. Fritz persuaded me they'd be a good investment, but I've never really taken to them to be honest.'

As she left, Deborah turned to me. 'I know she said she'd be fine, but if there is a problem, she'll need help.'

I nodded in agreement. 'I'll come too – though I'm only going as far as the gate.'

I gulped down the last of my tea and hurried after her, trying to keep up.

Kath was already half-way across the field, and we stopped at the gate to watch her as she reached the edge of the field and disappeared into the trees.

'What's she doing?' I said.

'Probably one of the young llamas has strayed away from the herd and into the wood. They can be really silly sometimes.' Deborah looked upset. 'They cost a lot of money, you know. Fritz hasn't been a help to her. Far from it. He's supposed to be the manager, but I'm not sure he's able to manage anything. Not from what I've seen.'

I hadn't been at Brydeshill long enough to form a firm opinion of Fritz, or any of them for that matter, but I thought about what Kath had said about the accounts. Was Fritz up to no good – was there a reason he'd left? If he'd been stealing from the business that was one possible explanation.

'I can't see Kath. Where has she gone?' Deborah stood up on the second bar of the gate, shading her eyes, straining to see. 'I'll go and find out what's happening.'

'Kath said to wait,' I reminded her, but it was too late. Deborah had jumped down from the gate and was busy unlocking it.

There was no point in trying to stop her. And she was right. Kath had been taking an unusually long time and if one of the young llamas was in trouble, she would need help. Even the young ones were strong.

'I'll wait here,' I said. 'If there's a problem, signal across and I'll go to find Gemma.'

But she was already out of earshot, almost running across to where the rest of the pack now grazed contentedly and even from this distance I could see that most of the food Deborah had left earlier had been eaten. This was most likely a great fuss about nothing.

But my feeling of relief was short-lived. There was a loud cry and Kath came hurrying out of the woods, stumbling towards Deborah who managed to catch her as she was about to fall. What on earth was going on?

Plucking up my courage I unlatched the gate and walked slowly towards them, keeping a wary eye out for any llamas that might try to attack me, but they herd kept their distance, intent on gobbling up any stray morsels of feed.

Deborah and Kath by now had reached me, Deborah supporting Kath with difficulty.

Before I could ask what was going on, Deborah looked up at me, wild-eyed. 'Mum, you'll have to phone the police.'

'What?' It was most unlikely the police would be interested in the llamas even if one was in difficulties.

‘Is it the llamas?’

Deborah shook her head. ‘No, no, it’s not that. Though it is why they were behaving so oddly.’

Kath cut in, taking deep breaths to steady herself. ‘It’s Fritz. He’s lying dead in the wood.’

‘Oh, good heavens. Did he have some kind of accident? Or did the llamas attack him.’

Deborah spoke. ‘No, it doesn’t look as if it’s been an accident. And certainly not the llamas.’

This was terrible news indeed. Whatever would happen next?

FIFTEEN

The police arrived quickly, siren blaring, disturbing the quietness as the patrol car roared up the hill from Rothesay. A second death on the premises was a concern much greater than the first, even if this also turned out to be an accident. What's more, it threw up all kinds of doubts about the death of Jose. I'd the impression Constable Brevin had some difficulty in believing that death had been no more than an accident in the confined space of the stable and this latest episode confirmed his suspicions.

Kath tried to reassure him when he muttered, 'Strange for there to be two deaths here in such a short time.'

'The first was an accident, of that I'm sure. Horses are powerful creatures and a kick from one of them could indeed be fatal.' Perhaps she thought if she repeated this often enough the police would believe her. On the other hand she ignored the unspoken question about why Jose had been at Brydeshill in the first place.

But this, this death, was of a different order altogether.

Fritz was lying on his back underneath one of the large oak trees and I tried not to look at his face. He lay almost securely snug in the tangle of roots that sat above ground, but as the primary examination started and he was turned over on to his front, the gash on his head seemed to show he'd been hit from behind with some force.

The police ordered us to stay back as they unrolled

the blue and white tape and secured it round several of the trees, closing off the scene completely.

'Better you don't come any nearer,' Constable Brevin said firmly. 'With the rain there's been lately we don't want any evidence trampled underfoot.'

It appeared as if Kath was determined to stand her ground as she remained perfectly still, staring at the body, until a stern command from the constable seemed to rouse her from her daze.

I shrank back immediately: I was there only because Kath had wanted someone to accompany her as she led the police over to where she'd found Fritz. I was reluctant, especially as I'd have to pass the llamas, but Deborah refused as soon as she was asked, shaking her head. 'I couldn't possibly,' she said in a whisper. 'It's too awful.'

So that was it. I had to brave the llamas, though I kept to the far side of Kath and of the police officers and was only too happy to obey the command to "move away" when asked.

'What do you think happened? Do you think it was an accident? That he fell and hit his head?' There was a note of hope in Kath's voice.

I'm no expert, but over the years I have seen enough dead people to think it likely Fritz's injuries had been no accident.

On the other hand, I didn't want to alarm Kath, so I made a non-committal answer. 'Mmm…anything is possible. We should know more when the police have finished a preliminary inspection.'

This seemed to satisfy her for the moment, and we walked back to the gate in silence.

'What on earth…' Deborah started to say, but I put my finger to my lips and nodded towards Kath.

Deborah made a face to acknowledge my silent

request for her to say no more and she followed Kath and me back to the farmhouse.

Kath slumped down in one of the easy chairs and put her head in her hands. ‘This is dreadful. What am I going to do now?’

‘Without Fritz?’ I said.

‘Yes, it will be difficult. There is so much work to do.’ She raised her head, a blank look crossing her face. ‘I mean, who will want to come here to ride now? It was bad enough with the first death but now…’

We sat around in the kitchen as Deborah made tea…and then more tea. From time to time I started an attempt at conversation, but eventually lapsed into silence. There was only one possible topic of conversation, but one we wanted to avoid.

A knock at the door startled us as the police came into the room. There were two of them, the Constable who had spoken to us in the woods and an older woman who introduced herself as Detective Inspector Lecky.

They sat down on the kitchen chairs opposite us and Constable Brevin pulled out his notebook and began to write, though we hadn’t said a word. He appeared to be suffering from a cold, as he kept sniffing and I was sorely tempted to lean over and offer him a tissue, then thought the better of it, though it continued to annoy me.

‘And when was the last time any of you saw…’ she glanced down at Constable Brevin’s notes, ‘…Fritz Hofferman?’

I looked over at Kath, but her gaze was rigidly fixed on the cup she clutched tightly in both hands.

Someone had to start so I said, ‘I last saw him two nights ago about eight o’clock when I went to check on the chickens, make sure they were securely locked up.'

'And what was he doing then?'

'Doing?'

'Yes, while you were locking up the chickens.' D I Lecky wrinkled her nose as she spoke. Perhaps she thought I looked unlikely to be the kind of person to be trusted with chickens.

'I don't work here,' I began, 'I'm here to …' but she interrupted impatiently, 'Yes, yes, but what was Fritz doing when you saw him.'

'He was helping bring in the horses,' I said.

'And you didn't see him after that?'

I hesitated. Should I tell her what happened? Or should I fudge the issue? That was the last time I saw him, but of course I did hear him after that. But she hadn't asked me that question.

She noticed my hesitation. 'Remember this is a suspicious death,' she said sternly. 'We need all the information if we are to find out what happened.'

I couldn't hold back. 'That was the last time I saw him,' I said, 'but I did hear him after that.

She raised her eyebrows. 'What happened then?'

I could put it off no longer and I recounted at some length the story of being unable to sleep and coming downstairs to make a hot drink, as much to give me time to think what I should say.

If DI Lecky was impatient at the time I was taking to get to the point, she didn't show it.

'He was in the yard,' I heard myself say.

'What was he doing there in the middle of the night?'

I shrugged. 'I don't know. He was going towards the arena, was in the shadows talking to someone I couldn't see, and I only recognised Fritz's voice. He has…had… a rather guttural accent.' I didn't mention the other man might have been Duncan. I was becoming less and less certain about that.

DI Lecky looked displeased with my answer, but instead of questioning me further, she turned her attention to Deborah.

'I last saw him earlier that morning at breakfast,' she said. 'I was busy for the rest of the day and our paths didn't cross.' She stopped. 'I might have seen him later, but I honestly can't remember.'

Kath seemed to be occupied peering into her cup as though surprised to find it empty.

'And you, Kath?'

For a moment it appeared as if Kath wasn't going to reply, but eventually she lifted her head, saying, 'I saw him mid-morning. He was helping Gemma in the stables, helping her supervise the volunteers who were mucking out. Then he came in at lunchtime. I don't remember if I saw him after that – I was busy all day.'

'And did you speak to him?'

'Oh, yes.' Kath's laugh was bitter. 'Indeed I did. But he didn't want to know, walked off, ignoring me.'

'So you had a quarrel then?' DI Lecky said.

Kath sighed. 'You could say that. You see, I was sure that lately he was up to something. And whatever it was, there was something not quite right.'

'What exactly do you mean?' DI Lecky frowned and I thought about those account books. Was Kath suspicious that Fritz might be defrauding her?

Kath tried to backtrack, her tone of voice showing she regretted her last words. 'Oh, nothing, I'm upset, that's all. When he disappeared I didn't worry at first, though I thought it strange he hadn't told me if he was going off the premises.' Then she added, almost wistfully, 'He was good with the horses, though. He's a great loss.'

Constable Brevin gave her a look which suggested he found her reply odd, then shook his head, snapping his notebook closed as the DI said, 'We can discuss this in greater detail later. If you could come down to the police station tomorrow morning and make a full statement.'

This was an order, not a request, but Kath didn't reply but stood with her head bowed, biting her lip.

Here was another question. Had Kath been honest about the last time she'd seen Fritz? But why would she lie?

SIXTEEN

Frustrated that I was getting nowhere – either with trying to find out more about the dead Spaniard or with my article, I considered telling Kath I couldn't think of any way I could now help. It was all very well Kath wanting me to find answers, but the police had made progress and we'd most likely hear the full story from them soon. What's more, I'd this impression she wasn't being entirely honest with me.

Yes, I felt sorry for Kath and the problems she was having at Brydeshill, but right now there was nothing I could do, no advice I could give. Perhaps I needed a break.

I thought about Tara. I'd take up her offer of visiting her again and this time I would enlist her help. It would be good to talk things over with someone with a different perspective, make me feel I hadn't entirely given up the search for answers.

Mind made up, I gave her a call.

'Of course, Alison, delighted to see you any time. I'm rather isolated here. It's fine most of the time, but it's always good to see you.'

'Great. I've to take a few photos for the article I'm working on and then I can come over.'

'Come about twelve for lunch,' she said and rang off.

Hoping I wouldn't have to enter into a long explanation about where I was going, I went in search of Kath. 'She's busy in the arena,' Gemma said when I asked. 'Even with so few people coming to ride, the horses still have to be exercised.'

Deborah was also there, busy putting Breeze through her paces but she kept her eyes on the horse as I whispered to her, having come up with what I thought was a good reason, 'Won't be long. As I'm going to be on the island for a little longer, I'm off to take photos for my article and I thought I might buy some postcards to send to friends.'

Just then Breeze decided to start pawing the sand and Deborah concentrated on calming her. 'She's fine,' she said as she saw the look of alarm on my face. 'It's just that she can be impatient if she's not exercised enough.'

As I was about to leave, Duncan came in. He stopped at the entrance and looked all around.

'There's Duncan,' I said. 'I hope none of the other horses has a problem.'

Deborah glanced over, then frowned. 'Yes, he was here in the arena when I brought Breeze in. He said he was looking for Gemma. I'd better see if I can help.'

As she shouted over to him, I left. I'd wasted enough time.

It was a relief to be away from Brydeshill for a while. I drove slowly down the steep winding road, enjoying another beautiful day. The verges bright with the pinkish purple of louse wort and yellow marsh marigolds and in the ditches where the winter rains had left the ground soggy, bog myrtle flourished. Spring would soon be over, and during the long summer days Bute would be at its best, welcoming tourists. I fervently hoped the mystery of the deaths at the stables would be solved much sooner than that.

Rothesay was busy, Montague Street thronged with shoppers. One of the best things about Bute is that no one seems to be in a hurry – a welcome change from the hustle and bustle of the streets of Glasgow.

At the Electric Bakery I purchased a cake to take over to Tara's, waiting patiently as the young lad in front of me made the momentous decision about whether to purchase an Empire biscuit or an apple slice.

The photos took much longer than expected. Many of the locations had changed greatly since the days of Bute as a prime holiday destination, but the museum would have older photos which would let me do a 'Then and Now' section. I glanced at my watch as I hurried back to the car. It was almost half past eleven but having given the excuse of purchasing postcards, I had to stop at the Discovery Centre to buy a few. I selected several at random from the display rack, hoping the couple in front of me wouldn't take too long. They appeared to be deciding on accommodation and as the minutes ticked away I thought I might have to abandon my proposed purchases. As I waited I thought about the history of this building, wondering if I might be able to say something about it in my article.

Time was passing but fortunately as I was about to sneak the postcards back on to the rack another assistant arrived, and I moved forward to complete my purchase. Perhaps she would know about the history.

'When was the Discovery Centre built?' I asked.

'Mmm, sometime in the 1920s, I think,' she said.

'Ah, too late for me,' and then had to explain my interest as she looked at me quizzically.

'There was a bandstand on the site much earlier,' she said. 'You could check that out. It was called the Winter Gardens when this building was constructed, and many famous entertainers performed here over the years.'

'It's certainly amazing,' I said, gazing around at the circular hall of cast iron with a wide, curving expanse of windows overlooking the bay.

'And look up at the domed roof with its exposed curving iron beams. It's beautifully made.'

I sighed. While it was good that the building had been successfully rescued after years of dereliction to act as the focus for Rothesay's improved waterfront it was too late for the year range of my article. Though I could mention the bandstand which originally stood on the site.

Aware the queue behind me was growing, I paid for my postcards and went to pick up my car for the drive to Tara's house.

But as I was about to unlock the car door, I heard a voice beside me.

'Hello, Alison. We meet again.'

I turned around to see Tyler grinning at me. He was holding a large bouquet of flowers, almost obscuring his face. 'For my mum's birthday, in case you're wondering.'

'Good to see you, Tyler.' I didn't want to appear rude, but I didn't have time to linger.

But Tyler was clearly in the mood for a chat. 'How are things up at Brydeshill?'

I hesitated, uncertain about how much he knew, if he'd heard about Fritz.

As though reading my mind, he added, 'I heard there's been another death. They must be very careless up there.' He chuckled, then stopped suddenly and made a face. Putting his hand to his mouth he said, 'Sorry, that wasn't called for.'

'What have you heard?' I asked, though I shouldn't

have been surprised how quickly news travels on the island.

He shrugged. 'Only that Fritz was found dead in the wood.'

'How did you hear?'

'Edwin Michel told me.'

'Edwin Michel? How did he find out?'

'I suppose Gemma told him.'

This wasn't making much sense. 'Why would Gemma do that.'

'Oh, they still keep in touch you know.'

'No, I don't know.'

'Edwin is Gemma's ex-husband. It was a perfectly amicable divorce – at least on Gemma's part. I'm not sure how happy Edwin was about it.'

How did Edwin hear I wondered, then said, 'Ah, Edwin is great friends with Duncan Bradstone, the vet.'

'What made you think that?' Tyler looked puzzled.

'I'm sure you told me they were often together, drinking in the Black Bull.'

'No, no,' Tyler shook his head. You've got it wrong. I was talking about Duncan and Fritz.'

When I thought about it, that made more sense given Kath's comment. 'It's exceedingly difficult for Kath…and the others,' was all I was prepared to say. This was a good moment to make my departure. 'Sorry to rush away, Tyler, but I'm going over to see a friend and I can't stay too long. I have to get back to feed the chickens.' I laughed, trying to make a joke of it, but Tyler didn't see it that way. 'I understand, Alison. Animals are a great responsibility. I had a dog when I was much younger, but it's such a lot of work and when they die – awful.'

I didn't think chickens somehow came into the

same category as a family pet, but I'd no intention of entering into a discussion about it.

'And I'm sure you want to get over to your mum's with those lovely flowers.'

Tyler seemed to recollect he was on an errand. 'Gosh, yes, she'll be expecting me. Will have the kettle on. That Fritz was well-known of course here on the island.' He winked.

With a wave and a smile, he hurried off and I stood staring after him, wondering what he meant by his last remark, but pleased I'd successfully deflected his questions about the deaths at the yard. Gossip and speculation would be rife on the island and I didn't want to add to it.

But Tyler was right. Although I didn't think "careless" was the correct word to describe what was going on, it was certainly very strange.

SEVENTEEN

Tara welcomed me with a broad smile. 'Oh, how kind to bring a cake for dessert, Alison. I usually do a batch bake at the weekend, but somehow last weekend was so chaotic, I didn't seem to find the time.'

'I'm not surprised. You seem to be busy.' I'd almost tripped over the pile of boxes marked 'Charity Shop' in the hallway and a scatter of children's toys made the living room equally hazardous.

'Yes,' she said, sighing and pushing back a strand of hair that had escaped from the ponytail she'd adopted, which made her look much younger.

After lunch we settled in Tara's living room with coffee and a generous slice of cake.

'Excuse the mess,' she said, deftly tossing some of the toys into a box in the corner. She slumped down on the chair opposite me. 'I seem to be so tired these days.'

'Understandable,' I said, 'with two young children to look after. And I see you're also attempting to do some clearing.'

'I suppose so,' she said, taking a gulp of coffee then making a face as she realised it was too hot.

Under cover of eating cake, I wondered how best to bring up the subject of Brydeshill and the events there without revealing Kath had asked me to help.

I needn't have worried. Tara was as keen as everyone else on the island to discuss what had happened.

'I heard about that second death… Fritz. Someone

said this one wasn't like the first. It wasn't an accident.'

Ah, so the first death was still thought to be accidental. That was interesting. 'No,' I said slowly, 'the police seem to think this one is suspicious.'

She hesitated before saying, 'I probably shouldn't tell you this, but I'd heard the police have been watching Fritz Hofferman for some time now.'

'Really?' Of what possible interest could Fritz be. I waited for her to continue.

'There's something odd about Brydeshill. Don't you think?' She nibbled at a piece of cake thoughtfully, looking at me, waiting for an answer.

'I'm sure that's no more than rumour, Tara. Certainly Brydeshill is having money troubles, but that's all.'

What did Tara know? I was intrigued by what she might be able tell me, but I'd have to be careful what I said.

But then she turned away. 'You're probably right. No more than island gossip. More coffee?'

While I wanted to hear more, I couldn't ask her directly and so I shook my head saying, 'No, thanks. I should be getting back. The chickens will be waiting.' If I'd not exactly grown fond of the chickens, I did feel some responsibility for them. In fact I'd given one or two of them names, though I kept that to myself.

As I left, she said, 'Do come back and visit me. We've still so much to talk about. Why don't we arrange the end of the week? If that suits you?'

Was there a promise in her words? Was she trying to tell me that she'd more to tell me, but not just yet? Whatever her reason, I said, 'Oh, I'd be delighted to do that, Tara. Although I'm managing fine with the chickens, I don't like to get too close to some of the horses, especially the large ones.'

Tara laughed. 'Oh, I'm sure you'll be okay, Alison. I rode for a while, even had my own horse, but when I had the children I didn't have time.'

I nodded in understanding. I realised now how much work went into looking after a horse.

As I left her standing in the doorway, I looked back to wave on the way to my car. I'd a strong suspicion she knew more than she was willing to reveal at this point. What was the story about the police and their interest in Fritz? That didn't ring true somehow. Surely it was no more than a guess. I should have told her the truth – that Kath had asked me to help.

With plenty of food for thought, I admit I wasn't concentrating on driving and almost without realising it, I found myself back in Rothesay.

The clock on the ferry terminal building showed I'd a spare half hour before I had to be back at Brydeshill. It was a lovely day and a walk along the prom as far as the Pavilion would give me a chance to think over what I knew so far.

I parked in Stuart Street opposite Rothesay Castle and began to walk down to Montague Street towards the prom. I hadn't gone far when I heard a voice call out, 'Hi, Alison,' and the sound of running footsteps as Duncan Bradstone caught up with me.

'Escaping the chickens?' he grinned.

'Not quite,' I said. 'And before you ask, I'm getting on fine with them.'

'Where are you going?' he said, falling into step beside me.

I shrugged. 'Just getting a breath of fresh air before I go back up to Brydeshill. It's such a beautiful day. Every time I come to Bute, intent on having a few days walking, I become caught up and have to change my plans.'

'Any word yet about that business with Fritz?'

'Nothing.' I shook my head.

'And nothing about the man found in the stables.'

'No, it's upsetting for everyone.'

Duncan nodded. 'Yes, I've asked Gemma to let me know if there's any news.'

'We all want to have this cleared up soon,' I said, then to change the subject, 'You're not an islander?'

Duncan said, 'I'm from Manchester originally and when I saw this post advertised I thought it would be a great way to make a lifestyle change. A relaxed pace of life and time to pursue my hobby of sailing.'

More for something to say, I commented. 'And the pace of life on the island is surely much slower than in Manchester.'

'Yes and no.' He gazed out over the water. 'There are so few vets on the island that we're really busy, especially at certain times of the year.'

'Ah.' That I could understand. 'So you have a boat.'

'Oh, yes, it's berthed out at the marina at Port Bannatyne. I sail her as often as I can.' For a moment he looked gloomy, then brightened up considerably as he added, 'But next weekend I've a locum booked. And I'll be off sailing up the Kyles. I like to get out on my boat as often as I can.'

'You've seen a fair bit of Scotland?'

'Yes, indeed. I've been to lots of places on the west coast I'd never have considered. Like Colonsay and…' He stopped. 'I'd better get back. I've a surgery in fifteen minutes and I'll need a cup of strong coffee before I start. Mrs Perty is coming back with her old cat and it's a bit of a struggle.'

'With Mrs Perty?' I said in astonishment, imagining

Duncan wrestling with one of his clients.

He roared with laughter and when he stopped he said, 'Oh, good gracious no. It's her cat Twinkle. He terrorises Mrs Perty and he's a nightmare in the surgery. He's an elderly cat the visits are becoming more frequent. And of all names Twinkle is the most unsuitable one she could have chosen.'

I sighed. 'It must be lovely to escape on your boat…away from everything.'

'Not as often as I'd like to. Still, mustn't complain.'

With a wave he loped off.

I stood for a minute looking after him. The island was a big enough change from Glasgow, let alone a city like Manchester. So many people came here to Bute on holiday and ended up staying. I'd often been tempted myself.

I quickened my pace towards the Pavilion, then crossed back to the prom to head for my car.

But suddenly I stopped, almost bumping into a young mother pushing a buggy along in the sunshine.

'Oops, sorry,' I said, and she smiled as she walked on towards the playpark. The child in the buggy was fast asleep.

I turned to look after Duncan, now a speck in the distance. There was something Fritz had said about Duncan. Something which scarcely registered at the time and now I couldn't recall what it was.

Ah, well, it would come back to me sooner or later. It probably wasn't anything important. My thoughts were in such a muddle right now, it wasn't surprising I couldn't recall the exact words.

In the meantime duty called.

EIGHTEEN

The police had been busy. This time it appeared they didn't want to leave anything to chance. While earlier inquiries suggested the incident in the stables had been an accident, the death of Fritz was most certainly murder. And that threw a whole new light on what had happened to Jose, encouraging the police to review the evidence.

It was Deborah who told me as she ran over as soon as I came out of my car. 'The police think the deaths of Jose and Fritz may be connected in some way,' she said, falling into step beside me.

'What makes them think that?'

She sighed. 'It's something Kath said. And when you think about it, there must have been some reason for Jose to come up here.'

'Such as…?'

She gave me a tight smile. 'Dunno. Maybe Fritz knew him, even though he denied it.'

This appeared a tenuous connection, no more than speculation so my reply was, 'Until there's some solid evidence, I don't think we should play guessing games.'

Deborah raised her eyebrows and sticking her hands in her pockets said, 'Guess you're right. I'd better go and sort out the work for the stable hands.' And with that she darted away across the yard, leaving me gazing after her. Despite what I'd said, was there a possibility she was right. That Fritz and Jose knew each other, and Jose had come to the stables to meet up with Fritz?

I shuddered. There was no time to dwell on this, but suddenly one of the constables appeared from the direction of the stables.

Fritz had had accommodation in the rooms built over the stables. Given this had once been the family home of the Michels in the days when horses were a necessity rather than a luxury, this had been where the junior groomsmen would have slept.

I hadn't been in these rooms, but I guessed they would have been made more comfortable in recent years, though who knew. There was little evidence money had been spent on renovations elsewhere.

The police presence in the yard and in the farmhouse had an unsettling effect on everyone…and on the animals. The DI remained tight-lipped about what they hoped to find, merely muttering whenever Kath tried to press for an update.

Gemma was in the farmhouse kitchen with Kath when I came in and held up her cup as she saw me. 'Tea?' she said.

I shook my head. I'd lost track of the number of cups of tea I'd brewed…and drunk.

'I don't know what they think might be of help in Fritz's rooms,' Kath grumbled. 'This is going to cause more bother. That's another livery gone.' She waved a piece of paper at me. 'Didn't have the courtesy to phone – just sent this curt letter.'

What could I say? The police were only trying to do their job and given the circumstances we might have to put up with their presence for some time yet.

Gemma was more direct. 'You should send an email to everyone, tell them not to panic. That this was something unlikely to happen again.'

Kath gave a hollow laugh. 'Do you think that would calm them? One death is bad enough – and now I'm not sure if that young man's death **was** an accident. If there's a killer on the loose who knows who'll be next?'

'Come on, Kath. You know that's not going to be the case, not with the police everywhere.'

Kath sniffed. 'You're sure of that, Gemma? '

'You can ask the police to leave someone on guard. Surely that would be a deterrent,' I said.'

Kath shook her head. 'That's not the problem. It's not only who killed Fritz…and possibly Jose. It's why would the young man be here? And why in that stable? Is there any significance in the one he chose?'

Neither Gemma nor I had an answer to these questions, but we were saved from further discussion as the door was flung open and Deborah came rushing in.

'Are the police still here? Is there any news?' She sounded out of breath, as though she'd been running.

'No, and there's not likely to be unless there's new evidence. The police aren't going to speculate with us, are they?' Kath said sharply.

Deborah looked crestfallen at this put down. 'No, I suppose not,' she said. 'But people are asking…'

'Who's asking?' Kath cut in. 'The best plan is to say nothing. Let's not fuel more gossip. There's enough of that around at the moment.'

Deborah turned on her heel and left without another word.

'You were a bit hard on her,' Gemma said in a low voice.

'Not in the least.' Kath sounded angry. 'You know how quickly rumour spreads. Before you know it all of Bute will have an opinion about what is going on, who the murderer might be, if they don't already.' She slumped down in her chair, weeping quietly.

Gemma went over and put an arm around Kath's shoulders. 'It will all work out. Just give it time. This is a great establishment and once all this is over, I'm sure you'll thrive again.'

Kath sniffed and raised her head, swallowing hard. 'I hope you're right, Gemma, but I'm not so sure.'

I looked on, feeling sorry for them, but there was nothing I could say that wouldn't sound banal. Despite Gemma's words of comfort, I didn't think it was possible life would return to normal any time soon. And what would Kath do then. If she decided to sell, who would want to buy?

And as we sat there in silence, I realised I'd been no help at all. Yes, none of this was Kath's fault. But she was right. The question was who had killed Fritz…and possibly Jose. And the other question which might well explain the deaths was…why?

NINETEEN

A loud bang awakened me from a nightmare filled with images of Fritz lying dead in the wood.

I lay still for a minute but there was no further noise, and I began to think it had been part of my dream.

It was difficult not to be affected by the feelings of gloom everywhere. It might have been a comfort if my article had been progressing well but my plans to write the first draft had sadly fallen by the wayside. I couldn't focus on the frivolities of Victorian seaside holidays when two suspicious deaths were as yet unsolved.

Sleep was now impossible. No matter how I tossed and turned, reshaped the pillows, I was still wide awake. I switched on the bedside light in the hope an hour of reading my book would distract me from disturbing thoughts and make me feel sleepy.

It didn't. Several chapters later I was wider awake than ever if that was possible. There was nothing else for it. I'd have to go down to the kitchen and make a milky drink. This was becoming a habit.

I put on my dressing gown, shivering in the cold morning air and crept downstairs. The only sound was the hum of the ancient fridge in the scullery and I remembered the kitchen didn't boast anything as modern as a microwave. I wasn't confident about fiddling with the controls of the range cooker. Judging from what I'd seen it had a mind of its own. A cup of tea would have to do.

Through the kitchen window I could see the first

light of dawn beginning to streak the sky with the promise of a sunny day and as I stood at the sink filling the kettle, I could hear the horses were already restless, anxious to be out of the confines of the stables.

I made tea and took it over to stand at the window, watching the sun creep up over the yard in a sky streaked with pink and purple, but as I was about to turn away a movement outside caught my eye. Something had disturbed the animals. Or rather someone.

I pulled the kitchen window curtain over a little more, to have a better view. Who was out in the yard this early in the morning? It wasn't likely to be one of the stable hands, the chickens were secure in their shelter and Kath always checked the llamas before finishing for the night.

As I continued to watch, the figure came out of the arena. Whoever it was, he or she bore no resemblance to anyone I recognised.

I felt angry at Kath. She'd refused to have a policeman posted at Brydeshill with a curt, 'We can manage fine, thank you. We're perfectly capable of looking after ourselves.' Even though it was clear this wasn't the case.

I moved back as the figure whirled around. From the bulky appearance it was likely to be a man, but it was difficult to be certain as he was dressed all in black with the hood of his parka pulled well down. If only he would look in my direction.

I stood for a minute, wondering what to do. Should I call Kath? Or phone the police?

But while I stood there dithering about making a decision the intruder disappeared and a few moments later I heard what sounded like the distant roar of a motorbike.

I turned quickly, too quickly, not seeing the black and white cat who'd decided to slink down from the cosy spot on the shelf beside the range cooker in the hope I might be a source of food. Years of having a cat should have taught me to be wary but all I could think about was the intruder. With an almighty thud, I tripped over the cat and landed full-length on the floor, spilling what was left of my tea.

I lay there for a minute, not daring to move, but there was no sound from elsewhere in the house. Everyone would still be asleep. Very gingerly I raised myself on one elbow and then knelt up with the aid of one of the kitchen chairs. With some difficulty I got to my feet, and much to my relief, no bones seemed to have been broken. But when I tried to walk, there was a shooting pain in my right foot, and I realised I must have twisted my ankle.

Hobbling over slowly I sat down on the easy chair in the corner to examine the damage more closely. My ankle was beginning to swell up at an alarming rate. Several minutes of poking and prodding convinced me my first thought had been correct. It wasn't broken, only sprained.

But my relief was short-lived. What should I do now? The kitchen clock said five thirty. Before long Kath would be coming downstairs. There was no possibility of making my way up the narrow stairs to my attic bedroom.

I thought about calling Deborah, then remembered my phone was lying beside the bed in my room. So that wasn't an option. There was no way of alerting anyone to my plight.

I wriggled back, trying to make myself as comfortable as possible after reaching over to drag one of the kitchen chairs into a position where I could lift my foot onto it.

Meanwhile the cat who'd been the cause of my accident had aloofly decided there would be no food forthcoming and had gone back up onto the shelf beside the range cooker, yawning and glaring at me in disappointment before dozing off to sleep once more. He didn't appear to be the least bit sorry for causing me this injury. But that's cats for you.

Before Simon and I started travelling we had our own cat, Motley, but the way he had settled in with our neighbour made me realise that where cats are concerned their only loyalty is food.

I stifled a feeling of self-pity. I hadn't even managed to finish my cup of tea before the accident, I'd no more idea who the intruder might have been, if indeed it had been an intruder and now I'd injured my ankle.

A quick look around the kitchen for something to help pass the time was futile. There wasn't as much as a book or a magazine to keep me company till one of the others made an appearance.

The pain was easing off a little as long as I didn't try to put any weight on it. This I discovered as I made a couple of attempts to stand up. I'd have to wait for the doctor's opinion, but if I'd sprained my ankle it would take some time to heal.

My immediate thought was, who's going to feed the chickens? Which showed how responsible I'd become for them. With Kath so short of staff this injury of mine was going to cause her more problems.

And to think my original plan had been to spend no more than two weeks on Bute. No matter what my intention, there was no way I'd be able to leave the island – or Brydeshill – any time soon. What a mess.

But as I sat there, with time to think about who might have been in the livery yard and why, it struck me.

If it was a stranger, why hadn’t the dogs barked?

TWENTY

I must have dozed off at some point because I was jerked back into wakefulness by the back door to the kitchen slamming as Gemma came striding into the room.

She stopped suddenly when she saw me. 'Alison, what are you doing up so early?'

I struggled in the chair, trying to find an easier position, but that only made my ankle more painful.

'I tripped over the cat,' I said, feeling decidedly sorry for myself and stifling a tear. 'And I think I've injured my ankle. I can't put any weight on it. It hurts when I try to stand,' and I said, gesturing to the floor, 'and watch your feet. I spilled my cup of tea.'

'Oh, you poor thing. Let me see.' Gemma said, taking a cloth from the draining board to wipe up the puddle of liquid before coming over to me.

Clasping my hands together, I said with a tight smile, 'Do you think that's a good idea?'

This provoked a grin. 'Don't worry, I'm not going to do anything. But I have updated my First Aid qualification recently and might be able to find out how bad it is.'

She knelt down beside me and I bit my lip as she gently prodded my ankle before standing up to say, 'Mmm. It's certainly very swollen. I think we should ask the doctor to have a look at it. I'll give him a call as soon as the surgery opens.'

She made no further comment as she went over to the range and lifted the kettle except to say, 'I guess you could do with another cup of tea since you didn't manage to finish the first one?'

'That's what caused the problem,' I said. 'I was wakened by a loud noise and couldn't get back to sleep. I decided a hot drink would help.' Not taking time to think about it, I added, 'And I was sure there was someone lurking in the yard again.'

Gemma didn't turn round. 'Nonsense, Alison. It must have been one of the stable hands.'

She busied herself sorting out the mugs and fetching milk from the refrigerator in the scullery as we waited for the water to boil. Kath appeared from the main part of the house, yawning and pulling her dressing gown round her. Before she could ask, Gemma nodded towards me. 'Alison tripped over one of the cats and she's injured her ankle.'

Kath shook her head. 'Those cats. They're both rescue cats, and you'd think they'd be grateful. But no, they're always causing trouble. And they're hopeless as mousers.' This was said in an affectionate tone which made me suspect she rather indulged them.

And indeed by now both cats were purring round Kath, but she shooed them away.

Kath gazed at my swollen ankle while Gemma helped me lift it onto a more suitable kitchen chair, with a cushion underneath as support. 'I'll check what time the surgery opens,' Kath said as she left the kitchen.

I tried again to talk to Gemma about the suspected prowler. 'I don't want to alarm Kath, but there was someone in the yard. I'm sure it wasn't one of the stable hands. And given what happened, my tripping over the cat, I'd no way of alerting anyone.'

Gemma shrugged. 'Are you sure? I didn't hear anything.'

‘Of course I am. I heard the sound of a motorbike being driven away.’

‘Mmm.’ It was clear Gemma didn’t believe my story. ‘The motorbike might have been one of the lads from the next farm along. Sounds can travel far in the silence here.’

About to protest, I thought better of it. Gemma clearly believed I’d been mistaken. Then, as if to stress her point, she said, ‘I’m sure you’re wrong, but I’ll ask the stable hands later. Don’t worry about it.’

‘We’ll have to make some other arrangement for you,’ Kath said, coming back into the room. ‘Even if it’s not serious, you won’t be able to climb those narrow stairs to the attic bedroom.’

Gemma handed me a large mug of tea. ‘Sip it slowly. It’s hot and we don’t want any more accidents.’

Her attempt at a joke didn’t make me feel any better and I was cross at having to take the blame for this unfortunate accident, when the cat was equally guilty. As though aware he had escaped culpability the black and white cat responsible for the mishap began serenely to lick his paws.

As Kath said, ‘We could use the small sitting room beside the front door. There’s a sofa bed there which should be comfortable for a few days,’ Deborah appeared in the kitchen, rumpled with sleep.

‘Gosh, is everyone up before me this morning. I thought I’d have time for a quiet breakfast.’

Once more I had to explain what had happened as she gazed in horror at my ankle.

Kath looked up at the kitchen clock. ‘I think I can phone the surgery now,’ she said. ‘Get Doctor Graham to have a look at that.’

‘Remember the clock is ten minutes fast,’ Deborah

said.

'Yes, but it's Wednesday,' Kath said. 'Ellen is the receptionist on duty today and she's an early bird. I'm sure she'll be there.'

I sat back and drank my tea as the three of them discussed my ankle as though I wasn't there. In a way it was a relief to place this problem into someone else's hands. I felt exhausted both through the throbbing pain and the lack of sleep.

I sat up suddenly, almost spilling my tea in the process. 'How will I manage down to the surgery?'

'We'll ask for a house call, but if that's not possible, we can help you into the van.' Kath looked round. 'I think there's a wheelchair somewhere.'

This sounded too much like a tricky operation. 'Please plead with the doctor to come here,' I said. 'Even if I have to wait.'

Gemma gulped down the remainder of her tea. 'I'd better get started. I can hear the horses already. As soon as they know someone is around, they begin to complain.'

'We'll soon be able to put them out full-time as long as they're rugged up,' Kath said as Gemma went out.

'What about the chickens?' I said.

'Don't worry. I'll feed them this morning. I'll go and get dressed now,' Deborah said.

Kath went into the hallway and I could hear her calling the doctor's surgery.

Whatever she said she must have been persuasive because she came back in a few minutes later. 'Ellen says she'll ask Doctor Graham to come over after his morning surgery. He should be here about 11. Can you last out till then?'

'Yes, I'll manage if I don't move around too much.'

Anything was better than contemplating a bumpy ride in a van down to Rothesay.

'Fine,' Kath said. 'I'm going over to the arena to check it out for today's lesson.'

Alone in the kitchen, there was so much to think about. The intruder, if it was an intruder, was almost forgotten – but not quite. I tried again as Gemma returned. 'Gemma, I'm certain there was someone in the yard early this morning. Did you have a chance to speak to the stable hands?'

She shook her head then said abruptly, 'Not yet. You might have been a bit muddled if you were sleepy. The dogs would have alerted us to an intruder.'

There was something else. Something I hadn't noticed in the concern about my ankle. Gemma had come in from the yard. Had she been out there, meeting the stranger? I dismissed this thought almost immediately. And as for the sound of the motorbike, Gemma was right. The roar had been distant. No more than one of the local farm hands returning home after a night out. I'd have to keep my imagination in check. That was a lot better than the alternative.

TWENTY-ONE

It was a relief that Kath managed to persuade Ellen, the receptionist, that Doctor Graham should come up to Brydeshill to have a look at my injury. In the meantime I'd have to try to keep as still as possible. Every time I moved a spasm of pain shot through my ankle.

While we waited for the doctor to arrive, Kath said, 'I'll see about clearing that downstairs room for you.'

'Sorry to give you this bother,' I said, meaning it. 'With everything you have to deal with, looking after an invalid is the last thing you need.'

She dismissed my concerns with a wave of her hand. 'No matter. It could have been a lot worse.'

Deborah and Gemma had gone off to organise the day's chores and Kath and I were alone in the kitchen. Now might be the time to check if I'd been mistaken about an intruder. But how best to approach the subject?

In the end, Kath gave me an opening. 'What made you come downstairs last night?' she said, as she moved about the kitchen, making a half-hearted attempt to clear up.

'I couldn't sleep, and I thought a hot drink might help,' I said, before going on quickly, 'and then I heard a noise outside…'

Kath whirled around. 'What kind of a noise?' she interrupted.

Taken aback by the sharpness of this question, I went on, 'I thought I heard someone prowling about in the stable yard and I was worried.'

Kath frowned. 'Well, it certainly wasn't me, but it could have been one of the stable hands, checking on the horses. Did you see who it was?'

'No, I tripped over the cat as I went to have a look. But by then whoever it was had gone.' I stopped, not mentioning hearing a motor bike revving up. By now I was convinced I'd been mistaken, and Gemma's suggestion was right. In the silence the noise could well have carried from some distance.

Saved by the bell, I thought, as the back door opened, and Doctor Graham came bustling into the kitchen. He was a small, fussy man and I didn't have much confidence in the way he tutted and shook his head as he examined my ankle. But I was wrong to doubt him and he smiled reassuringly as he made his diagnosis.

'No bones broken, I'm glad to say.' He shook his head again. 'But you'll have to have that strapped up and rest it for a few days. After that, if you behave,' this said with a twinkle in his eye, 'you should be able to start moving around. But I'd stay out of the way of any cats if I were you. Remember RICE.'

Kath and I stared at him in puzzlement. Did he mean I should put rice on my swollen ankle? How would that help?

He chuckled as he saw the look on our faces. 'It means Rest, Ice, Compression, Elevation. Best way to treat the problem.' He wagged his finger. 'But you'll have to be patient. I'll leave you a prescription for a compression bandage and for some painkillers.'

While all this was going on the cat that had been the cause of the accident stood up, stretched then settled back down to sleep, all the while regarding us with what could only be a look of contempt.

Doctor Graham snapped his bag closed and said, 'I

must be off. I've another couple of house calls to make. Let me know if your ankle gets worse, but if you do as I say, you'll be right as rain in a few days.'

I squirmed back in the chair, flinching a little as the pain caught me. This was going to be a difficult few days.

'Right. Time to get the bedroom sorted,' Kath said.

'Sorry to be such a nuisance,' I apologised again, but Kath laughed. 'Honestly, Alison, I've stopped worrying. I'm not sure what else can go wrong now.'

She stopped as Gemma put her head round the door. 'All well, Alison?'

'Yes, thanks,' I said, 'though I'll feel a lot better once I have the painkillers.'

'Avoid the cats, that's my advice,' she grinned, turning to leave.

'Just a minute, Gemma,' Kath said. 'Were you out in the stable yard early this morning? Alison thought she heard a noise.'

Gemma stood still, her body angled away from us. 'Why do you ask?' she said, after a pause.

'Alison thought she saw someone lurking around.'

Gemma turned to face us. She smiled, but the smile didn't reach her eyes. 'No, I think Alison must have been imagining it. There are always noises during the night. She isn't used to it.'

Kath frowned. 'We're all on edge right now. The slightest thing upsets us.'

Why did I not believe Gemma? But then again, surely I'd have recognised her? And if she was the person in the yard, why would she not have said. Then I thought, if it was Gemma, it would explain why the dogs didn't bark.

TWENTY-TWO

Kath enlisted Deborah to help me move along to the small bedsitting room, a slow process, and I was glad to sink in to the chair by the window while Kath fussed around to make sure I elevated my leg as prescribed. Deborah had thoughtfully brought one of the easy chairs from the kitchen and positioned it beside the window with a footstool in front.

'It's rather basic,' Kath said, 'but it's only for a few days until you can climb the stairs again.'

I nodded in agreement. I was lucky there was a spare room, and it was nowhere near as spartan as Kath had suggested.

For one thing, its position in the house gave a view over most of the yard, through to the fields so I wouldn't feel quite so alone, being able to watch the comings and goings.

I'd be under strict guard for a few days to make sure I did as the doctor said. Not that I minded. The way my ankle felt, sitting in the easy chair with my leg up was about all I could manage.

'I'm going down to Rothesay to collect your prescription,' Deborah said. 'I'll pop into Print Point and bring you back some books. I know you'll fret if you've nothing to do.'

That wasn't strictly true. I'd arranged to have several items brought down from the attic bedroom, including my laptop. A new idea to add to my article had occurred to me, one that I could do with online research. And in my current situation that seemed a good way to spend the time. Always assuming the

Wi-Fi behaved. There was a randomness about the signal on the island as I'd discovered to my cost on more than one occasion.

'We'll leave you to rest now,' Kath said, adjusting the large bag of frozen peas she'd strapped to my ankle in the absence of ice. 'Deborah will buy a large bag of ice when she's in town.'

I nodded and lay back, glad of the opportunity to be on my own.

Once they had both left, exhaustion overtook me and despite the pain in my ankle, I must have dozed off.

I wakened with a start a while later. A glance at my watch told me I'd been asleep for over an hour and I struggled up into a more comfortable position. The bag of peas had dislodged itself while I'd been asleep and by stretching carefully I managed to retrieve it from the floor where it had fallen. By now of course, the peas were a wet, slippy mush and I dropped the bag back to the floor, wondering how long it would be before Deborah returned.

As though she'd read my mind, the bedroom door opened and my daughter came bouncing in, in her usual ebullient style.

'I've got everything,' she said, breathlessly as though she'd been running. 'Let's get you sorted.'

Compression bandage snugly in place, a couple of painkillers administered, and I began to feel much better.

'Perhaps I'll be able to move about by tomorrow,' I said hopefully.

Deborah looked horrified. 'You heard what Doctor Graham said. It will be a few days before you can do that. You need to rest your ankle.'

Then, as I made a face, she adopted a stern tone.

'Do you want to cause more problems? Do as you're told for once, Mum.'

She was right, of course, but I didn't feel the blame lay with me. It had all been to do with that wretched cat.

Although I'd anticipated differently, the day passed quickly. Deborah had brought me a good selection of books from the Print Point, the painkillers worked well, and I dozed a lot, each time I wakened feeling a little better. Noises drifted in from the yard, the sound of neighing and of the horses' hooves on the cobblestones as they were led out to the fields, or to be ridden. There were shouts and bursts of laughter as riders called to one other, the buzz of a distant tractor, and late in the afternoon the screech of tyres as a car drew up outside the farmhouse.

I heard the car doors slam and then voices I recognised. The police had returned. I only hoped they didn't want to interview me again. I didn't feel up to it. But I wasn't destined to escape a grilling, despite my injuries.

Kath ushered DI Lecky and Constable Brevin into the room. 'The police would like a word with you again, Alison.'

Positioning herself behind the police, she made a face, but I wasn't sure if it was a warning of some kind that I couldn't interpret, or a general show of dislike that they had turned up again.

No matter how Kath felt she'd be glad to have the case solved as soon as possible and the yard back to a semblance of normality.

She didn't wait around, but left saying, 'Give me a shout if you need anything.' Perhaps she'd had enough of talking to policemen.

I felt strangely vulnerable, sitting there, unable to

move as they both stared at me. As there were no other seats in the room, they had to stand and the sight of them towering over me only made me feel worse, guilty even, though I'd nothing to be guilty about.

To my relief, Gemma came in. She leaned over me and whispered, 'Kath thought you might need support,' as DI Lecky watched us.

'If you could just go over again what happened when Fritz was found?' she said, her expression impossible to read. Did she believe I was holding something back.

I closed my eyes, as much to give the impression that I was concentrating as to block out the sight of DI Lecky and Constable Brevin in front of me.

Oddly, they didn't enquire why I was sitting with my ankle strapped up, but possibly Kath had tried to deter them from interviewing me by telling them of my plight. If she had, they were ignoring it.

I recounted the way in which Deborah and I had gone to feed the llamas, but I'd held back, being rather afraid of them. And how she had gone over to help Kath when she learned Fritz had been found dead over by the little wood on the far side of the field where the llamas were. I gave as much detail as I could remember and when I opened my eyes it was to see Constable Brevin staring at me, a frown on his face.

'And you saw nothing suspicious? No one anywhere nearby? No strangers?'

I shook my head. 'No, there was no one.'

DI Lecky glanced at her colleague, who was busy making notes.

Now I was beginning to feel angry. Surely they couldn't think that I, or Deborah and I, had anything to do with Fritz's death. 'I've told you all I know. Is there any reason why you think I might be holding something back?'

The police officers exchanged another glance. Really, this was getting ridiculous. What's more, my ankle was beginning to throb again, and I wanted them gone so that I could take another couple of painkillers and drift back to sleep.

Constable Brevin stood flicking his pencil back and forth and I thought that now I'd told them what I knew, they would leave. But no. There was yet another question from the DI.

'Can you give me the exact time you and your daughter began to walk over to the wood?'

'No. Deborah went ahead to help Kath, but you must understand, Inspector, that we weren't keeping a note of the time. And I didn't go as far as the wood…I waited at the gate. I didn't think the llamas and I would get on.'

My attempt at a joke was met with a stony silence, so I sighed and tried again. 'I guess, and it is only a guess, that it must have been about four o'clock. I feed the chickens twice a day so was before the second feed.'

Prompted by a desire to have them on their way as soon as possible, I said again, 'So it must have been around four o'clock.'

DI Lecky sniffed. 'Interesting. You say Fritz was seen working in the stables the previous evening. Doesn't leave much time between that and when he disappeared, does it?'

'You're not suggesting I killed him, are you?' The angry words were out before I could stop myself. 'That would be a ridiculous suggestion. For one thing, why would I be meeting him in the woods?' I still wasn't willing to say I thought I'd heard Fritz the night before – I was becoming more and more uncertain about what I'd seen and heard and there was no point in muddying the waters.

Constable Brevin looked down at his notebook before lifting his head to nod to the DI as she said, 'I'm not suggesting anything. I'm merely trying to establish the facts. That's the most important thing right now.'

Constable Brevin snapped his notebook shut, as the DI added, 'We'll leave it there for the moment, but we might ask you to come to the police station to make a statement.'

'How can she do that?' Gemma said, pointing to my ankle. 'She's been told to rest.'

DI Lecky showed no sympathy for my plight. 'I'm sure we'll find a way round it.'

She beckoned to the constable, who was so deeply engaged in staring at Gemma he didn't notice.

'Constable Brevin,' the DI called over. 'Time to go and leave these people in peace. You can examine the lady's answers later.'

Constable Brevin blushed as he turned away from Gemma to follow DI Lecky .

As they left, DI Lecky looked back to say, 'Fritz was found in the wood, but it's most likely he was killed elsewhere,' leaving us gazing after her in shock.

As the policemen went out, Kath and Deborah came bustling in.

'What on earth are they thinking,' Kath said angrily. 'Imagine suspecting any of us of being involved in the death of Fritz. That's ridiculous.'

I didn't reply. The possibility that someone at Brydeshill was implicated was too dreadful to consider. But whatever had happened to him the explanation surely lay at the yard.

It was Deborah who helped by changing the subject. ‘You mentioned cleaning up the arena. Let me help you.’

Kath looked at her blankly. Her mind was clearly still on Fritz. ‘What? Oh, yes, of course. Best to do that now.’

She and Deborah went off to sort out what would be a lengthy task, leaving me alone with Gemma.

‘You seem to know Constable Brevin well,’ I said, more by way of conversation than any real curiosity.

She laughed. ‘We were at school together, at Rothesay Academy. The old one, the remains of which you can see on the way up here.’

‘Oh, yes, I did notice a couple of derelict buildings. But it looks quite modern.’

‘Mmm – but there were problems. You might remember the issues with buildings constructed in the late 50s and 60s.’

‘Indeed I do,’ I replied, thinking of the number of solid Victorian buildings in Glasgow which had been demolished in the name of progress, only for the buildings replacing them to be bulldozed because they were so poorly constructed.

‘Don’t be thinking there’s any romance between Phil Brevin and me,’ Gemma said. ‘Oh, he would like there to be, but I’m not interested.’

‘Too busy with the horses,’ I smiled.

‘Something like that,’ she replied, neatly side-stepping the question. Then she said, ‘Did you tell the police everything you know?’

I thought this a strange question, but I’d no intention of confiding in Gemma. ‘I’m sure they’ll want to interview us again at some point.’

Gemma shook her head. 'Speaking of the horses, I'd better go and help the stable hands. We have a couple of the volunteers in today and while they're willing, they need to be supervised.'

Mmm – perhaps there wasn't any hint of romance with Phil, but possibly Duncan was a different matter.

As I watched her go, shifting a little in my seat to try to find a comfortable position, I wondered how long the volunteers would last. Most of those I'd seen were youngsters and their parents might not be happy to let them stay on in a yard where two deaths had taken place, one of them a murder.

Then I thought – was there a reason Gemma had come in while I was being interviewed by the police. Did she want to find out what I'd say to them?

TWENTY-THREE

One advantage of this enforced idleness was that it gave me plenty of time to think. People popped in and out to see me: Kath to check I was comfortable, Gemma to update me on what was happening with the chickens (she'd now taken over that task) and Deborah to make sure I was doing as I was told. I even had a visit from the cats, but I can't say I was pleased about that, given the circumstances.

There was news about Jose, and it was Deborah who brought it.

'There's been progress about that man found in the stables,' she said, fidgeting with the top button of her jacket.

'I knew they'd be able to find out more about him. The world is such a small place nowadays.'

She sighed. 'You remember he was found in Topper's stable? And no one could work out what he was doing there?'

I nodded, waiting for her to continue.

'Well,' she went on, 'it's been discovered he must have been on the island the evening before he was found dead. The story is that one of the CalMac employees distinctly remembers him on the last ferry, because there was a bit of hassle in the onboard cafe. His English wasn't too good, so he held up the queue as he searched for the right money to pay for his coffee.'

'And is there any word about why he was on the island? Why he came to Brydeshill?'

She shook her head, disappointed perhaps that there

was so little to tell. 'There's lots of gossip, but no one knows for sure.'

'And where did he come from? Was he living somewhere in Britain before coming here to Bute?'

'No. They've managed to track him on a flight from Malaga a few days before. But there's no word yet on where he was between arriving at Glasgow airport and travelling down to the ferry at Wemyss Bay.'

This was a puzzle indeed. 'Perhaps the police do know more but aren't telling Kath. That's the most probable explanation.'

Deborah shrugged. 'Someone must know about him. It's not likely he would decide on a whim to come up here, even if his plan was to have a holiday on Bute. If I hear anything else, I'll let you know.'

Off she went to help with the horses. There were now only a few remaining in livery, though the stable horses, Marvel, Topper, and Sparky and Caffrey still had to be looked after. Pixie and J were getting more attention from their owners, if that was possible. And though Felix and Breeze were out all the time, it was as though all the horses sensed the feelings of tension.

Kath had reluctantly cancelled the Wednesday night classes though so far it was still worthwhile to run the Saturday morning class. One thing was for sure. She couldn't continue if there was little or no income. Deborah was increasingly worried. 'And those ledger books are still lying on the table, pushed to one side. I think Kath can't bear to look at them.'

There was an air of quiet frustration. As there had been no progress with either death, everyone believed they must be linked, though no one said.

And there were other questions. How had the young man come up to the stables? There was no sign of a car anywhere nearby according to Kath. It wasn't impossible that he'd walked, though Brydeshill was a fair distance from the ferry terminal.

I opened my laptop and tried to ease myself into a comfortable position. There was nothing I could do from here, no way I could help. But I could attempt to make progress with my article.

Try as I might, I couldn't concentrate. My mind kept drifting back to the two deaths, to what possible connection there might be between them. It was perfectly possible the police knew what had happened – there was no reason for them to share information with us, or even Kath. After all, we might be suspects.

I closed my laptop. Much as I hate not being able to solve a mystery, I felt disappointed that I'd not been able to make progress with this one. And I wasn't likely to find out more until I was able to get out and about again.

Deep in thought, I came to with a start as I heard my phone ring. It took me a minute or two to realise what it was, and rummage through my bag to find it. Drat! I'd missed the call.

It was Tara, so I rang her back immediately. A chat would be a welcome distraction.

'Sorry I missed you,' I said.

'I thought we could arrange for you to come over again,' she said. 'Unless you're being kept too busy at Brydeshill.'

I explained what had happened, trying to make light of my accident, but she wasn't reassured.

'How awful,' she kept saying. 'That's such a nuisance.'

Which didn't make me feel any better.

'I'm sure I'll be fine soon,' I said. 'If I do as I've been told.'

She chuckled. 'That's going to be hard for you,

Alison. I was going to suggest you might like to come over at the weekend, stay over if you can be spared. I suppose that's not possible now.'

This conversation was making me more and more depressed. It was bad enough having to spend more time at Brydeshill than I'd originally intended, but now I was missing out on a weekend with Tara.

There was a silence, then Tara said, 'Are you mobile? I could come over to Brydeshill and collect you. We've a comfortable spare room with an ensuite.'

I didn't hesitate. I was of no use here right now. The feeding of the chickens had easily been incorporated into the daily routine – which made me suspect the job had been organised as a way of making me feel useful.

'I'd love that,' I said. 'I'm sure I can manage into the car,' crossing my fingers. Then a thought occurred to me. 'As long as it won't be an inconvenience for you? With a husband and the children to look after are you sure you don't have enough to do without me?'

'Of course not,' Tara said. 'Warren is taking the children over to the mainland to visit his parents so that gives us lots of time to chat. I'll pick you up about four o'clock. No arguments.'

I'd no intention of arguing with her. I was only too grateful for her suggestion. I'd have to tell Deborah and Kath but surely there could be no objection. They might well be glad to have me out of the way, one problem fewer to deal with.

About to phone Deborah and explain what was happening, I was forestalled by a loud rap on the door. Before I could say, 'Come in,' the door was flung wide open and Deborah came running in. She stood there, breathing heavily.

'Whatever's the matter?' I said, alarmed by this sudden appearance.

'There's been news,' she said.

Dramatic as ever, I thought, but instead I said, 'News? About what?'

She paused, clearly for effect. Even though she was desperate to tell me, she wanted to spin out the story.

'The police phoned Kath a few minutes ago.' She stopped.

'Oh, for goodness sake, Deborah,' I said, trying to conceal the impatience in my voice. 'Just tell me what's happened.'

'The police have found a car and it appears to be the one that young man was driving. His passport and driving licence were in the glovebox.'

'Where did they find it?'

'It was parked a couple of miles down the road, hidden in the overgrown bushes in the car park of the old Rothesay Academy.'

'How did they think to look there?'

'They didn't. At least not initially. A crowd of lads were playing about round the old school, the one built in the 1950s, and they spotted it. The car was clearly not any old wreck. It was a hire car which helped in identifying it as the one Jose was driving. He'd hired it from a company in Glasgow.'

'But why did it take so long for the police to find it?'

'A bit of luck. The boys shouldn't have been there, these old school buildings are extremely dangerous and strictly out of bounds, but you know what boys are like. They thought it suspicious a new car should be parked there and went back to check the next day to find it hadn't been moved. One of the boys ripped his trousers climbing out over the fence and had no option but to confess to his mum. The car was well hidden, at the far end of the car park, where the bushes have run rampant.'

That was indeed odd. If that car did belong to Jose, it could only mean he'd parked it there and walked the rest of the way up to the stables. Why on earth would he do that? This mystery about Jose was becoming increasingly complicated and I told myself sternly that I should stay out of it, leave it to the police. But then again, Kath had asked me to help. Besides, who can resist a challenge? Not me.

TWENTY-FOUR

Despite the inconvenience of my ankle, I was relieved to be going away from Brydeshill. This latest information about Jose's car had confused rather than cleared up the story.

With increasing impatience I watched the hands of the clock creep round ever so slowly till it was time for Tara to collect me.

'Gosh, made it at last,' she said as she came rushing in to the kitchen. 'It took so long to organise the children. They took ages deciding which toys to take. They were so excited,' she continued. 'Warren's mum and dad spoil them rotten and they love going there.'

With considerable effort and with help from Deborah, I managed to manoeuvre myself into her car, luckily a large jeep. Deborah had found a small overnight bag and Kath had contributed a walking stick 'To help you move around,' she said. I'd a suspicion the walking stick had belonged to Fritz, but I accepted it gratefully. Although I could feel an improvement in my ankle already, I wanted to be fit and well as soon as possible.

I won't say the journey was pleasant, despite the view. The weather had turned drier and warmer and Tara wound down her window to catch a cooling breeze. This time as a passenger I could look out over the fields to the bay in the far distance, watch the ferry coming in. Crowds of daffodils still crowded the verges, but here and there the first bluebells and red campion were beginning to peep through.

Even so, despite these distractions, over the bumpier parts of the road I could feel my ankle become increasingly painful and I tried not to flinch less Tara thought this a comment on her driving.

She chattered non-stop as she drove along.

'Do you have many friends on the island?' I asked.

She turned to face me, then looked away, grabbing the steering wheel tightly. 'Yes, but it's so difficult to make time to see anyone and there's the problem of living out in the country.'

That I could understand, and my mind wandered as she went on, 'Do you remember my good friend Meg? I shared a flat with her when you and I were working together on the book about the Rothesay Pavilion.'

I smiled. 'Of course I do.'

'She went off the island last year after her wedding to a doctor who lives and works in Glasgow. He was here on a golfing holiday with friends and that's how they met up.' She made a face as she said this.

'You don't approve of the marriage? Of her choice of husband?'

She shook her head. 'It's not that. It's just that I miss her. We've been friends all through school. On the island you get to know people in your class so well – none of the schools have as many pupils as those on the mainland. And Meg and I have so much shared history. There's no one else I can confide in in quite the same way.'

'Yes, I understand that. My friend Susie Littlejohn married an American and went to live in the States, in California. We've been friends since college.'

We fell silent, lost in our own thoughts. Susie's decision to marry and return to America with her husband was the right one for her, but I did miss her.

As we made our way down the hill to turn towards town, the old Rothesay Academy came into view. This time as a passenger I'd a better view of all three buildings.

We passed the first one, stoutly built of grey stone and I spied the date 1938 above the main door.

'Gosh,' I said. 'I didn't notice that before. I've only caught a glimpse while driving. That's the same year as the Rothesay Pavilion was built.'

'Yes,' Tara said, and I took a deep breath as she followed my gaze. 'The original Victorian building, overlooking Rothesay Bay, was extended and modernised in 1910 and again in 1938.'

'Why did they close it? Too expensive to update it, I expect.'

Tara laughed. 'No, it burned down in 1954 and was replaced by the one next to it in 1959. You can see that was a bit of a monstrosity, in the typical style of that time, though the views over the bay were good. That's the one I attended. The new building at Townhead is a joint campus site with Rothesay Primary School and Argyll College.'

I turned back to have a last look. Although the location was spectacular, the utilitarian shape of the building lacked any curves or adornments to break up the starkness: it hadn't stood the test of time as well as the original.

'Wait!' I said.

Tara jammed on the brakes with a little squeal. 'What is it? What's wrong?'

'Sorry, I didn't mean to startle you, but could we go and have a look at that car the police found? The one belonging to Jose?'

Tara sounded unhappy at this suggestion. 'Do you think so? Surely the police will have towed it away by now, or at the very least placed a guard around it?'

'Mmm. Possibly. But it won't take a moment to check.'

She nodded reluctantly and started up the car again, moving across to go into the old car park, saying, 'If there's a policeman about, we'll make a quick exit. I don't want to have to make up a story to explain why we're here.'

'I'll say we made a wrong turn,' I said.

She raised her eyebrows. Even I had to agree this would be a dumb excuse. 'Look,' I said, pointing to the blue and white tape fluttering in the far corner of the carpark, 'there's no policeman here. We won't have to think of an excuse.'

'There will be no car either,' Tara said again as she came to a stop. 'The police will have taken it away for examination.' She didn't say so, but I'd the impression she thought this was one of my hare-brained schemes.

'I suppose so.' I felt deflated, but I'd no idea why. What did I expect to find that the police hadn't?

'I don't think you should become involved, Alison. Let the police handle this one.'

About to say, 'But I am involved,' I decided it would be better to remain silent. And it would only take a moment or two to check. I said, 'Let me have a quick look at where the car was found and then I'll be satisfied.'

Tara made no reply as I opened the passenger door, but she stepped out and came round to help me. 'This isn't a good idea, Alison. The paving stones are uneven and broken. You don't want another accident.'

'I won't be long,' I said, pulling up the walking stick Kath had given me and leaning heavily on it as I went across to find the spot where the car had been. Tara stood beside her car, watching me.

In this corner of the car park, where the bushes had been left to grow unchecked, it was clear to see where Jose's car had been parked. Years of neglect had all but obscured the parking bays, but the recent rain meant the tyre tracks had left a deep imprint.

I made my way around slowly, grateful to have the walking stick to help me, but there was nothing to see. Tara was right. The police would already have searched the area thoroughly.

Disappointed and about to turn away and hobble back over to the car where Tara stood watching me with some amusement, my eye caught sight of something glinting in the sunshine, among the dead leaves and litter. It's only an old bottle top I thought, but something made me look again and I strained awkwardly to bend down for a closer look. It was a broken bit of metal of some kind and appeared to be part of a small circle. With some difficulty I managed to stoop low enough to retrieve it. It looked insignificant, unimportant and I turned it over in my hand. The surface was worn smooth, but there was the faintest of inscriptions on the other side. Without thinking, I slipped it into my pocket. Most likely it was something dropped by one of the pupils who'd attended this school long ago and I wondered about the child who had lost it, if it had been of any value to him or her.

This had been a waste of time. I don't know what I'd expected to find. Some significant clue perhaps? That wasn't likely. These days police search methods were so thorough there was little room for amateurs.

As I started to move towards the car, I could see Tara tapping her foot impatiently.

‘Sorry,’ I said.

She raised her eyebrows as I tried to hurry towards her, then slowed as she held up her hand. ‘Don’t rush. There’s plenty of time.’

‘Did you find anything?’ she asked as I came up to her, obviously expecting the answer would be no.

‘Let’s go,’ was all I said, sliding the walking stick on to the back seat and manoeuvring my way carefully into the passenger seat.

Tara started up the car, and we drove straight to her house. I was so looking forward to the weekend away.

TWENTY-FIVE

A weekend at Tara's restored my good humour and my ankle felt much better. And in spite of several prompts, it was as if Tara deliberately avoided the subject of the deaths of Jose and of Fritz.

But my feeling of wellbeing didn't last long after I returned to Brydeshill.

Firstly, I'd the impression Kath was disappointed I hadn't managed to find out more about the death in Topper's stable and if it had anything to do with Fritz's murder.

Secondly, the morning after returning I slept later than intended and came to with a start. I jumped out of bed and bustled through to the kitchen, watching out for the cats.

Two cups of coffee later, I still felt groggy, out of sorts. I did want to be able to report progress to Kath, but I'd nothing new to tell her.

No mention had been made of the intruder I thought I'd spotted in the yard several nights before. I had to find a way to raise the subject of the intruder again with Gemma, find out if she'd done as promised and checked with the stable hands. But the decision was luckily taken out of my hands.

I was alone in the kitchen, the others occupied by the many tasks around the yard. Things seemed to have quietened down and Kath was looking more cheerful. None of the other owners had suggested moving their horses and though there were several empty stables, she seemed more upbeat saying, 'I'm sure we can build up the business again, especially once we're into summer. People have short memories.'

With my ankle feeling so much better, I was more than willing to take on the task of feeding the chickens once more. In a funny kind of way I'd missed looking after them and with everyone having so much work to do, I'd be glad to help. What's more, I'd given up any hope of returning to Glasgow any time soon.

The kitchen door opened, and Kath, Deborah and Gemma came in for lunch, chatting animatedly.

In the end all my agonising about how to approach the subject was for nothing, because as we were eating lunch, Deborah said, 'What did the police say about the intruder the other night, Gemma?'

Ah, so Deborah had also heard someone. 'I wasn't imagining it, then?'

Ignoring my comment, 'Nothing much,' Gemma said. 'They didn't seem particularly interested to be honest.' She didn't look up but kept staring at her plate.

'It wasn't one of the stable hands?' I said.

'No, it wasn't,' Gemma mumbled.

Deborah turned to me. 'I told Kath that when I thought about it, I was sure I'd heard a noise. Gemma and I asked everyone, but there was no one here out and about at that time of the morning. I insisted Gemma phone the police.'

'You also heard something, Alison?' Kath said.

'I..I... thought I might have heard, seen, someone, but then again, thought it could be my imagination.' I didn't say that Gemma had tried to convince me of this.

Kath chewed at a fingernail as I continued, 'I only caught a fleeting glimpse of someone in a dark coat with a hood before he or she went towards the arena. By the time I looked again whoever it was had disappeared.'

'You would know,' Kath said, 'being on the ground floor you'd have a much better view.' She paused. 'Gemma told me about it, what you thought you'd seen. Still, no harm done…there's nothing missing, no evidence there was anyone here. Gemma said she'd phoned the police.'

Deborah said, 'The police will probably want to speak to you. You'd be better to phone them now. There's always someone on duty at the station in Rothesay.'

'There's no need for you to bother about that,' Gemma jumped in. 'I've told them and I'm sure that's enough. They've plenty to do investigating everything else that's happened here.'

Deborah didn't look happy at this suggestion. 'I think they'll want to hear what everyone has to say. Mum should call…'

This seemed to annoy Gemma even more. 'A waste of time. They have all the information they need.'

To divert attention, I said, 'My ankle is much better. I'll be able to go back to feeding the chickens if that would be of help.'

Kath didn't reply, but Gemma said, looking pleased by this interruption, 'Brilliant. One job fewer for me to do. I can't seem to get on with them.'

As soon as we'd finished coffee, I stood up and mindful of Deborah's insistence, said, 'I'll phone the police station now,' but before I could do so, Gemma said, 'There's no urgency. I've told you – I've already talked to them. Let me handle it. If they want to interview you, they'll let you know. The conversation I had with PC Brevin was short. He says they'll be back in touch.'

I couldn't understand why Gemma was trying to discourage me from making the phone call. But on the other hand I didn't want to press her, not until I'd checked it out, had a look around the riding arena. The intruder I'd spotted had most certainly come from there.

'Strange the police haven't followed it up,' Deborah said, looking directly at Gemma. 'Why do you think that is, Gemma?'

'I'm sure they're busy trying to find a murderer rather than someone just lurking about the yard. Someone who was probably one of the stable hands who didn't want to admit to it,' Gemma muttered as Kath said, sounding firm. 'Alison, it's best to let Gemma handle it. We don't want the police getting confused by a whole lot of different stories.'

Deborah made a face. 'I don't think that's likely. Surely they'll want to gather as much evidence as they can, have as much information as we can give them?'

Gemma stood up. She sounded angry. 'I think we've more to be concerned about. Like how we keep the place going. We want to retain the remaining liveries. Police on the premises will only upset everyone more and …'

Kath interrupted, shaking her head. 'Leave it, Deborah. The police will be in touch with us when they're ready. So Constable Brevin assured Gemma. Meantime we must do all we can to make sure the business picks up again. That'll take all our energies.'

Deborah shrugged, but I could tell she wasn't happy. Even so there was nothing to stop me phoning the police on the pretext of corroborating the story.

Then again, perhaps better to wait till the police

contacted me. I was already involved enough in the problems of Brydeshill.

There was a knock on the kitchen door and Duncan came breezing in. 'Any chance of coffee?'

A look of alarm crossed Kath's face. 'What's wrong now?'

He grinned and pushed back a lock of hair that flopped over his eyes. 'I'm on my way to Westhill and thought I'd pop in.' He pushed the lock of hair back again. 'I'll have to find time to visit the barber, but I'm so busy.'

'Maybe if you didn't spend so much time sailing your boat,' Kath said tartly, but there was a smile on her face. Probably relief that she didn't have to spend yet more money on vet's fees.

As Kath went to take the coffee pot from the stove, Gemma stood up, yawned and stretched. 'Must go,' she said. 'Loads to do today. That new livery is coming in.'

As Gemma reached the door she turned back, and I caught her exchanging a look with Duncan. An almost imperceptible nod. What was that about?

TWENTY-SIX

I went to bed early, not long after dinner. I didn't want to continue discussing the business of the intruder, but I was determined to find an excuse to investigate the arena. There must be, or have been, something there that the prowler wanted. And Gemma was right about the contact with the police. Far better to have one person as the link. Though it was strange they hadn't been in touch.

I'd only just settled down with my book, when the bulb on the bedside lamp flickered several times before going out with a pop. My first inclination was to snuggle down and try to sleep. I'd only a couple of chapters left. But then I knew I'd find it difficult to drop off if I didn't find out how the story ended.

The others would still be in the kitchen and I considered asking Kath for a light bulb, but I couldn't face further speculation about the problems at Brydeshill.

There might be a bulb in one of the drawers in the tallboy in the corner. It was worth a try and if not I'd abandon my book and try to sleep. I pulled open the curtains and moonlight flooded the room, giving me enough light to see.

The tallboy was an old-fashioned piece of furniture, made of solid dark mahogany, with a top that flipped up to display various sized compartments for storing toiletries with a mirror inset into the lid. It had been a long time since I'd seen one of these. I remembered my uncle having one in his bedroom at my grandmother's house. A confirmed bachelor, he remained living with his parents until they died. He was a precise man, who loved order and stability and couldn't tolerate change of any kind. Unfortunately, none of these family traits passed down to me. Then again, perhaps that was why he never married.

That being his personality, this item of furniture suited him perfectly. A place for everything with the flip-open top large enough to contain personal items, always to hand, but out of sight.

It took a little tugging to open the top before I remembered there was usually a press button on the lid and I felt around until I located it.

There was a groan as it creaked open. Kath may well have given the room a perfunctory dust while preparing it for me, but it was clear the inside of this piece of furniture hadn't been touched in some time, as a thin film of dust covered the inside. But the tallboy contained little of interest. Whoever this had belonged to, he had taken all his possessions with him.

There was a knock at the door and Deborah came bouncing in.

'What are you doing here in the dark?' she said, stopping with her hand on the door handle. She turned round and flicked on the overhead light. I blinked as the harsh light came on.

'I'm looking for a light bulb for the lamp,' I said.

'What made you think you'd find one there? You should have asked Kath.'

'I know, but I didn't want to bother her.'

Deborah raised her eyebrows in that way she has of saying, 'Why not?'

As I shrugged, she said, 'I'll get one for you. I don't think it's a good idea to go stumbling round in the dark.' She didn't say 'since you've had one accident already,' but that's what she meant.

I sat down on the edge of the bed. 'Thanks. But why did you come in?'

'Oh, yes,' she said. 'I wanted to check how you were feeling. It's not like you to go to bed so early. I know you offered to feed the chickens in the morning, but if you're not up to it, just say. I don't mind doing it for a few days.'

'I'm perfectly fine,' I said. 'If I have to stay here for a while longer I'll be glad to have something to occupy me.'

'I thought you were at last making progress in writing your article about holidays in Victorian Bute. Surely that's plenty to be going on with?'

'Yes and no,' I admitted. 'I still seem to lack the motivation somehow. I'm aiming to have it finished by the end of June, so I'll devote all my time to it when I get back to Glasgow.'

She grinned. 'I can understand that. Bute always seems like another world.' As she went out she said, 'I'll get that light bulb for you. I know you're lost without your bedtime reading.'

'Wait,' I said, catching her by her sleeve. 'Has there been any word on the night time intruder? Any phone calls from the police?'

Deborah frowned. 'No. That is a bit odd, isn't it? When I asked her again after you'd gone to bed, Gemma kept saying it could only be one of the stable hands who wouldn't own up. Why would that be? Nothing seems amiss.'

'And isn't it strange the police haven't been back to check?

And why would one of the stable hands be reluctant to admit being out in the livery yard?'

'There could be any number of reasons,' Deborah

said, ‘I did say there was no option but to contact the police again in case there was an intruder…’

‘That is peculiar.’ I could think of no explanation for Gemma’s reluctance to chase this up, unless she was concerned another police visit wouldn’t be good for business.

‘Do you want me to mention it again to Kath?’ Deborah looked uncertain.

‘Certainly not. If the police had been in touch, I’m sure Kath would have told us.’ I had my own reasons for not contacting the police. I wanted to check out the arena first.

But Deborah wasn’t so easily deterred. ‘What do you think? With two deaths on the premises you’d think the police would treat this as urgent.’

Now I was sorry I’d raised the subject, so I made a pretence of yawning, saying, ‘Oh, I’m far too tired to think about it all now. I’m sure Kath and Gemma will sort it out. There’s probably a perfectly simple explanation.’

‘Right,’ Deborah said. ‘I’ll get that light bulb for you.’

As she left, I climbed back into bed. Best to make her believe I was ready to go to sleep. Once the lamp was functioning again, Deborah could put off the overhead light on her way out.

But as I lay there, my eyes closed against the glare, I couldn’t help but wonder what was going on at Brydeshill. And why, after two suspicious deaths, no one appeared to be worried about a prowler.

TWENTY-SEVEN

Thanks to Deborah's efforts in securing a replacement light bulb I was able to finish my book, but I didn't feel sleepy. Perhaps going to bed early hadn't been a good idea.

I kept going over and over what I'd seen several nights previously. Why would someone, even one of the stable hands, be wandering around in the middle of the night? And why would anyone be in the arena? I'd have to find a way to check the other cupboard but finding a time might prove difficult as the arena was in use most of the day.

I'd offered to feed the chickens, so I'd have to be up bright and early. I already felt badly about how little I'd contributed recently, knowing how hard pressed everyone was. I couldn't afford to sleep late again.

This was becoming ridiculous, I thought, as I set the alarm on my phone. My original purpose in coming over to Bute to complete the research and finish my article, visit Deborah, and have the opportunity for fresh air and exercise was no more than a distant ambition. When I learned of the first death I should have insisted Deborah come back to Glasgow with me, leaving the police to deal with the situation.

In the meantime what I needed was a book to divert me. I'd have a look in the bookcase in the hope there might be something there to capture my interest and I got out of bed to browse the shelves.

Many of the first books I pulled out were ancient, several of them with pages yellowed with age. These hadn't been read in a long time, that much was evident. A few were improving tracts and the choice of novels was limited. Many seemed to be novels with a horsey theme, not really to my taste.

Then on the bottom shelf I spied a copy of an Agatha Christie novel. I was sure I'd read it before, but so long ago I was unlikely to remember the plot. It had clearly been a favourite read of someone in the household because it was well-thumbed. Perhaps there were others who liked a change from novels that reminded them of work.

I settled down with the book I'd chosen. Tomorrow I'd be back to working. With plenty of fresh air and hopefully the opportunity for a proper walk there should be no problem about sleeping.

I started to read, but my mind kept drifting, thinking about how I might manage to have a look in the cupboards in the arena without being spotted. I didn't want to go exploring at night. With that last episode of the prowler I'd seen (or thought I'd seen) still fresh in my mind, I was extra wary.

That was an issue for later, and I went back to the book. There was something in the middle, poking a little over the top of the page and I pulled it out to find a single folded page of old-fashioned writing paper, pale blue and very thin. It was too flimsy to be regular writing paper and then I realised what it was. It was airmail paper, the kind people used in the days when not only did people write letters regularly, but to send a letter abroad was expensive, so lightweight paper and envelopes were common.

This reminder of the past made me smile. Should I open it? The paper had been written on: I could see the mark of the pen through the paper.

Oh, well, I thought, it can't be anything important if it's been used as a bookmark and I unfolded it carefully, the creases a sign it had been nestling between the pages for some time.

At first I wasn't sure what I was looking at. Then in a flash of recognition I understood. The letter was written in Spanish. My ability in the language is slight, mainly consisting of what I learned on a short course I signed up for several years ago, before Simon and I went on a grand tour of Spanish cities. But I could recognise many of the words, mainly because they were repeated over and over.

I picked out enough to have a flavour of what the letter was about. It had been written from Granada almost twenty years ago. And the sentiment expressed was undying love in tones of desperation.

I couldn't quite make out the signature, but at a best guess the name was Antonio.

And what's more, the letter was addressed to Kath.

TWENTY-EIGHT

Now intrigued, I scanned the letter several times, trying to pick out more phrases here and then, but then I stopped, feeling guilty to be reading something so personal. I slid the letter back and put the book down on the bedside table.

Eventually I fell into a troubled sleep, wakening as dawn filtered through the curtains, feeling tired and headachy.

There was no point in lingering. I'd promised to go back to the job of feeding the chickens and as I gingerly stood up, it was to feel to my great relief that my ankle had returned to normal. I'd probably have to be cautious for a day or two longer, but unless I did something foolish, it felt as good as new.

The kitchen was quiet when I went in, thank goodness. I wasn't in the mood for chat, but by the sight of the breakfast dishes lying in the sink, the others were out and about in the yard.

I selected the largest mug from the rack and luckily there was still coffee in the pot. I sat down at the kitchen table, ignoring the boxes of cereal and the tempting freshly baked loaf and home-made jam.

I couldn't face anything to eat. I was too confused about the letter I'd discovered. If it really did belong to Kath, she had been in Granada many years ago. On holiday? Working? I knew nothing about her previous life.

But if the letter to her was written in Spanish, I had to assume she had at least a smattering of the language. Else why would this Antonio write to her in

Spanish? And from the little I could understand, this was a love letter.

No matter how much this puzzle played on my mind, it would have to wait till later and unless I could think of a good tactic. I couldn't ask Kath directly without revealing I'd been reading the letter.

Annoyed that I hadn't just put it back in one of the other books, I rinsed out my mug (I couldn't bear to add it to the pile of dirty dishes) and, pulling on my boots, I off to see the chickens, foolishly wondering if they'd missed me. Perhaps I was becoming more accustomed to country life than I'd thought I would.

There was a great deal of activity in the yard, though there was still no work taking place on the site of the proposed new arena. If money was as tight as everyone said there was little chance Kath would be able to find the money to complete this before winter. And the current option, the old barn, didn't look as if it would survive much longer.

Two of the horse owners had turned up early and Kath was taking a private lesson in the arena. As far as I could tell, there had been no further cancellations and I guessed she was making a great effort to keep everything as normal as possible. It did mean there was no possibility of getting in to the arena to have a look, I thought, as I opened the entrance to the coop, and the chickens came scrambling out. I didn't delude myself that this was anything other than cupboard love, as I scattered the scraps mixed with feed.

While they were busy pecking away at the food, giving no sign whatsoever of having missed me, I lifted the basket and began to ferret around to collect the eggs. Perhaps if Simon and I settled somewhere semi-rural, I could buy chickens of my own. A thought quickly dismissed.

As I straightened up, pleased that once again there was a plentiful supply of eggs, I spied Gemma over in the far corner of the yard, at the entrance to the field with the llamas, chatting to a man with his back to me. There was something familiar about him, but I couldn't recall what it might be. As I continued collecting the eggs, I glanced over from time to time, hoping he might turn around and I'd recognise him. It was only when I'd finished and came out of the coop, the basket laden with eggs, that Gemma started to walk across with him towards the farmhouse.

They stopped as I moved in front of them, cheerfully saying, 'Good Morning,' so that I could have a good look at the stranger.

'Oh, hello, Alison,' Gemma replied. 'Have you seen Kath?'

'I think she's in the arena,' I said. 'From the sound of it as I passed, she's taking a lesson.'

I stared at the man, realising I had seen him somewhere before, hoping Gemma would take this as a hint to introduce us. It seemed I was mistaken, until she suddenly said, 'Oh, this is Edwin Michel.'

Of course. This was the man Tyler had introduced me to last time I'd been down in Rothesay, the previous owner of Brydeshill.

The words were out before I could help myself. 'What brings you back to the old family home?'

For a moment he looked taken aback, then he laughed, 'Oh, I'm not back to claim the inheritance, for sure. We were glad to be able to sell the place to someone who could make something of it. It had no future as a dairy farm. I run a completely different business now.'

I mumbled something non-committal in reply, holding up the basket of eggs. 'I'll take these into the pantry and sort them out.' Kath sold some of the eggs to the local butcher's shop and it was a daily task to make sure the best of them arrived in perfect condition. The income was a useful supplement to what she could earn from the stables.

Gemma and Edwin continued walking towards the arena, chatting animatedly. They clearly knew each other well, another sign of the closeness of the community on an island such as this.

I stood staring after them as they crossed the yard. Yes, I now remembered Edwin from that meeting in Rothesay, but there was more to it than that, although for the life of me I didn't know what.

But as they almost reached the arena I had a sudden thought. It was Edwin's back view that looked familiar, reminded me of someone. Then it came to me. The height, the way he walked. I recollected the prowler I'd seen in the yard a couple of nights ago and with a shock of recognition I realised it might well have been him.

But if it was, what could he possibly have wanted, back at the old family place, that he couldn't have discussed openly with Kath? There had to be some reason he was prowling around the yard.

The basket of eggs was beginning to weigh heavily on my arm, and I crossed to the farmhouse, pondering this turn of events. And unsure what I should do about it. Between this latest development and the problem of the letter, I'd plenty to think about.

TWENTY-NINE

Curious as I was about Edwin Michel and the reason for his visit, I had to ignore my concerns that he might have been the prowler. That didn't make sense when it was clear he could come and go as he pleased.

That might be something I could do to move matters along. If I could find an opportunity to chat with him, casually drop a few words about the intruder into the conversation, I might be able to find out if my guess was correct.

Then, almost immediately I realised this was no more than wishful thinking unless he made another visit to Brydeshill soon.

I deposited the eggs in the pantry, swiftly sorting them by size into the cartons conveniently set out on the table for that purpose. Perhaps I was getting better at this. I hoped so, as I wasn't much use as an investigator.

As I stacked the last of the boxes, ready to be put in the strong wicker basket stored under the table, I decided I'd have a word with Kath, using the excuse of offering to take the day's supply down to Rothesay. There wasn't much else to do around here right now and a long day stretched ahead of me. I could escape for a couple of hours to have lunch at the Ettrick Bay tearoom and a walk along the shore.

Besides, it would give me a pretext to avoid going back to writing my article. I couldn't think how I'd make progress any time soon. I'd come to a halt again and might have to abandon all pretence of work while

I was here. I told myself I'd make up for lost time when I returned to Glasgow, though I wasn't sure how the editor would react to a request to extend the deadline.

As I closed the door of the farmhouse behind me, Gemma and Edwin were coming out of the arena, chatting to Kath. One of the young girls who'd been having a lesson was leading her pony out to the field and I heard Kath call, 'Well done, Ruby. You're improving.'

Ruby turned bright pink at this compliment. I'd a feeling Kath was a hard taskmistress, and such praise wasn't readily given.

About to tell Kath of my offer to take the eggs into town, I suddenly thought this might be a good opportunity to have a look in the arena. Edwin had left and Kath had gone into the farmhouse with Gemma and Deborah saying, 'Time for a break.'

I waved over to them and pretended to be fiddling with the door to the coop. Gemma waved back calling, 'Are you having a problem, Alison?' and I stood up replying, 'Not at all. Everything's fine,' in case she decided to come over to help. Kath was too deep in conversation with Deborah to notice and I stood and watched as they walked off. As soon as they disappeared indoors, I strode across the yard and slipped as quickly as I could into the arena.

I stood still for a moment, gazing around me. There was nothing much to see in this huge barn. The sand on the floor had been raked over after the riding lesson, the wooden railings round the perimeter were hastily patched in places, tied up with rope, and over in the far corner stood the cupboards holding the spare pieces of riding gear where Deborah had found me a pair of boots.

I made my way across the expanse of the arena trying for all the world to look as if there was something terribly interesting about the place, hoping to think of a reason for being there should I be asked. Finally I decided to say the boots Deborah had found for me were hurting and I'd remembered there were spares in one of the cupboards. It seemed as good an idea as any.

Ignoring the cupboard where Deborah had found wellingtons for me, I stopped in front of the other one. The one Fritz had made such a fuss about.

Both cupboards were tall and sturdy, apparently made many years ago and though plainly built and shabby through years of use, the craftmanship of past generations was unmistakable. They looked out of place here, most likely to have come from a country house sale. They were certainly too big to have been in the farmhouse.

I pulled at the door of this second one, but it refused to budge. I should have thought of this. Given Fritz's insistence it would also be locked. Not that there was anything of value here if the other cupboard full of riding gear was anything to go by, but even so.

There was a sudden noise. I stopped, listening intently, before moving quickly across to the first cupboard. But the noise must be from outside. No one came into the arena.

I'd have to be quick. Already I was beginning to fret about being found lurking here, excuse or not.

I reached up for the key to unlock this one as I'd seen Deborah do. Unfortunately, as I opened the door I pulled too eagerly at the handle and the contents came tumbling out, showering me with an assortment of old boots, riding hats, and various bits of tack. As I staggered back a snaffle bit caught me on the hand, drawing blood and I landed with a thud on the ground, momentarily dazed.

My first reaction was to laugh. I must have looked quite a sight, sitting there surrounded by all this riding gear. I licked the wound on my hand, trying to remember when I'd last had a tetanus injection.

Getting to my feet rather shakily I began to put everything back in the cupboard, trying to remember from my earlier visit if they had been stored in a particular order. Then I stopped. Why was I doing this before having a proper look? I'd no expectation I'd find anything, but now that I was here, I might as well check through.

I began to remove the riding gear bit by bit and placed everything on the ground. But I was in for a disappointment. There was nothing of interest and solid as the cupboard was, its plainness precluded any secret compartments. The other cupboard might be more productive, but as it was securely locked there was no way I'd be able to inspect the contents unless I could find the key.

I finished putting everything on the shelves as best I could, closed it securely then stood looking at the other cupboard for a few moments, thinking about the last time I'd been here, when Fritz had come in and found us. He'd been furious, far angrier than the occasion merited. If the other cupboard also contained no more than riding equipment, why would he be so upset? And why would it be securely locked?

Closing my eyes, I tried to recollect the scene: Deborah and I at the cupboard, searching through for a suitable pair of boots. Then Fritz had appeared. He'd come in from the far side of the arena and from that viewpoint what had he seen? I hurried over to the side entrance, went out and then came in quickly as

Fritz had done. I'd been so taken aback by Fritz's reaction, it was difficult to recall the exact sequence of events.

Yes, that was it. I'd been standing beside Deborah, partly blocking the view. That must be what had happened. From a first glance Fritz might well have thought we were looking in the second cupboard.

He'd come in quickly, said something about having to keep the cupboards locked. He'd made a mistake about which one we were searching. Wait a minute. After he'd made so much fuss, he'd calmed down, then walked over to the box bench at the far end. By then Deborah had her back to him, was looking at me and making a face at Fritz's response. Was there some reason he'd been so anxious to check the box bench?

Perhaps that's where the key was hidden. Buoyed up by this thought, I was suddenly distracted by someone clearing their throat, and opened my eyes to find Gemma standing staring at me. I'd been so engrossed I hadn't heard her come in. Duncan was standing at the entrance watching us with some amusement as Gemma said, 'Are you okay, Alison? What's going on?'

What possible explanation could I give for my strange behaviour?

THIRTY

Duncan shouted over, 'Tell Kath I'll check out that horse she's interested in and phone her.'

He waved goodbye as Gemma and I stood staring at each other in silence. Then we both began to speak at once.

'Can I help you, Alison,' Gemma said.

I muttered, 'I thought I might find some boots here…the ones Deborah found for me are pinching, and I really need a sturdy pair for being around the yard…'

Gemma cut in. 'Did you think they might jump out of the cupboard.?'

'No, no, I couldn't…'I searched for an explanation. 'I couldn't remember which cupboard they were in. I was hoping that if I closed my eyes it might come to me.'

Even to me this sounded a lame excuse. Gemma didn't reply but bent down to pick up something from the ground. 'What's this?'

Damn! It was the snaffle bit. I hadn't noticed it in the rush to close the cupboard. 'No idea,' I said, pulling my sleeve down to disguise my injured hand. 'Looks like something to do with the horses, perhaps?'

She moved over and I edged out of the way as she tugged at the cupboard door. 'It belongs in here, I think.'

She let out a little shriek. 'Look at the mess. What's happened?'

I could feel my cheeks burning, but I didn't speak.

Anything I might say would only make matters worse.

'Kath had better not see the state of this,' she muttered, beginning to rearrange the riding gear on the shelves.

'I'd better go,' I said. 'I have to take the eggs into Rothesay. I'll think about the boots later.' I realised I hadn't cleared this with Kath, but even if I didn't do the egg run, I had to get out of here. And I didn't mention the key was in the lock.

Gemma seemed not to notice, too intent on sorting out the mess I'd left by cramming everything back into the cupboard any old how. I did think this fuss about this cupboard was a bit much, considering how untidy the farmhouse was. It appeared it was a different matter with the animals and the riding equipment: they had priority.

I fled the arena without a backward glance. Gemma didn't acknowledge my departure, busy finishing rearranging everything, all the while muttering to herself. I should have owned up to being responsible for the mess, but it was too late now.

As I hurried to collect my coat and bag I spotted Kath coming out of the farmhouse with Deborah. Here was my chance to have a proper excuse to slip away.

'I'm going into town. Do you want me to take the eggs with me? It would save you a trip.'

'That would be really helpful, Alison,' Kath said, her eyes shining. 'There's so much to do here. Thanks to Edwin it looks as if we'll have a couple of new liveries and I have to sort out the stables for them.'

Ah, that had been the reason for Edwin's visit. This was good news indeed and I dismissed any idea I had that he had been the prowler.

I hurried indoors and collected the eggs, stowing them carefully in the large wicker basket and taking my time to carry it to my car.

As I accelerated away, Gemma emerged from the arena. I saw her go over and speak to Kath, the look on her face probably a sign of her annoyance at the chaos of the cupboard. I wasn't going to linger long enough to hear Kath's reaction. I could only hope that by the time I returned, peace would have been restored and the problem of the cupboard forgotten.

I breathed a sigh of relief as I hit the main road down into Rothesay. At the old Academy, the blue and white tape was still there, tattered and broken as it fluttered in the breeze. The daffodils which had provided such a welcome splash of colour were beginning to fade and wood anemones peeped out along the verges. The first of the bluebells were in bloom, mixed with froths of wild garlic, welcome signs of the change of seasons.

I concentrated on the road, remembering how we'd tried to make boring car journeys more tolerable when the children were young by encouraging them to look for a rare white bluebell, said to indicate where a fairy had been. Deborah played the game for a while, but Maura and her brother, Alastair, soon became wise to this trick.

As I drove along, I wound down the window the better to enjoy the feel of the warm air. Spring had been late in coming this year after a winter marked by grey skies and unusually heavy rain, even for the west coast. There had been torrential downpours in many areas and several times the trains from Central Station in Glasgow had been cancelled because of flooding on the line. But all that was now forgotten in the blue skies and soft winds of late Spring. Perhaps we'd have one of those exceptional west coast summers which happen from time to time. We could only hope.

So absorbed was I in enjoying this afternoon of freedom, that I reached the bottom of the main road without realising and turned left to go down to the mini roundabout. The butcher's shop I was heading for was on the far side of Rothesay, opposite the Albert Pier and I parked outside, ignoring the yellow lines. I didn't want to risk any accidents crossing from the parking bays with my precious cargo.

The town was busy, the ferry had just berthed, disgorging a new group of day trippers. Although the island isn't large there seem to be increasing numbers of visitors who come over to walk in the quiet of the beaches and the woods, leaving those in immediate need of coffee or something more substantial to head immediately for one of the many cafes or pubs.

I spied a family of mum, dad and two young children walking along the prom towards the Pavilion, each clutching a generous ice cream cone. It might well have been the family who'd been in front of me in the ferry queue at Wemyss Bay. Nothing says holidays like ice cream. I might even be tempted myself.

The butcher was pleased to see me. 'Just in time,' he laughed. 'I've almost run out. There seem to be a lot of people who've come over to the island in camper vans or who've booked into self-catering and decided they need lots of eggs. And my usual supplier's been held up and won't be here till tomorrow afternoon.'

Glad to have been of help, I came out of the shop with a spring in my step. I crossed back to my car and sat there, wondering where to go next. The police seemed no nearer to finding out why Jose had been found in the stable or who was responsible for the death of Fritz.

I wasn't in the mood for going back to Brydeshill right away but wasn't sure if I wanted to stay in town. Abandoning my original plan of lunch at the Ettrick Bay tearoom, which I suspected would be thronged with visitors, Tara came to mind.

We'd worked so well together before and she had a sharp mind, forensic even. If I told her the full story and how Kath had asked for my help, she might be able to come up with some ideas to help me make sense of the events at Brydeshill.

Decision made, I started up the car and leaving the bustle of the town behind, I turned the car to drive to Tara's house. As I approached the bend to St Ninian's Bay, I did think it might have been an idea to phone first, then told myself if she wasn't at home, I could go for a walk along the beach out as far as the old, ruined church.

While Rothesay was busy, in this part of the island there was little traffic, and I reached the side road leading to her house more quickly than anticipated.

Then I realised it was almost twelve o'clock. I'd been so wrapped up in debating how much I should tell her about the situation at Brydeshill that the idea of bringing a sandwich for lunch hadn't occurred to me. Too late now.

As I drew up in the courtyard in front of the house, once the parking area for the farmyard machinery, and now gravelled over with white chippings and adorned with several large pots brimming with tulips of all colours, there was no sign of her car. There was additional parking at the back of the house, and I crossed my fingers that's where it would be.

I drew up on the far side of the yard, underneath a

row of trees that would provide some shade. It had become increasingly hot, far hotter than you would expect for this time of year. I crunched through the gravel to the front door before knocking loudly.

Nothing. No response. I knocked again, this time pressing my ear to the door as if that would do any good, considering how thick this door was.

Tara might be in the kitchen or out in the garden and I walked quickly around to the back of the house to check.

She wasn't in the garden, but her car was there and beside it was an ancient black car that looked familiar, very like the car belonging to Edwin Michel.

The kitchen was a new extension, running along the whole width of the house, the original tiny kitchen having been converted into a utility room. One of the features of this new part of the house was the full-length sliding glass doors through which the kitchen could be seen clearly.

Yes, indeed, Tara was in the kitchen sitting on one of the chairs by the scrubbed pine table. She was chatting to someone who had his back to me. I recognised him and I shrank back, hoping I hadn't been spotted. What should I do? Just leave quickly and perhaps phone her later? Too late. She'd spotted me and stood up, hurrying over to slide open one of the glass doors.

'Why, Alison,' she said, 'what a surprise. I'm delighted to see you. Come in.'

She stood back to let me pass through to the kitchen. I nodded to the man sitting in the other chair, wondering what on earth he was doing here. I was right – it was Edwin Michel.

Now might be my chance to find out if he'd been the intruder in the stables.

THIRTY-ONE

'Have you met Edwin Michel?' Tara said, as Edwin stood up to greet me.

'Yes, we met recently,' he said with a tight smile, gripping the back of the chair.

'Edwin was in my class at school,' Tara went on.

Aware of Edwin watching me carefully, as though waiting expectantly for me to say something about his visit to Brydeshill, I made a non-committal response.

'Come into the sitting room,' she said. 'It's more comfortable.'

We followed her through, and I opted for a seat from where I could watch Edwin.

'I'd love a glass of water if it's not too much trouble,' I said. 'I've been into Rothesay and I meant to buy a bottle of water there. It's such a lovely day, I thought I'd go for a drive round the island.'

Tara leapt up. 'Of course, of course. How remiss of me. I was so surprised to see you, I forgot my duties as hostess.' Luckily, she didn't express surprise that it appeared I'd driven all the way out to Straad in search of a glass of water.

She hurried off into the kitchen, leaving me alone with Edwin. If I didn't speak now I might not have another opportunity. But before I could think how to begin, Edwin started with, 'Tara and I have known each other for a long time. We went to Rothesay Academy together. Tara's been back and forth to the island for many years, but now she and her husband are settled here it seemed a good idea to renew a friendship.'

This seemed a long explanation. Perhaps was it an excuse for his being here? And he must have known that Tara's husband wouldn't be at home at this time of day.

I coughed to hide my confusion, telling myself that this was no more than my imagination at work again. Even if there was something going on with Tara and Edwin, it was no concern of mine.

Tara came back into the room carrying a tray with glasses, a jug of water and a bottle of orange squash. 'I wasn't sure if you'd prefer this,' she said. 'And I've put the kettle on for tea. You'll have time for another cup, won't you, Edwin?'

Please let him say yes, I thought, wondering if I could tactfully ask a question that might identify him as the intruder the other night. There was no possibility of discussing this with Edwin while Tara was there, so I'd have to think of a way to get her out of the room once more. Nothing came to mind. Too late. I'd missed the opportunity.

Would Tara be able to help? I could try my plan of confiding in her, but if they were such friends, went back to schooldays, she might not be interested in hearing my theories, might have a loyalty to Edwin.

Edwin stood up saying, 'Thanks, Tara, but I must be going. I've an appointment with my lawyer in half an hour and it will take me that time to drive into Rothesay. I've to collect some papers from the house first. I was in London all last week on business and I'm rather behind with all the paperwork.'

'I'll see you out,' Tara said. She gestured to the tray. 'Help yourself, Alison. I'll only be a few minutes.'

'Goodbye, Alison,' Edwin said. 'No doubt we'll meet up again.'

I smiled but didn't reply as he caught my hand in a limp handshake. I don't know why but he made me feel a bit creepy. And unless he was lying, he had a perfect alibi. There was no way he could have been the prowler at the stables if he'd been off the island for a week.

I heard Tara and Edwin stop at the front door, talking in soft voices, but I couldn't make out what they were saying, though I sidled towards the lounge door, listening intently. As I heard the front door slam I hastened back to my seat, taking a moment to pour myself a glass of water.

When Tara came back I was sitting sipping the water. And I still hadn't been able to think of an excuse for my visit, so I said, 'I'd love that cup of tea if it's still on offer.'

'Of course,' Tara said, though she looked a little surprised at the note of insistence in my voice. Why had I not thought this through before dashing over to Tara for advice?

I needn't have worried. When she returned a few minutes later, carrying another tray laden with a teapot, mugs and a plate containing a selection of what looked like home-made cakes, she said, 'I'm glad you appeared, Alison, else Edwin Michel might have been here all afternoon. I wasn't sure how I'd manage to get rid of him.'

'But I thought you were the best of friends?'

She made a face. 'That's what he likes to think. He must have a short memory. Yes, we were at school together, but that's as far as it went. He was a bit of a bully and most people couldn't stand him to be honest.'

'That does surprise me. So why did he come over then?'

‘He wanted to have a chat to Warren, though goodness knows why. He’s said he’ll come back at the weekend when Warren is here.’ She smiled. ‘We might have to find an excuse to go to the mainland for the day, make sure we’re not at home.’

It was time for a decision. I could put it off no longer. Should I tell Tara about what was happening at Brydeshill or not?

But as she poured me a cup of tea, offering the cakes in a way which would have been rude to refuse one, she said, ‘And then there was all that trouble about the sale of Brydeshill.’

This added a new dimension to the problem, and I decided it would be best to wait, hear what Tara had to say, before confiding in her.

‘What kind of trouble?’

She sat down on the chair opposite me and took a long gulp of her tea, before leaning over to add extra milk.

‘Well,’ she said, ‘I’m not sure if I should tell you. I don’t want to spread gossip.’

But I knew from the expression on her face that she would tell me the full story.

THIRTY-TWO

What Tara had to say was intriguing, and difficult to make sense of. 'Kath paid more than she should for Brydeshill?'

'Yes.' Tara sighed. 'I didn't want involved, and now Edwin has told me the story, I'm concerned how Kath will make enough money to survive and…' She left the rest unsaid.

'And why would Edwin tell you?'

She shrugged. 'No idea. I want as little as possible to do with him. I think he likes it when someone is in trouble. He was gleeful about the amount of money he made from the sale. And he keeps going back to Brydeshill from what I hear. Perhaps he feels he still has a stake in it. It shows you what kind of a man he is.'

'You mean because he keeps returning?'

Tara grimaced. 'He's one of those people who like to hang on. When we were at school together he was always lurking on the edge of one of the groups. You know what teenagers are like.' She sighed. 'I guess I felt sorry for him. Big mistake. And then when he found out I was back living on the island permanently, he turned up out of the blue. He's been "popping in" on a regular basis ever since. He's impossible to put off. The only good thing is that he's often off the island with his business concerns.'

This seemed a strange way to behave, even for as friendly a place as Bute, but I had to take Tara at her word. Besides, I'd now decided to confide in her my suspicions about the yard.

She crossed her arms and stared at me. 'Lovely as it is to see you, Alison, is there a particular reason for your visit?'

Swallowing hard, I said, 'There is something I want to discuss with you, Tara.' And almost without stopping for breath, I filled her in on the details of what had happened at Brydeshill. Though for some reason I didn't add in the bit about Edwin's visit earlier in the day. It wasn't relevant, particularly now it was clear he had an alibi.

She sat in silence as I went through the sequence of events, occasionally frowning.

As I finished my story, laying emphasis on why I was so worried about everything, she leaned forward.

'I know you won't want to hear this, Alison, especially with your fondness for getting involved, but don't you think on this occasion you'd be better to leave this to the police? Whatever happened to that young man, we know Fritz's death was murder. Keep out of it.'

She sounded stern and I didn't reply, rather taken aback at the tone of her voice. She was right, of course. Every time I came to the island I seemed to have this knack of becoming entangled in some problem or other.

'This time my plan was to visit to Deborah,' I protested. 'I hadn't seen her for some time, and it seemed the ideal opportunity to combine that with the chance to do some research on the island. I was booked into The Ferry Rest, but they had a problem with a burst pipe and had to cancel all the bookings. To be honest, I was grateful that Kath agreed to give me a room at Brydeshill. And when she asked me for help, I couldn't say no.'

Tara nodded. 'Yes, poor Hettie. There's been a lot

of damage from what I hear. And right at the beginning of the holiday season. Rotten luck.' She seemed to recollect I was in the middle of my story. 'Go on, Alison,' she said.

'Then, just before I arrived there was that business with the dead man in the stable…and then Fritz. I couldn't leave seeing how upset Kath was. And I had agreed to do what I could to help.'

Tara sighed. 'From what I gather, that might have been your original intention, but you seem to have become an invaluable member of staff.'

About to protest again, I bit back the words, thinking of how much I'd become part of Brydeshill. On this occasion, Tara was right. But as soon as I could, I'd be off.

I sipped my tea to give me time to think before saying, 'These deaths must surely be linked in some way? You know the island, know Kath.'

'Yes,' Tara said, 'but it's like the situation with Edwin. We were all at school together, but that's a long time ago. And I don't know much about the livery business, though I do love horses.' She looked wistful. 'Perhaps one day I'll be able to have a horse of my own again.'

I wanted to take her back to the conversation about Brydeshill. 'I'm sure you've heard what people are saying about what might have happened.' One thing about Tara was that she had a sharp mind, was able to see sense where often I could only see muddle. And there's no way she wouldn't have heard the island gossip about recent events.

She lifted the teapot and looked over at me, but I shook my head. She poured herself a second cup, slowly and deliberately.

I waited in silence, resisting the temptation to speak

and eventually she sat back with a sigh. 'Schooldays seem so long ago, Alison. We were all different people then. After sixth year we all went our separate ways. Some people can't wait to get off the island, head for the city lights.'

'I suppose the problem is for some kinds of qualification you have to go to a college or a university on the mainland. Lots of people come back, though. The grass is always greener, as they say.'

She laughed. 'That's so true. Some of us found that living on Bute had many compensations. I couldn't imagine myself anywhere else now.'

'Not even if Warren were to be offered a plum post in another part of the country?' I said, thinking of my own situation and the complications with my marriage through the various jobs Simon had ended up doing.

'Oh, I think we'd find a way through,' she said. 'And the island is such a great place to bring up children.'

We were drifting away from the topic and I was making no progress in finding out what Tara knew, hoping there might be a clue in any gossip she'd heard.

'You didn't know Fritz?'

She shook her head. 'No, he came to the island to work for Edwin and he wasn't off the farm much, from what I know. I only met him once or twice recently when he was in town with Kath, buying supplies for the yard. I don't know anything about him really.'

'But Kath and Edwin – you know what they did after school.'

'Oh, yes. Edwin left to take up a job on the

mainland, but his father died suddenly, and he had to come back to manage Brydeshill. His heart wasn't in it though and after struggling for years he sold it to Kath. She'd come back to the island by then. If she can't make it a going concern I guess it will go back on the market.'

'Oh, where did Kath go after school? One of the cities? College?'

'No, no, Kath was the most adventurous of us all. Straight after school she headed off to Spain, to Granada, to take up a post as a guide for one of the tourist companies there. Her parents were strict, and she seized the opportunity to leave as soon as she could. To be honest we were surprised when she returned. And when she bought Brydeshill. She had worked during the school holidays at the local stables – the ones on the other side of the island – and that's where she was employed when she returned to Bute. But even so it's a big leap to owning your own place.'

I waited for her to continue, sipping my tea slowly.

Tara grinned. 'Yes, we were all surprised by her decision. Though she seems to know what she's doing.'

But it wasn't the business of buying Brydeshill that had surprised me. If Kath had spent time working in Spain as a tourist guide, why had she claimed she knew little Spanish? And how did that tie in with the letter I'd found?

THIRTY-THREE

There was too much conflicting information, too many puzzles and more confused than ever, I left after an hour of general chit-chat with Tara. She hadn't been much help, to be honest, though the visit had cheered me up. And she had made it clear she thought I shouldn't involve myself one minute longer in the events at Brydeshill. But how could I not? There was no way out now. I had to find out what was happening, what the story was, before I could go back to Glasgow.

After leaving Tara's, I wasn't inclined to go back to Brydeshill immediately. I'd have a walk to clear my head, mull over what Tara had told me.

It was some time since I'd been to the area round by Mount Stuart and I seemed to remember there was a path along a quiet beach there near Kerrylamont Farm that came out at Kilchattan Bay. Someone had mentioned it to me ages ago, and it was one of the many places on the island on my list to explore. Why not now?

I left my car in the car park at Mount Stuart and headed for the farm, only about half a mile south of the main house. I seemed to remember it had once been the home farm for Mount Stuart House, serving the family well over many generations. Now the buildings were no longer in use, but they were being repurposed, though given their historic status, it might be some time before all were occupied again. I guessed it would probably end up as a mixture of small workshops, largely craft, which was the usual way of making best use of such large spaces.

There were so many hidden walks like this on the island. Most of the tourists who came to Bute didn't stray far from the main routes and even the most adventurous preferred the West Island way to exploring less well-known areas.

The old home farm was much bigger than I'd imagined, and I skirted round the perimeter before quickening my pace up the track to the Bruchag Road, and then walking briskly towards Kilchattan along the curve of the narrow beach of white sand. In one of the fields of barley a lone tree stood, its greening branches reaching for the sky and I wondered why it alone had been spared.

A few minutes later I came out at Kilchattan, congratulating myself on completing what had been a rather demanding walk in places where the terrain was rough and uneven. I determined that while I was on Bute, I'd try to explore other hidden places on the island and on the way back to Brydeshill I'd stop off in town to buy a large-scale map.

Lost in thought, idly watching a trio of gulls as they squabbled over a leftover chip wrapper which they had snatched from the litter bin, I was startled to hear a voice beside me.

'Out for a walk?' It was Duncan Bradstone. Then, seeing the look of surprise on my face, he added with a smile, 'Sorry if I alarmed you. I can see you were absorbed in watching the antics of those seagulls.'

'You get so used to the quiet here – I've just been to Kerrylamont and there wasn't another person in sight.'

He looked puzzled, then said, 'Ah, White Sands beach. Yes, I know it. It's only one of so many beautiful walks on the island.'

‘My plan is to buy a map in town and try to find time to explore more of the island before I go back to Glasgow.’

‘You’re leaving soon, then?’

‘It’s difficult,’ I said. ‘I’d hoped there would be some progress with finding out about the deaths, that I could leave, but nothing much seems to be happening. Or the police aren’t saying.’

He turned away to look out over the bay. ‘Yes, strange business. Do you think there’s a link between both deaths?’

‘There must be. It’s unlikely there would be two such incidents in the same place...and one so close after the other.’

‘Mmm.’ He turned back to look at me. ‘Why don’t you and Deborah come over for dinner one night? I’m sure it would give you a break from all this nonsense.’

‘That would be excellent,’ I said, assuming he was doing no more than making polite conversation, but he reached into his jacket pocket and pulled out a business card. ‘I’ve a pen somewhere,’ he said, feeling about in his other pockets before finding one. He hastily scribbled on the card. ‘This is my home number. The one on the card is the business number of the surgery. Give me a call tomorrow when you’ve asked Deborah and we’ll arrange something.’

‘Thank you,’ I said, the thought flashing through my mind that perhaps he had an interest in my daughter. Nonsense. I’d seen him with Gemma. That was where his attention lay. Even so, I was sure Deborah would be delighted to accept the invitation, but better to ask her first.

‘Not at all. And it will do me good to have a bit of company. I’m still a newcomer here and with such a busy job, there are few opportunities for socialising.'

'What sort of time were you thinking of?' I said.

'Say about 7.30? I don't finish surgery until 7 so that gives me enough time to close and get home. And now I'd better be off. I've been attending to a calf having problems feeding and now I'm on my way to see to a sick horse. Probably not much wrong with her, but always good to check it out. I look forward to your phone call.'

With that he strolled off and I watched as he unlocked his car and climbed in, giving me a quick toot of the horn as he passed me on the way out of Kilchattan.

This time I took the shorter way round by the road. During my walk Mount Stuart had become busy: as I drove down towards the main road, two large tourist coaches passed me, and there were several cyclists making their way slowly up the steep incline towards Kilchattan.

I stopped in town for the map I'd promised myself, and to buy some goodies from the Electric Bakery, before a quick glance at the clock on the tower of the ferry terminal told me it was time to go back.

Much refreshed by my day out, I drove the few miles back feeling lighter of heart. And Duncan's invitation would be an opportunity for Deborah and me to escape Brydeshill for a while.

Surely the police would find out the truth about the two deaths and identify the culprit or culprits. Then I'd be able to leave, go back to Glasgow. I shouldn't have been so optimistic.

THIRTY-FOUR

At first I thought it was just the usual activity in the yard. In the past couple of days, several more riders had returned and there was a horse I didn't recognise being led out from one of the stables. I chuckled to myself. I was becoming quite the expert.

'Mum!' Deborah came over, leading Caffrey. 'Where have you been?'

'Over to see Tara and then I went for a walk. I'm back in plenty of time to feed the chickens.' This was intended as a joke, but she didn't respond.

'The police were back, closeted with Kath for ages.'

'Did they want to interview everyone again?' I might have to go down to the police station in Rothesay if they did want to speak to me.

She shook her head. 'They left about an hour ago, but when I went in to see Kath, she wouldn't answer my questions. She might be willing to talk to you because she wouldn't say anything to me. We have to know what's going on.'

'Okay. I'll try, but she might have information she doesn't want to share just yet.'

Deborah sighed. 'We only want to help.'

'What are you doing?'

She laughed. 'Can't you see? Caffrey has been having a great time rolling in the mud.'

Leaving her grooming Caffrey, I crossed the yard to the farmhouse. Kath was sitting in the kitchen, staring dully into space and it appeared she'd been sitting in that position for some time. The accounts ledgers still occupied the far end of the table and from the look of them, they hadn't been touched.

Unsure of where to begin, I decided it was best to be direct and I sat down opposite her saying, 'Deborah says the police have been back, but only to see you. What did they want?'

This had the desired effect, because she looked up, startled, and said, 'It was all most peculiar. I didn't know what to make of it. They quizzed me about what I was doing in the years before I bought Brydeshill. I've no idea what that had to do with anything.'

Since hearing the story from Tara, I'd fretted about how to introduce the subject of the letter. Here was the ideal opportunity.

'Did they want to know about your time in Spain?'

Her head jerked up. 'What do you mean? How do you know about that?'

'I was looking for a book to read and came across a letter to you from someone in Spain, written a good number of years ago.'

She started to say, 'What gave you that idea…' but her voice tailed off.

'I've been to visit Tara and she told me that immediately after leaving Rothesay Academy you went to Spain to work as a tourist guide.'

A sullen look crossed her face. 'So?'

'The letter is in the room next door,' I said, standing up. 'I'll fetch it now.'

Before she could stop me I scurried into the bedroom and pulled the letter out from the book on the bedside table.

When I came back into the kitchen, Kath hadn't moved, but she looked up anxiously.

Without a moment's hesitation, I unfolded the letter, smoothing it out as I laid it in front of her.

She picked it up with trembling hands. 'I'd forgotten all about this. I must have put it there – out of sight, out of mind.'

'Is that what the police wanted to ask you about? All those years ago in Spain? What has it to do with what's been happening? Why would the police be interested in your past?'

I stopped, aware I was chattering on without giving her time to reply. We sat in silence as Kath read the letter through. 'It was so long ago,' she said, sighing. 'One of those episodes you put to the back of your mind, try to forget and get on with your life.' She waved the letter in the air. 'This is my life now. You can't let the past dictate what happens in the present.'

This was fine, but she was avoiding the issue about how this letter might relate to the events at Brydeshill.

'Perhaps you should show this letter to the police. That might help with the case.'

Now she looked puzzled. 'How would that help? All it would do is muddy the waters. It's of no significance.' She gave a hollow laugh. 'A youthful love affair. I can scarcely remember what he looked like.'

'That might be true,' I persisted, 'but the police must have some interest in your past. How did they find out you'd spent time in Spain?'

'How do they find out anything nowadays,' she said, staring down at the floor, avoiding my gaze. 'There are records everywhere. Nothing is private now.'

I wanted more information. 'What did you do in Spain? Were you there long?'

It looked as if she wasn't going to tell me, that she didn't trust me sufficiently, but finally she looked up from the letter, saying, 'I spent several years there as a tourist guide. You know what it's like. I was young, eager to leave the island and experience life. And when the opportunity came up…'She stopped. 'But it was all so long ago, so far away.' She gazed at the letter then folded it over, perhaps recalling painful events from her past.

Suddenly, as though coming to a decision, she crumpled the letter and threw it deftly into the wastepaper basket. 'Best forgotten. I've told the police what they need to know.'

And with that she stood up and strode purposefully out of the room, leaving me looking after her.

But as soon as she was out of sight, I retrieved the letter from the wastepaper basket. There was more to this story than Kath was telling me. I'd have to find a way of getting at the truth…and sooner rather than later.

THIRTY-FIVE

The puzzle of the locked cupboard in the riding arena nagged away at me. There must be some reason Fritz had been so anxious to keep us out of there. But right now there was no opportunity to investigate. Life around the stables was starting to become busier. After a sudden downturn because of what had happened, riders were beginning to return, at first in small numbers then almost without warning all the classes were fully booked.

Kath had been able to restart individual lessons with several private clients, only a couple of the livery stables remained empty.

There was no word about finding a replacement for Fritz. I suspected Kath was torn between feeling she should wait, given the circumstances, and the need to keep the business going. The vet students Duncan had suggested hadn't yet arrived, an appeal for more volunteers had brought no response and everyone was working non-stop to keep up with demand.

It was becoming light earlier now and as I wakened with the early morning sun filtering through the curtains and the sound of the dawn chorus, I lay listening for a while, thinking how peaceful it sounded. I was still in the ground floor bedroom. No one had suggested I might return to the attic room and I'd deliberately avoided the subject.

This might be a good opportunity to have another look in the arena. If I was quick I should be able to check the cupboards before any of the stable hands appeared. I dressed quickly, remembering to pull on a sweater against the early morning chill and crept out through the kitchen making sure to avoid any obstacles. There were advantages to having a room on the ground floor and I ignored the temptation to stop for coffee, reckoning the sound of the kettle might disturb someone.

The ginger cat stretched lazily as I came through then jumped down, meowing loudly, no doubt in search of food. Ignoring this plea and deftly skirting round him, I opened the back door, hoping it wouldn't squeak too much and deliberately leaving it on the latch.

For a moment I hesitated, remembering recent events, but decided to take the chance. From what I recalled you had to tug it hard to close it fully and the resulting loud bang was sure to be heard.

Outdoors, I paused. There was no one about as I came out into the yard and although Baron and Nyx greeted me enthusiastically, they soon bounded off in search of something more interesting.

The morning was fresh, but that kind of day where the heat builds up. The horses seemed quiet, probably still dozing, unused to someone being about at this early hour, though there was a whickering from Marvel's stable. A gentle reminder I'd have to be quick. And the longer I lingered here, the more likely the animals would create a fuss, and someone would come to investigate.

I hurried to the arena, not pausing to look back. In here the smell of stale sawdust was pungent, acrid. Gemma would clean it, rake it over later, but for the moment I tried to take shallow breaths as I crossed to the cupboard.

Having been interrupted first time round, this time I was determined to find the key to the second cupboard. The first one I could discount, the cupboard with riding gear, but the other was the cupboard Fritz had seemed so anxious about. But finding a way of opening it was another matter. I stood and stared at it, hoping inspiration would strike me. Where might the key be hidden? I was sure it was somewhere convenient, else why would Fritz have made such a fuss when he saw me there? Which could only mean this was a cupboard where more than one person had access.

Brooding about this, I began to search around, stretching up to feel along the top of this cupboard. But I wasn't tall enough to reach far enough back. I'd have to find a ladder. I scanned the arena, but there was no ladder and nothing obvious that would serve instead.

What a nuisance. I only needed a little help. In the far corner I spied a couple of three-step mounting blocks which were part of the equipment to help riders on to a horse. Worth a try, I thought and pushed the nearest one over. But even balancing rather dangerously on the top step on tiptoe I was unable to reach to the back of the top of the cupboard.

Frustrated and aware time was slipping away, I stepped down from the mounting block, trying to think where else a key might be hidden. After all, I reasoned, Fritz hadn't been much taller than I am, so it was unlikely he'd have hidden the key somewhere inaccessible.

But another look around the arena gave no clue to a likely hiding place. What a waste of time and effort. Feeling defeated, I sat down on the mounting block, aware of sounds from the yard. Someone was up and about. There was no point in lingering. I'd be better going back to the farmhouse for breakfast. Kath and the others would be up soon, if they weren't already, and I didn't want to have to think up another excuse for being in the arena.

I lifted the mounting block and carried it over to put it back beside the others. But as I replaced it, I noticed the bench box beside it. This was where Fritz had been standing when he'd been so cross with Deborah, and I quickly lifted the lid. But it was empty.

Why should I be surprised? If this had been the hiding place, Fritz would have realised we'd seen him and hidden the key somewhere else. I looked again at the mounting blocks. The one I'd been using to stand on had what looked like a lid on top. Perhaps it wasn't just a mounting block after all. I fiddled around with the lid, prising it this way and that till with a satisfying click, it opened. It was a narrow opening, but inside there was a small box, a box which wasn't locked. And there was a key. This must be it. But as I lifted it out, I heard a voice calling, 'Hello, hello, who's there?'

I stood clutching the key, unable to move. It was Gemma. What should I do now and what explanation could I give this time?

THIRTY-SIX

As Gemma came striding into the stables, I scurried over to put the key back where I'd found it, checking the mounting block as I did so. Good! I'd remembered to close the top securely. Then I thought, what if Gemma is involved in whatever is going on here? Will she realise what I've been doing?

This was going through my mind as I ran over and, grabbing the key from the top of the boot cupboard, I quickly unlocked it and pretended to be rummaging about among the stack of boots, shoes, and other riding gear.

As Gemma approached me, I grabbed the first boot in front of me, holding it up to examine it closely.

'Oh, it's you, Alison. You're up bright and early.' She looked puzzled. 'Is there a problem? I thought you'd found a suitable pair of boots last time.'

'Yes,' I said. 'But I'm trying to find a pair of boots to wear round the yard. All this recent rain has made everywhere so muddy and…'Aware I was chattering on to no purpose, I turned away to hide my confusion. 'The other one of this must be in here somewhere.'

'Unless you plan to take up riding, I don't think those boots will be of any use.'

'Oh, really,' I said, giving a false laugh. 'What do I know.' I replaced the boot in the cupboard. 'I guess most of the boots in here are for riding?'

Gemma frowned at me. 'Yes, of course they are. There are a few pairs of wellingtons and I thought you'd found some that fitted. I saw you wearing them round the yard. What's happened to them?'

Suddenly inspired, I said, 'With all the rain, I thought it might be a good idea to have a spare pair. In case the others got wet.'

She clearly thought I was even more ignorant of country matters than she'd believed. Then, plainly tiring of this silly conversation, she turned on her heel and began to walk away, saying, 'With everything that's happened you can't be too careful. See you later.'

Sighing with relief, I sat down on the bench beside the cupboards. Another missed opportunity. Trouble was, if the livery yard became busier, if there were more people around, there would be fewer chances to explore.

No point in sitting here brooding and I made my way slowly back to the farmhouse. Kath was in the kitchen and there was a delicious aroma of coffee and of bacon sizzling in the pan on top of the stove.

'Gosh, that smells good,' I said, suddenly realising how hungry I was.

'Plenty for everyone,' Kath said, looking up from buttering thick slices of home-made bread.

One thing I would miss about here was the quality of the food. Or perhaps a contributing factor was the fresh air and exercise. Whatever the reason, I made short work of the bacon sandwich and large mug of coffee she placed before me.

'I must go and feed the chickens,' I said, rising reluctantly as she offered me a second cup of coffee.

'You're becoming too attached to those chickens,' she said with a grin. She appeared to have recovered her good humour. There had been no further discussion about the letter, and I couldn't think of a way to broach the subject again.

And while I was keen to do so, I didn't dare to raise

the subject of the police investigation, hoping she'd tell us if there had been any news about either of the deaths.

Out in the yard, I stood watching: several horses were being led into the arena by their young owners. Deborah came up beside me. 'Good to see things are beginning to return to normal.' She was also happier than I'd seen her in days. 'The Pony Club competitions will be starting soon and it's important to get the practice in. Kath's taking a dressage class today.'

Then she laughed. 'You should think about learning to ride. I hear you were trying out some of the spare riding boots for size.'

So Gemma had told Deborah about my visit to the arena. It was impossible to keep anything secret here. I'd have to be careful and choose my time carefully if I was to find out what was in that cupboard. And I was now more determined than ever.

'You know that's a joke, Deborah,' I said as she went off, chortling to herself.

Meanwhile there were the chickens to attend to.

THIRTY-SEVEN

The afternoon wore on, the time passing quickly, although there was much less to do than usual. Perhaps I was slowing down to a simpler way of life. I pottered round the yard, gave Deborah a hand topping up the horses' hay nets (I drew the line at helping muck out the stables), had a chat with a couple of the owners and checked the chickens.

Now at a loose end, I thought I might take some time out to find a sunny area in the garden behind the farmhouse to read my book. My article was no further forward, but I convinced myself I'd be able to work flat out when I was back in Glasgow…unless I was suddenly seized by inspiration.

The old stone of the building reflected the heat, making this spot an ideal suntrap. I settled down to read, but my mind kept wandering back to the deaths and I found it difficult to concentrate. Any question about progress brought a strange response from Kath, given she'd asked me to help. 'I'll tell you as soon as I know anything,' she snapped, and I didn't have the inclination to pursue the matter. Perhaps she was disappointed in me, had expected too much. And so far I'd been no help at all.

Was it no more than coincidence that the young man found dead in the stable was Spanish? Then again, it might well be. I thought about the letter I'd found. But the young man couldn't have been known to Kath. If Kath had been in Spain as a tourist guide, that must have been almost twenty years ago, judging by the date on the letter.

Why should I be surprised that a Spaniard had come to Bute? Odd, yes, that he'd been found dead in the stables but not that he was on the island. People now holidayed in Scotland from all over the world and many visited Bute as part of their itinerary.

There was another dilemma. Was there a connection between Jose and Fritz? The only link that came to mind was that he was also foreign. Had Jose come to the island to find Fritz for some reason? It was all too much of a puzzle, especially for a warm afternoon like this.

As it became hotter and hotter in this little corner, I felt myself slowly drifting off to sleep, lulled by the hum of bees, the distant neighing of one of the horses. That early morning start was beginning to catch up with me.

Suddenly I heard voices and came to with a jolt, letting my book slide to the ground. Silence. I must have been dreaming. But then as I bent to pick up my book, they came again. Someone must have opened the kitchen window in the farmhouse.

At first I could hear only a murmur and it was impossible to make out who was speaking. But a few moments later the talk became more heated and voices were raised. One of the speakers was unmistakeable – it was Gemma and the other was a man's voice.

I considered moving away rather than eavesdropping. It was difficult enough explaining to Gemma about being in the riding arena and I didn't want to appear as if I was now listening to a private conversation. But if I tried to creep away I might be noticed and that would be equally bad: I was immediately under the window and any movement would be detected.

Sad to say, curiosity got the better of me and I kept perfectly still as the conversation continued.

'This is a nonsensical request. How can I…'I heard Gemma say, but the remainder of her words were lost as she turned away or moved about.

The man replied, 'I'm only asking what we agreed. We had…' Again the words were lost.

It was incredibly frustrating, only hearing part of the discussion but as I waited there was a murmur of conversation before voices were raised again. I heard Gemma say, 'There has to be a time limit. You have to understand after what happened, I can't go on.'

The man gave a low laugh. 'Stop worrying. Business is picking up again. It'll work out.'

'You don't understand,' Gemma said with a sob in her voice.

Their voices dropped once more, and I couldn't make out the rest of the words.

Suddenly I heard the man say, 'I'll be in touch later. Just stop worrying. It's all going to be fine.' Then the kitchen door slammed with some force and I instinctively drew back. I had only a moment or two to decide. Should I stay hidden till I was certain the man had left. Dare I peep round the corner to see who was coming out of the farmhouse.

There was no decision to be made, not really. I had to find out who had been having this conversation with Gemma. Scarcely daring to breathe, I stood up and crept on tiptoe to peek out round the side of the building, ready to draw back at any moment.

At first I could only make out a back view, but as he walked down the path from the farmhouse towards the yard he turned around briefly to glance back.

Of course I knew him. I'd met him recently while on my walk at Kilchattan Bay.

It was Duncan Bradstone, the vet. What had they been talking about? It was something to do with money, that was for sure.

Then I realised there could only be one explanation. Now it all made sense. Duncan had been at Brydeshill several times to attend to one of the horses that had gone lame. He'd come over today to collect his fee for the work he'd done, but Kath was in no position to pay him despite his belief the business was returning to profit. Had Gemma been pleading for more time? Things at Brydeshill must be much worse than Kath was willing to disclose.

THIRTY-EIGHT

It was a strange kind of day: showers and cold one minute, bright sunshine the next. After three weeks on the island I was beginning to feel claustrophobic, and I'd have to make a choice soon. I couldn't stay on indefinitely. There was a more settled air at Brydeshill, and no matter what the outcome of the recent deaths, there was a determination that the business would continue. Soon I'd be able to pack up and return home.

I caught up with Deborah as she came downstairs next morning.

'I think I'll go back to Glasgow next week,' I said, watching for her reaction. 'I can come back over if the police want to interview me again.'

I was relieved to see her smile as she said, 'I guess you can't stay on indefinitely. To be honest, I might move on also. This job was only supposed to be a temporary post, to help out. I didn't envisage being here as long as this.'

This wasn't what I'd expected. It might not be a well-paid job here at Brydeshill, and certainly there were no opportunities to use the skills acquired on the many courses Deborah had attended, but at least it was a job.

'What will you do if you leave here?' I frowned.

She shrugged but didn't meet my gaze as she said, 'Declan messaged me a few days ago to say there's a new gallery opening in Glasgow.' She stopped and the next words came out in a rush. '…and he wondered if I'd like to apply for the post of manager.'

‘Is it opening soon?’ I said, making an effort to sound positive rather than critical of yet another change of employment.

‘Oh, the gallery opens at the beginning of September. I think the interview might be next week. I’m waiting for a reply to my application. I’ve told Kath I’ll have to be off island for a couple of days.’ She sighed. ‘It’s been interesting working here, but Kath knew it wasn’t more than a short-term solution. And this gallery sounds exciting, promoting new talent. Much more in line with what I want to do in the future. It’s a permanent position.’

My hope was that this might be the turning point for my daughter, so I said, ‘That sounds promising. Lots of luck with the interview.’

Then I wondered how Kath would react to the news, to having to look for a replacement. Not your difficulty, I told myself. Aloud I said, ‘I’m going to Rothesay to pick up a few bits and pieces.’

It didn’t take long to find what I wanted in Rothesay, mostly because the shopping was only an excuse to get away for a while. Stopping to chat with several people I knew passed a good half hour. I suspected they wanted me to provide an update about the deaths at the yard, but I could honestly say I’d nothing to report.

My plan had been to go into the Kettledrum for coffee but when I looked in most of the tables were occupied and Helmi’s, the Syrian café, proved no less busy. I wasn’t in the mood to return to Brydeshill and decided to drive over to Ettrick Bay. If the tearoom there was crowded, I’d buy coffee and cake to take out, being optimistic about a break in the weather.

As I drove into Port Bannatyne, I caught a glimpse of several yachts creaming down the Kyles. There must be a boat race on, and I slid into a parking space near the bus stop. I'd walk along to the end of the village to sit on one of the many memorial benches dotted along the edge of the promenade to watch. The sight of the yachts gliding calmly down towards the Kyles, sails billowing in the breeze, was soothing – the kind of therapy I needed right now.

As I sat there, lost in contemplation, a shadow fell across the grass and I heard someone say, 'We meet again.' I looked up to see Duncan Bradstone towering over me. With a guilty start I remembered the conversation I'd overheard. And I hadn't yet phoned him about the dinner he'd suggested.

He pointed to the yachts. 'I should have been out there today, but I've a full list of calls.'

'Do you do much racing?' I enquired, as much out of politeness as interest.

He shook his head. 'Not as much as I'd like, to be honest. There are so few vet practices on the island, we're always busy.'

'Are you on a call now?' I was struggling for a topic of conversation, but Duncan seemed in no mood to leave.

'I'm on a break – my yacht is berthed in the Marina here at Port Bannatyne and I'm popping over to do a quick check. She's been here for most of the winter and I'm trying to get her ready for the summer. I intend to have a long holiday this year. I feel I deserve it.'

I stood up. 'Talking of having a break, I have to move also. I did intend to go to Ettrick Bay for coffee, but the morning seems to have slipped away. I'll have lunch there. And then I'll have to get back to Brydeshill.'

'Those chickens, I guess?'

‘Exactly. Somehow I’ve become responsible for them.’

We said good bye. Thank goodness he hadn’t mentioned dinner again. With a last look at the yachts, now disappearing round the headland to sail up the Kyles, I stood up to walk over to my car. A glance back to watch Duncan as he reached the edge of the Marina saw him stopping as someone came out of the boatyard, pointing towards the lines of boats berthed there.

As I drove past I couldn’t resist slowing down, in time to see Duncan walk down the pontoon to jump up onto a very smart blue and white boat, its polished wood and shiny brass rails a testimony to hours of loving care. Perhaps he was being modest when he’d said he had work to do on his boat. I knew little about yachts, but this must have cost a pretty penny.

As I drove towards Ettrick Bay, I was still thinking about this luxurious vessel belonging to Duncan. But what did I know? There could be any number of reasons why a vet owned a boat like this. Then I remembered what Fritz had said – something about Duncan making lots of money. Was that possible with a veterinary practice?

But all thoughts of Duncan and his elegant boat were dismissed as I drove along the Ettrickdale Road, past the old Smithy and on to the car park at the Tearoom.

For the next hour I’d forget all about the problems at Brydeshill and enjoy the peace and tranquillity of the bay.

THIRTY-NINE

Lunch at the Ettrick Bay tearoom and a walk along the sands by the Kirkmichael Road put me in a better frame of mind and I returned to the yard determined to make a fresh start on my article. No more excuses, I told myself sternly. I'd plenty of material and should surely be able to finish the first draft, especially now I had a date in mind for returning to Glasgow.

The yard was quiet when I drove in, the chickens drowsing in the still air and the heat of the afternoon. In the summer field, the horses were also quiet, contentedly nibbling at the grass. Felix looked up as I approached, tossing his head as though in recognition.

There were no classes that afternoon, judging by the empty arena and although I spied a couple of owners over by the stable block, I guessed Kath and the rest of the staff must be in the farmhouse having a late lunch.

As I locked the car, a thought struck me. This might be the ideal time to try once more to investigate the second cupboard. I glanced around, but apart from the owners I'd spied earlier, now busy chatting as they groomed their horses, there was no sign of anyone else.

I walked quickly over to the arena, glancing back from time to time to check I hadn't been spotted. But I needn't have worried and I reached the entrance and slipped inside without being seen.

Even so, I stopped at the entrance for a moment. It would just be my luck to find out I'd made a mistake. There were always jobs to be done: preparations, clearing up after classes, sorting out equipment. But no, it was as deserted here as it was in the outside yard. There was one last problem. If someone did come in, what excuse could I use this time? Ah, then it came to me. I could say I'd dropped my watch last time I'd been here. A flimsy excuse, but hopefully I wouldn't have to use it.

To be on the safe side, I took off my watch and slipped it into my jacket pocket before making my way round the side of the arena towards the cupboards.

But first I went straight to the mounting blocks on the far side of the arena.

Drat? Which one had the key? They all looked the same and having been in use since my last attempt to investigate, they were no longer in the same positions. How stupid. I should have thought of a way to remember the correct one last time, but I'd been so anxious to get away.

As luck would have it, the first two proved unsuccessful, but the third time I struck lucky and almost dropped the key in my haste to open the cupboard.

Aware speed was of the essence, I tried the key in the second cupboard. But no matter which way I turned it, the lock wouldn't budge. Hoping one more try would be more successful, I pushed the key into the lock and turned it with as much force as I could muster. But my vigour was almost my downfall, as the cupboard door swung open suddenly, almost knocking me over.

Slightly winded, I took a minute to catch my breath before opening the other door and examining the contents.

But I was in for a disappointment. All I could see

were boxes of varying sizes, stacked tightly on all the shelves. I picked up the one nearest, then the one next to that, but they were no more than standard cardboard containers, the kind you can find in any stationer's shop selling envelopes. They were securely sealed and there was no way to have a look inside one and then reseal it. I lifted one, shook it, but though it was reasonably heavy, it didn't make more noise than a muffled thud. Whatever was in them, I couldn't guess.

What a waste of time. Deeply disappointed, I was about to close the cupboard and return the key to its hiding place in the mounting block, when I stopped. Why on earth would Fritz be so angry about piles of boxes? And why go to the trouble of hiding the key?

I stared at the boxes, then pulled aside two on the middle shelf. Something caught my eye. Right at the back was a manilla envelope, so small as to be easily missed. Which may well have been what had happened. I pulled it out and opened it. Inside was a notebook.

Another glance around to make certain there was no one else in the arena and I began to flick through. The notebook contained several pages with a series of numbers and what looked like hieroglyphics neatly set out in columns. They looked for all the world like random scribbles and a series of numbers. Could they be phone numbers? But none of the entries looked like a dialling code, so that wasn't likely.

What should I do? This might mean nothing, or it might be important. Why bother to keep a cupboard like this locked unless what was inside was of value. And if it was a clue, I'd need a lot more time to make any sense of it.

Aware of time running on, I pulled out my phone,

taking a screenshot of the pages before slipping the notebook back into the envelope and replacing it in the cupboard. It was a moment's work to lock the cupboard and replace the key in its hiding place in the mounting block before hurrying back out into the yard, my heart thudding. I took a moment to breathe deeply to calm my nerves before striding towards the stables, trying my best to appear unflustered.

The owners who'd been chatting at the stable block came towards me, leading their horses out to the field, nodding politely but showing no inclination to stop. Just as well, as the guilty expression on my face would surely have aroused their suspicions.

Congratulating myself on a kind of success, even though I'd no idea what it all meant, I strode purposefully towards the farmhouse. All I had to do now was decipher the information from the notebook. Easy to say, but it might prove a lot more difficult to do. I'd no idea where to begin.

FORTY

Absorbed as I was in trying to make sense of the information in the notebook I'd found in the cupboard in the riding arena, the issue of the Spanish love letter and what it meant to Kath had slipped to the back of my mind. Not for long, though.

First things first. Determined to make progress while I was still in the mood, I went back to my room to write my article. By dinner time I felt a lot more cheerful. I'd come up with an idea which would make a good introduction to the article, had managed to draft a rough outline, and identified gaps where more research was needed.

When I came into the kitchen, humming to myself, Kath, Gemma, and Deborah were already seated round the table. There was a smell of something spicy in the air.

'Someone has been busy,' I said.

'Sit down and enjoy.' Kath smiled, handing me a plate. She seemed more relaxed.

But as we were about to eat, the phone rang.

'Who is it now?' Kath said crossly, pausing in the middle of dishing up the hearty stew she'd prepared. 'I don't want to speak to anyone right now.'

'It might be the police with news,' Deborah said, getting to her feet and pushing back her chair.

'Then you answer it. If it's the police I'll take the call. If not, I won't.' Kath went back to ladling out the stew as Gemma cut slices from the freshly baked loaf.

Deborah made a face, but she went out into the hallway to answer the call. Despite Kath's reluctance, despite her pretence, I could see she was straining to hear who was phoning, but Deborah had pulled the door over and all we could make out were muffled exclamations.

A few minutes later, Deborah came back, saying, 'I really think you need to take this, Kath. As far as I can make out the caller is phoning from Spain and he's asking about Jose.'

Kath dropped the ladle, making little splashes of gravy on the kitchen table as she sprang to her feet. 'What did he say?' she said, not waiting for an answer as she hurried out of the room.

'You'd better hear for yourself,' Deborah called after her, but by then Kath was out of range.

'What's going on?' I said.

Deborah shrugged. 'I'm not sure,' she said. 'It was a terrible line, but I did manage to hear enough to understand he's connected to Jose and is trying to find out what happened. The police have been in touch with him.'

'That must mean the police have found out more about Jose.'

'Guess so.' Gemma said. These were the first words she'd spoken during the discussion and I wondered why she'd been so quiet. She took a few mouthfuls of her stew, then sat back and pushed her plate away.

'I'm going out for a ride,' she said, standing up. 'Topper isn't getting enough exercise and he's becoming far too fat.'

'Don't you want to wait and hear what Kath has to say?' Deborah said. 'Surely we'd all like one of the mysterious deaths cleared up.'

'No doubt Kath will give us all the details,' Gemma said, slamming the door to the kitchen behind her.

Deborah looked over at me and raised her

eyebrows, but before she could comment on Gemma's sudden departure we heard the phone receiver being replaced none too gently and Kath came back into the kitchen.

Deborah looked as if she was about to speak, but I put my finger to my lips, warning her. Better to let Kath tell us in her own good time.

The silence stretched out and at last she said in a puzzled voice, 'That's someone claiming to be Jose's father. The police asked him to come over to identify the body.'

'Your Spanish must be good if you understood all of that,' Deborah said.

Kath looked at her blankly, then seemed to collect herself. 'A combination of his English and my smattering of Spanish got us there.'

Why was Kath pretending that she had only a basic understanding of the language when it was clear her time in Granada must have made her reasonably fluent? Perhaps the arrival of Jose's father would shed light on the mystery.

FORTY-ONE

More problems were to follow. Possibly Kath thought Jose's father would come to Bute, identify the body, answer all relevant questions from the police and then head back to Spain. And that would be the end of the matter. Except of course it didn't answer the important question of why Jose had been in Topper's stable.

But it didn't work out like that. There followed a couple of anxious days as we waited for more news. Then early one morning a police car drew up as we were finishing breakfast. We were all on edge and at the sound of a loud knock on the kitchen door Kath jumped to her feet, almost spilling her mug of tea in the process.

She glanced out of the window. 'That's the police again.' She hurried out, closely followed by Gemma.

'Aren't you going too?' I said to Deborah.

'In a minute.' She reached over for another slice of toast and began buttering it slowly. 'Why don't you go,' she said. 'I know you're desperate to find out what's happening.'

This I couldn't deny, but it might be better to wait.

But before I could make a move, Kath and Gemma came back into the kitchen followed by two police officers, Constable Brevin, and a young woman constable I didn't recognise. Behind them came a tall, distinguished looking man of middle years.

'This is Jose's father, Diego Molina Sanchez,' Kath said, frowning. There was a sharpness in her tone I couldn't quite work out. She should be pleased that at last there might be an answer to the many questions about the young Spaniard.

Diego made a little bow, saying, 'I had to see where it happened. Where my son was…' he stopped. 'Where my son died.'

Deborah and I muttered condolences, as Constable Brevin said, 'We won't be too long. This is difficult for everyone.'

About to offer tea to allow us time to come to grips with this sudden turn of events, Kath stopped me. 'Let's do it now,' she said, 'and then perhaps you can have something to eat before you leave.' She was ashen-faced, trembling, and held on tightly to the back of the chair to steady herself.

There was a murmur of agreement and we watched in silence as Kath, Diego and the police officers went out to the stables to undertake this sad task.

'We'd better organise food, in case they're hungry,' I said to Deborah and we set to, using the rest of the bacon in the fridge and cracking eggs into a large bowl.

Neither of us was in the mood for chat. Being busy helped the time pass, but even so it seemed ages before the small party came back from the stables.

Diego covered his face with both hands, and Constable Brevin guided him to one of the easy chairs.

'That was not easy,' Diego said, looking up. 'Poor boy, to die all alone like that, without his parents.'

'How is your wife coping?' I said and he looked up at me blankly for a few moments. 'She isn't with you?'

'She died last year,' he said, blinking away a tear. We waited in silence as he pulled out a large handkerchief from his pocket and wiped his face.

'That is what makes it more difficult. Jose was a lovely young man, *muy agradable*, everyone liked him. Why did he have to come here? All for nothing.'

'Or why was he found in the stables,' muttered Constable Brevin, but no one answered him. We were too busy thinking what we could say to comfort Diego. To have lost his wife so recently and now his son was such a cruel blow.

Though Diego accepted the offer of breakfast, it was out of politeness as he did no more than push the food around on his plate, though he did have several cups of coffee in quick succession.

Gemma came in, closing the door quietly behind her and went over to whisper to Kath, 'That's the horses turned out for the day.' But it appeared Kath scarcely registered what she was saying.

A heavy silence hung in the air: trivial conversation seemed inappropriate, yet we didn't want to contribute to his grief by asking about Jose.

Finally Diego pushed his plate away and said, 'Do you have any idea why he was here? And why he was in the stables? There seems to be no explanation for it.'

Kath shook her head. 'We're as baffled as you are. And the police can't find a motive for murder. I'm sure it must have been an accident.' She glanced over at Constable Brevin, but he didn't look up.

Kath shrugged. 'There has been a major investigation,' and Constable Brevin nodded as she went on, '...appeals made. You'll have seen the posters in the shops and on the ferry, but apart from the couple of pubs where he enquired about Brydeshill, and the CalMac employee in the onboard café, no one has come forward to say they knew him.'

'Not quite true.' Diego drummed his fingers on the

table. 'The police say that a couple on the ferry remember seeing him.'

Kath looked as if she was biting back tears. 'But I found him early in the morning. He must have been on a ferry the night before.'

Diego nodded. 'That is so. The couple say Jose was on the last ferry that night – the one that leaves Wemyss Bay about 8 o'clock.'

'But that would mean he was in town no later than nine o'clock,' Deborah butted in.

Diego turned to look at her. 'The police have traced him to a couple of places where he went in to ask about Brydeshill. Including the Black Bull, where he had a meal.'

Ah, so he must have lingered in town.

'Perhaps he walked up to Brydeshill – that would account for the time discrepancy. If he stopped off for something to eat and then came up later…' My voice tailed off as I caught Kath looking at me strangely. She was right of course. Even if that had been the sequence of events, there was still no way of explaining why he ended up in the stable.

'Are the couple on the ferry sure it was Jose?'

'Oh, yes,' Diego said. They were behind him in the queue at the onboard café and remembered how he struggled with the unfamiliar money. They had to step in to help him. The person in the café was becoming impatient as he was holding up the queue.'

There was a silence, broken by Deborah saying, 'I must say your English is good.'

Diego made a bow. 'Thank you. My company does a lot of business with America. But then Kath's Spanish is equally good.'

I looked over at Kath, who had turned away to hide the blush spreading across her face. What was this about? When I'd shown her the letter, she'd claimed she spoke little Spanish. And again last night when she spoke to Diego on the phone. She'd alleged Diego didn't speak much English, yet here he was happily and fluently conversing with us.

But there was another surprise a few moments later. Deborah, sensing the atmosphere in the room, tried to break into the conversation.

'Was Jose your only child?' she said.

'What? Oh, sorry.' Diego's thoughts were clearly elsewhere. This had apparently upset him, and I motioned to Deborah not to continue. He would tell us in his own good time.

But Diego collected himself and said in a quiet voice. 'Yes. In fact he was not our son. We adopted him as a baby. My wife and I could not have children, so we adopted Jose when he was only a few months old. We could not have loved him more if he had been our natural son.'

'Oh, that's even worse. How old was he?'

Diego sighed. 'He would have been eighteen years old on the 21st of August.'

There was a gasp from Kath as Deborah said, 'How awful. And you've no idea why he came over to Bute.'

Diego fiddled with his coffee spoon, averting his eyes. 'I do have a good idea.'

'But you said…'Deborah began, only to be interrupted by Gemma, 'And have you told the police?'

Diego looked up and nodded. 'Yes, I did. It seems the most likely explanation.'

The room was silent, no one spoke or even stirred, waiting for Diego to continue. Surely now he was here he'd be willing to reveal what he knew.

Then, as everyone else gazed expectantly at Diego, I happened to glance over to where Kath was sitting in the far corner. Tears were streaming down her face as she sat there, quietly sobbing. What had Diego said about the death of Jose to affect her so badly?

FORTY-TWO

Suddenly Diego noticed how distressed Kath was.

'Something has upset you about my visit?' he said.

Kath lifted her tear-stained face and sniffed loudly. 'Where did you adopt Jose?'

'He was left as a baby in the care of a convent, Las Hermanas de La Sancta Vida, in Granada.'

'So the mother had handed him over? Why? There must have been a good reason.' Deborah frowned.

Diego gave a faint smile, drumming his fingers on the table as he replied to Deborah's comment. 'Well, not so much "handed him over" as abandoned him. He was found early one morning as one of the Sisters went to the front gate to collect the bread left by *el panadero*, the baker, on his rounds. She found him standing there, scratching his head, and looking at a bundle lying at the corner of the overhanging porch.'

'And this was Jose? Just left like that?'

'Ah, yes.' Then Diego went on quickly. 'But the baby was well cared for, clean and had been well fed. Whoever left him knew he would be found and taken in.'

'Even so, to desert your child like that.' Deborah sounded appalled.

A shadow crossed Diego's face. 'To you it sounds very callous, but you have to understand this is not such an unusual event.'

Diego made it sound as if babies were abandoned as Jose had been every day, but I knew what he meant. A desperate mother, unable for whatever reason to care for her child, would have sought out the best place of safety. But what an awful thing to have to do. With three children of my own, I couldn't imagine the agonies the mother had gone through, how frantic with worry she'd been to give up her son.

Gemma, who had been sitting quietly throughout this story, suddenly chimed in with, 'So you adopted Jose? But how does that have anything to do with why Jose suddenly appeared here.'

Diego sighed and there was another long silence while I watched him.

At last he said, slowly and carefully, 'Part of this story was our fault. A bad decision made by myself and my wife. We loved him very much, he had been our son for so long that we did not think of him as belonging to anyone else.'

'Ah,' said Gemma, 'so you didn't tell him he was adopted?'

Diego shrugged. 'We thought about it often, talked about it, but somehow the time never seemed right. And what good would it have done? We had no information to give him about his real family. He was happy with us, ready to take on the family business when I retired. He was *nuestro hijo,* our son, no matter what the story about his original family. Why upset everything for someone who had no interest in him?'

'But everyone has the right to know where they come from. Who their real family might be. What you have done is cruel.' Gemma sounded angry.

'But perfectly understandable,' Deborah said, rushing in to cover any awkwardness.

Diego looked upset, but it soon became clear it was nothing to do with Gemma's outburst.

'You are right of course. We should have told him many years ago, been honest with him. As it was, when he found out he was terribly angry. That day I will never forget.' Diego put his head in his hands, clearly remembering the episode with sadness.

'How did he find out?' The words were out before I could stop myself. If the circumstances had been as Diego suggested, then surely there must have been a catalyst, something that prompted the discovery that he had been adopted.

Diego reached into his pocket and pulled out an envelope. Opening it carefully, he extracted the object inside. It was a slim silver chain, broken in two.

'When Jose was found in the stable here, this was around his neck. But there is something missing. When he was *abandonado*, abandoned as a baby, there was a small half disc attached to this chain. We kept it, kept it safe, or so I thought. But when my wife died, I found it too painful to clear out some of her possessions and Jose offered to sort out her belongings. He found this silver chain and the half-moon disc in one of the boxes in the attic.' He gave a wry laugh. 'I'd forgotten all about it, hadn't thought about it in years.'

'But Jose wouldn't know what it was, surely?'

'No, but grief stricken as I was, I couldn't help myself when he asked me about it. I blurted out the truth without thinking.'

'So what happened to the disc?'

Diego shrugged. 'No idea – when he was found the disc was missing. There was only the broken chain.'

My heart began to thump as a memory stirred. What was it I'd found down in the car park of the old Academy? I'd forgotten about it, put it into my pocket without thinking.

'I might have some idea what happened to it.' I scrabbled in my pocket and pulled it out.

'*Eso es*! Yes, that's it!' Diego shouted. 'Where did you find it?'

'In the Academy car park – the chain must have broken, and the disc fell off.'

Engrossed as we were in this story, no one had noticed Kath slip out of the room.

As we sat there, unsure what to say next, since we couldn't explain this, she returned.

Slowly she opened her hand and held up a silver chain with a half disc. It looked like the one I'd found.

What on earth was this?

She sniffed, wiped away a tear and said, her voice croaking with emotion. 'I think you'll discover that this is the other half of that disc.'

FORTY-THREE

There was a silence in the room as we tried to make sense of this revelation. I didn't dare look at the others. They would be as perplexed as I was. Why would Kath have this other half of the disc found with Jose as a baby?

Deborah was the first to speak. 'I think you need to explain, Kath.' Her voice was low, and at first I thought Kath hadn't heard, but she eventually raised her head, saying, 'Can't you guess? Jose was the baby I abandoned at the door of the convent in Granada eighteen years ago.'

'I don't understand,' Gemma said, frowning. 'What's the story of the disc? How does that work?'

Diego stroked his beard, almost as a gesture of comfort. If this was a shock to us, it must be a terrible blow to him. 'We always wondered about that. We kept the disc in case.' He stopped. 'Or rather, I insisted we keep it. My wife was not so sure. She said it was nothing to do with us, nothing to do with Jose. He was now our son and dwelling on the past would only bring grief. How right she was. Now, because of that disc, I have lost my only son.'

Gemma cut in. 'There is an explanation, then. An explanation for his trip to Scotland, his journey to Bute.'

This might explain one thing, but it raised other issues.

'But how would Jose know to come to Bute? How would he have that information,' I said. It seemed far-fetched, that of all the places in Scotland Jose would decide to come to Bute and ever stranger, to come to Brydeshill.

'It's what's written on the disc,' Diego said, holding it up.

I couldn't see it clearly from this distance. 'What does it say,' I said, determined to pursue the answer.

'You can see for yourself.' He slid the disc half across the table to me and it fell to the ground with a clatter.

As I bent to pick it up, out of the corner of my eye I saw Kath watching me carefully.

I lifted the disc. 'Perhaps it would be better if you had a look at this first,' I said, holding it out to her.

She shook her head. 'I know what it says. You read it.'

The writing was tiny, almost microscopic, and I had to screw up my eyes to decipher it.

Kath. O'Doonan
Always a loving mother.
And underneath there was half of a map of the Isle of Bute

Kath came over and laid the other half of the disc on the table, sliding them together as I laid it down. They fitted perfectly.

'You can see what my half says,' she muttered, lifting it, and holding it out to me.

Joseph O'Doonan
Always a beloved son
21st August
Underneath was the other half of the map of Bute, this time clearly identifying its location.

Still puzzled, I said, 'How come Jose knew this was about him? Surely you could have said it was just something you had in the house?'

Diego wiped away a tear. 'It was kept in a box with the name of the convent on it, the little shoes he was wearing and a tiny Scottish flag.'

There was a pause and then he went on, with some difficulty, 'And the birthday date being the same as Jose's was enough to start the conversation. I was tempted to lie, but in the end I had to tell the truth.'

'Even so, eighteen years is a long time.'

Diego shook his head again. 'Jose was *tan enojado*, so angry, that we had kept the information from him.' He shuddered as though recollecting a terrible quarrel. He didn't have to say more. I could imagine the scene. Jose's realisation that the story about his real birth mother had been kept from him all this time, that he had been lied to.

'What happened then?' Gemma glanced over at Kath, who was sitting still as a statue.

Diego shrugged. 'There was nothing I could say to repair the damage. All those years of happiness gone in an instant. All because I would not listen to my wife.'

Stifling a sob, he said, 'Nothing would do then, but Jose would go to the convent, try to find out *la verdad*, the truth.'

'And they were able to help? After all this time?' Deborah chimed in.

'The convent kept good records. There was the hope that although Jose had been left, the mother would come back for him. She did not return and eventually the baby had to be placed for adoption. And once Jose had this information it was only a matter of using the internet to track his mother down.' He shook his head. 'Nothing is secret now – nothing.'

'I had no choice!' Kath's voice filled the room, startling all of us. 'Don't you understand. I was young and alone in Granada, thinking the father of my child would marry me. But for all his protestations of love, I was deserted.'

She paused, before continuing in a stronger voice, 'Oh, he thought it over later, wanted us to be reconciled, wrote letter after letter, but by then it was too late. A good friend took me in, and I managed to get medical help through her. But when the baby was born I couldn't continue to stay with her. I had to go home. And I couldn't bring the baby back with me. My parents were strict – that was why I left in the first place. I had nowhere else to go.'

She began to weep quietly, and Gemma went over to put her arm around her shoulders. 'It's okay, Kath. I'm sure it seemed the right decision at the time.'

'I always hoped we'd meet up some day,' Kath said between sobs. 'But I'd no idea how to trace him.'

Diego stood up. 'It seems he knew how to find you.' He sounded angry. 'You forfeited all rights when you left him in the care of the Sisters. He was our son, not yours.'

Kath pulled a tissue from her pocket and wiped her eyes. 'Yes, I know you did your best for him, gave him the life I couldn't have. But he was still my son.'

This was the story then. Jose had tracked Kath down using the scanty information on his half of the disc. How easy it is to find someone these days, using the internet and only a few clues.

But what had happened to Jose once he arrived at Brydeshill? Why had he not immediately knocked on the door? There had to be a reason he'd gone into the stables.

And it certainly didn't explain what had happened to Fritz and whether his death was in any way linked to Jose's arrival at the yard.

FORTY-FOUR

Diego left soon after the discovery that Kath was Jose's birth mother, scarcely able to speak. We sat in silence, each with our own thoughts. He and his wife had adopted Jose, had given him a good home and to have that snatched away from you in such a manner seemed most unfair.

Kath had tried to reason with him as he stood up saying, 'I have had enough of this talk. None of it will bring Jose back.'

'But it wasn't my fault,' Kath said, jumping up to face him. 'I had no idea what had happened to him. I could only hope the Sisters would make sure he was well cared for. As indeed he was.'

This plea fell on deaf ears. I suspected it wasn't so much that Diego was enraged with Kath as with himself. If he and his wife had been honest with Jose, it was possible that, although Jose would have wanted to find his birth mother eventually, the quest could have had a much happier outcome. Easy to say, but they must have thought it the right decision at the time.

As Diego and the two police officers left Kath sank back down on to the chair. 'What more could I have done,' she said, but it was clear she was talking to herself and didn't expect an answer.

Remembering there had been no contact about the intruder, I slipped out after them to catch up with Constable Brevin. 'I thought someone would have come back to us to ask about the prowler Gemma reported.'

Constable Brevin stared at me. 'What prowler? What report? We've had no word about any intruder apart from the one about Jose.'

'But Gemma reported it.'

He shook his head. 'You must be mistaken. Sorry, I have to go.'

I couldn't understand this. Why had Gemma lied to us?

As I re-entered the room, 'Deborah and I will see to the horses,' Gemma said and together they hurried off, leaving me alone with Kath.

There was an awkward pause. Kath sat slumped in the chair, deep in thought and to be honest I'd no idea what to say that wouldn't sound banal.

When she finally spoke it was in a flat voice, sighing as she said, 'This is such an awful business. I expect Diego will want Jose's body returned to Spain for burial, but I would prefer he stayed here on the island, near me.'

To me this sounded unlikely, given the circumstances, but I knew little about adoption laws in Britain, far less what might apply in Spain. All I could do was mumble some words of comfort, but from the faraway look on her face, I don't think she registered what I was saying.

But no matter how badly Kath was feeling about the situation I couldn't let the moment pass without a question. 'Terrible as this business about Jose is, do you think it has anything to do with the death of Fritz? Do you think they're connected?'

She looked up, as though suddenly remembering I was there, and a bewildered look crossed her face. She shrugged, moving her chair closer to the table. 'What makes you think that, Alison? You believe Fritz and Jose knew each other? I don't see how that is possible. Fritz has been working here for many years. How could Jose possibly have known him?'

I'd no answer and Kath wasn't convinced there might be a link. 'No idea,' I said lamely. 'But they were both killed here.'

'The circumstances are completely different. I'm sure, have to believe, Jose's death was an accident, but Fritz was murdered.' Her voice rose as she came to the end of the sentence, bewilderment giving way to anger as she added, 'What right has Diego to be blaming me for what happened? He has no idea of the difficulty I found myself in, young and alone in Granada. If it hadn't been for my good friend, Maria Elena, I don't know how I would have coped. I might have taken drastic action.'

Not wanting to upset her more, I didn't ask what she meant by "drastic action," but I could sympathise with the plight she had found herself in all those years ago.

'Perhaps it's time to move on,' I ventured tentatively. 'We can't change the past, much as we might want to.'

For a moment it appeared she was going to rebuke me for being unfeeling. Instead she sat back, her shoulders slumped, putting her head in her hands. 'You're right of course, Alison. This has been terrible, much worse than the death of Fritz. At least the police are dealing with that. I just wish this meeting had been more amicable.'

'It might happen yet,' I ventured. 'He's understandably upset right now, but it might be worth making an attempt to speak to him again before he leaves the island. Give him time.'

'Do you think so?' For the first time since Diego's arrival she sounded optimistic. 'That would be as much as I'd want, as much as I could expect. I understand how angry he is, but to leave it like this…' Her voice tailed off.

'Don't give up hope,' I urged her. 'You know where he's staying. Why don't you leave things to settle for a day or two, then try to contact him?'

Her look of uncertainty made it clear she didn't think it would be as easy as I was suggesting, but she nodded. 'I suppose it's worth a try. Better than not doing anything. You're right, you can never change the past, but you can make the future better.'

'Exactly,' I said, eager to take advantage of this more positive attitude. 'But remember he's only on the island for another few days.'

This seemed to confuse her, and she drummed her fingers on the table. She had regained her composure, and this was more like the assertive Kath I knew. 'You're right. It's worth one last try. When he leaves here I may never see him again. And I don't want to have this as my last memory of Jose.'

'If you need someone to go with you, I'm happy to help.'

She nodded her appreciation. 'Thanks, Alison, but this is something I have to do on my own. Lay the ghosts of the past to rest.'

FORTY-FIVE

Kath was true to her word, because when I came through to the kitchen the next morning, there was a note on the table.

'Thanks for your support yesterday. I've decided not to wait but have gone over to the hotel to try to see Diego. Deborah and Gemma will look after the llamas this morning.
Kath.'

A part of me was pleased she'd decided to try to make peace with Diego, another part apprehensive she hadn't thought it through. Much would depend on her approach. We'd hear soon enough if her visit had been a success and meantime there was work to do.

I might even miss this, I thought as I strewed the feed around in front of the chickens. At first I'd been a bit afraid of them, but now I felt quite at home, standing my ground as they came clucking and pecking around.

As I came out of the coop saying, 'That's all for now, girls. It's all finished,' I rattled the bucket to confirm my words. Then I chuckled to myself. What on earth was I doing chatting to them like this?

Still smiling, I came back across the yard towards the farmhouse. There was a large 4 x 4 parked by the door, a car I didn't recognise. What was happening now?

As I approached, the front door to the farmhouse sprang open and Duncan Bradstone came storming out. He stopped abruptly when he saw me standing there and the scowl on his face quickly turned to a smile.

Behind him came Gemma saying, 'It's got to be sorted as …' She also stopped on catching sight of me, but unlike Duncan she made no pretence of being other than very cross.

I racked my brains for something to say but the best I could come up with was, 'I've been feeding the chickens. They are so lovely, so friendly.'

Duncan and Gemma stared at me. Duncan was the first to speak. 'Glad you've become so enamoured of them, Alison.'

Realising how stupid this comment of mine sounded, I tried to change the subject but somehow this only made things worse. 'Is there some problem with the horses again? They do seem to have had a run of bad luck.'

'No, of course not. Duncan came over to have a word about…' Gemma said.

'…about the last bill,' Duncan jumped in.

Gemma shook her head, but she didn't speak.

'Anyway,' Duncan said, beginning to walk briskly towards his car, 'remember to tell Kath I called and that I'm sure we'll be able to sort things out.'

Gemma mumbled something I couldn't catch in reply and with a nod to me, Duncan beeped the fob to open the car door.

Gemma and I stood together looking after him. 'I didn't recognise the car,' I said.

'Mmm, it's new,' Gemma said, continuing to gaze after Duncan as he roared off down the drive way, his large 4x4 making easy work of the potholes.

Was Kath in such financial difficulties that the vet had to come up to Brydeshill again to remind her about what she owed? Surely that was a sign the bills hadn't been paid for some time. But why discuss this with Gemma?

As though she could read my mind, Gemma said, 'In spite of how it sounds, there's not a problem with the livery bills. Duncan just wanted to make sure that Kath was happy with the last treatment he prescribed for Pixie.' This had the ring of an untruth about it as I thought back to the conversation I'd overheard in the farmhouse kitchen. But then again, Gemma was probably being loyal to Kath.

I knew little about Kath's finances, except that times were hard, but it immediately struck me as a strange way to behave, confirming this was no more than an excuse. Surely if there had been any problem about one of the horses, it would have been up to Kath to phone Duncan? And as Kath wasn't around, was it appropriate to discuss the financial situation with one of the employees.

Gemma turned on her heel, saying, 'I must get on. There's so much to do around here and there's no likelihood of a replacement for Fritz any time soon.'

She strode off towards the stable block, the tenseness of her back indicating to me that she was angry about something and I didn't think it was only because there would be no replacement for Fritz.

I should have been more aware. And one of the clues should have been that swanky new 4 x 4 belonging to Duncan. When I thought about that, and about the flash boat anchored out at the marina at Port Bannatyne, I wondered how there could be enough business on the island to give him an income that would allow him to live in such style. Most of the establishments on the island had to live frugally. The decline in rural employment had been accelerating in recent years, no matter how hard people worked.

Of course. Hadn't Duncan told me he'd worked in Manchester? That would explain it. House prices on Bute would be a lot less than in Manchester. Or he may have been left money by his parents. There could be any number of possibilities.

Stop speculating, I said to myself, shrugging off my doubts. Even so the puzzle kept nagging away at me. When Kath returned, I'd have to check if Gemma had told her about Duncan's visit. As yet I wasn't sure how I'd approach that without seeming too interfering, but I'd find a way.

FORTY-SIX

As things turned out, there was no opportunity to bring up the subject of Duncan's visit with Kath. But the more I thought about it, the number of visits he'd been paying to the livery yard seemed excessive. What's more, he'd spent a lot of the time talking to Gemma.

There might of course be a perfectly simple reason for his regular visits if it was true he had a romantic interest in Gemma. Just as well we hadn't followed up his invitation to dinner. Deborah might have misunderstood the offer.

The more I thought about it, the more likely it seemed. Gemma was an attractive young woman, and he was a single man. And there was a reason for his frequent visits to the stables. With Kath being so short-handed, there were few opportunities for Gemma to get away.

I'd found the answer to one problem that had been nagging away at me, but what about the others?

And now, if Kath was correct, the mystery of what had happened to Jose was cleared up. But there remained the problem of finding out why he'd been in the stable. And who had killed Fritz. The police appeared to be making progress. I had this firm belief they were near to making an arrest, but why would they tell Kath?

I felt almost light-hearted as I worked in the scullery, chopping, and sorting the scraps of food with regular chicken feed, ready to give them their last feed of the day. For such small creatures they could consume a great deal.

And in a few days I'd be on my way back to Glasgow, I thought as I made my way across the yard, swinging the bucket and humming to myself. Deborah was much happier, and I suspected she'd soon be leaving also. She hadn't told Kath as far as I knew, but my hope was that the job interview would go well. Kath had indicated there might be a couple of new stable hands starting soon, girls who lived locally, which would also save on accommodation costs.

It was later than usual when I fed the chickens, and I could hear them clucking and scratching as I approached.

'Yes, sorry I'm late, girls,' I said, stepping into the coop, then casting a look around in case someone might have heard me talking to them. I began to think Duncan was right – I might be more attached to them than I'd thought, might even miss them when I left the island. But then there were a lot of things I would miss. Tara sprang to mind as I opened the gate to go into the coop. I made a resolution to keep in touch with her this time. It was all too easy to let friendships slip in the maelstrom of day-to-day living.

As the chickens greedily gobbled the food, as though they hadn't been fed in weeks, I stood looking at the sun beginning to set over the bay far below. It was a beautiful evening, one of those west coast sunsets that comes from time to time when the day has been a disappointing one of rain. Now the sky was streaked pink and purple, the half-moon a faint glimmer in the sky.

Reluctant to go indoors, I stood there breathing deeply as the last of the light faded. I'd come back to Bute, that was for sure, but next time it would be for a proper holiday.

Apart from a couple of visits to catch up with Tara and one or two solitary walks, I'd had little time for recreation during my stay on the island. I shivered as the cool of the evening caught me, the breeze from the bay taking the heat out of the day. I yawned as I waited for the chickens to finish before locking them in. It had been another long day and I was looking forward to an early night. There was a feeling things were settling down and I felt a tremendous sense of relief.

The last of the light faded as I began to walk slowly towards the farmhouse, still deep in thought. Fleetingly I caught a glimpse of a figure slipping out of the stable block. This couldn't be another intruder. I stopped, unsure what to do. The figure was clad in black and I stepped to the side of the arena, drawing back as the figure moved towards me. Holding my breath, I very slowly peeped around, ready to move out of sight in an instant.

But whoever this was, he or she hadn't noticed me and continued to the top of the road out of Brydeshill. Just before the old wooden gate at the end of the private road, the figure stopped and looked back. At that moment, the moon sailed out from behind the clouds. It was Gemma.

What on earth was she doing dressed like that, I wondered, slipping back again into the shadows. And where was she going?

My curiosity piqued, I had to find out what she was doing. She must be heading out of the yard and on to the road to Rothesay. Perhaps it was her intention to walk into town. Then I reminded myself that to someone as fit as Gemma the walk wouldn't be as challenging as it was to a townie like me. But why not take her car?

I couldn't think of a reason for her attempting to sneak out in this way. My pulse quickened. There was no option. I had to find out where she was going and what she was up to. I might have the wrong idea, but I thought of the times I'd seen her meet Duncan. Were they as innocent as they'd said?

If there was a problem about the payments for Duncan's visits, he'd have gone directly to Kath and not involved Gemma. And if there was a romantic attachment there was no need to keep it secret.

It took no more than a minute for me to make up my mind. I slid the empty bucket in behind the coop and started to follow her, keeping close to the side of the road in the shelter of the trees.

At first I thought I'd lost her. I crept to the end of the road, but as I looked around I couldn't spot her. Had she turned back, and I hadn't noticed? Then I caught a glimpse of movement over by the trees a little way down towards the main road.

Given the dark clothing she was wearing, it would be difficult to follow her in this area where there were no streetlights, but there was only one road down with no other side roads off, so if I proceeded cautiously and carefully, I'd be fine.

I wasn't cut out for this kind of snooping and as I moved forward a couple of twigs snapped beneath my feet and I stopped, holding my breath, fearful they'd betray my presence. I waited with bated breath. But it seemed Gemma hadn't noticed because she continued on her way, quickening her pace, looking neither to left nor right. Now that she was out of the range of the yard, her stride was confident as she headed for her destination.

But where could that be? And why would she do

that at this time of night, dressed as she was. And it wasn't sensible to undertake a walk like this in the dark, on a road where there were no streetlights.

After about a mile, I began to tire of this pursuit, cross at myself for starting on it. Of what concern was Gemma's evening walk to me.

Suddenly she stopped and moved to the side of the road. I heard a low, 'Damn' and she lifted her foot to examine her ankle. She must have stepped into one of the ditches. I crouched down behind a row of hedges, watching and waiting. There was a flicker of light. She was using her mobile phone. I could do one of two things. I could continue to follow her, or I could turn back now while there wasn't so much ground to cover. The thought of being back in a cosy bed with my book was appealing. Much more attractive than being out here in the darkness following Gemma.

On the other hand, if she went as far as Rothesay, I could get a taxi back to Brydeshill from there. Then I realised I didn't have any money. In my haste not to lose sight of Gemma, I hadn't thought to run back for my bag. Or even my coat as I shivered in the cooling night air. I clutched my thin jacket round me.

But even as I considered this, Gemma started to walk quickly again and I decided to continue to follow her, promising myself I'd go no further than the town. This part of the road at least had the merit of being downhill all the way. One of the taxi drivers would surely be kind enough to take me back and trust me to pay him.

I stood up, stretching to ease the cramp in my legs from crouching down and rubbed my ankle, hoping it wouldn't start playing up again.

But I soon discovered Gemma wasn't going as far as Rothesay. In the few minutes I'd let my attention wander, she'd disappeared once more, and I hurried to catch up with her. Once I knew her destination, I'd look for a taxi. No question.

But there was still no sign of her. I'd lost concentration for no more than a few seconds. She couldn't be far away.

At this point in the road there were streetlights, and I peered this way and that trying to spot her. Then suddenly there she was, turning left to the stairs leading to the car park of the disused Rothesay Academy building. Why would she be here?

There was no help for it. Despite my misgivings, I had to follow her and find out what she was up to.

FORTY-SEVEN

The sensible part of me said that I should have turned back when I had the chance. But then I'd told myself Gemma must be up to no good, that I owed it to Kath to find out what was going on. But that wasn't the reason.

This was yet another example of my foolishness and even as I crept down towards the derelict 50s building, I could hear Simon's voice in my head, 'Please don't get yourself involved in any more trouble, Alison.' But I ignored this, the way he worried about my aptitude for getting into difficult situations, promising I'd only check out what Gemma was doing here and then leave quickly before I was spotted. I'd no intention of confronting her. Besides of all the places I thought she might have been going, this one hadn't figured.

This building, set high on the hill overlooking the town, had once echoed to the footsteps of generations of children. Now the former school looked to be in a perilous state. Most of the windows were broken, remnants of old curtains flapping like so many birds, reminding me of the seagulls that screeched and whirled everywhere on the island. Gemma had disappeared again and as I approached the main entrance, it appeared to be securely locked, with a large iron bar firmly across the front door.

Even were it possible to get in this way, Gemma hadn't had enough time to do so. There must be another way in.

I ran down the stairs to try at the back of the

building, thinking if this one was like others built in this era there should be a place where deliveries could be unloaded near the kitchens. Not that I'd much hope it would be any easier to enter here, but Gemma must know of a way in and I might be lucky enough to discover it.

Sure enough, there was a double door with the sign 'All Deliveries Here' in faded letters prominently displayed above the peeling paint. I cast a fearful look around, but I was alone.

The doors were closed, but as I pushed gently one of them gave way easily and I slipped inside.

I stopped, trying to get my bearings. My guess had been correct. I was in a large, high-ceilinged room which must once have been the school kitchen. A couple of range-style cookers stood against the far wall and several Formica topped preparation tables filled the middle of the room. There was a look of disorder, as if the place had been abandoned in a great hurry. Ancient cardboard boxes, crumbling and musty, lay piled up in a corner. Dampness was a theme here: mould growing on the ceiling, the scratched lino squishy underfoot.

On the far side near the inner door, two ancient giant-sized refrigerators stood sentinel. I'd no wish to explore them: the rank smell was enough to tell me there might still be remnants of food lurking within from days long past.

And though this place had been long derelict, it had a ghostly air as though a crowd of children might suddenly come rushing round the corner, laughing and jostling. A feeling made stronger as I opened the door in the far wall and found myself in a long, dark corridor. The light from the streetlamp did little to illuminate this part of the building and without a torch it would be foolish to risk exploring any further.

What's more, I'd no idea where Gemma had gone. It was possible she hadn't come into the school but had headed for one of the other buildings in the grounds. As usual, I'd made assumptions.

I stopped, wondering what to do next. Then I heard a noise, a sound of a door slamming in the distance.

Intrigued to find out what was going on, I crept forward. There was something odd about this. Why would Gemma come down here at night? There was, as far as I could tell, nothing to be seen here apart from the detritus of long ago, items of no value.

I felt an urge to sneeze coming on, caused by the dust which lay everywhere and took a deep breath, hoping that would stop it. I didn't want to alert Gemma to my presence.

What harm could it do to walk along to the end of this corridor? That way I might find which of the doors had been slammed. Screwing up my courage, I started to move forward, but I hadn't moved more than a few yards when there was another sound behind me. Oh, no. Someone else had come in.

A feeling of terror seized me. I should have left when I'd had the chance.

I had to decide what to do next… and quickly.

The corridor was long and doors leading off could only be the old classrooms. If I could slip into one, I might yet be okay. Whoever had come in wouldn't be expecting to find me here and that might give me an advantage.

I tried the door handle of the first room, but it refused to budge.

My heart began to thud and moving swiftly on, scarcely daring to breathe, I tried the next one, pulling and tugging as I heard the footsteps coming nearer.

To my horror this handle came away in my hand and fell to the floor with a clatter.

I stopped, holding my breath.

Whoever had come in would realise I was here – the noise I was making trying to get into one of the classrooms was loud enough.

This was impossible. But where else could I hide?

One last turn and the door handle of the last classroom on the right gave way suddenly. Scarcely able to breath, I slipped into the room and as quietly as I could, pulling the door to with not a moment to spare.

This door was one of the old-fashioned kind – solid below but with frosted glass panels on the top half except for one made of clear glass. My instinct was to duck down behind the solid panel and make sure I was hidden. But that part of me eager to find out what was going on couldn't resist lifting my head high enough to peep through the glass panel.

But the panel, though made of clear glass, had not been cleaned in a long time and it was like looking through fog.

I scrabbled in my pocket and found a tissue. A quick scrub made the view slightly clearer and a moment later, a figure I recognised come striding past.

It was Duncan Bradstone.

That decided it. Whatever the reason for Gemma and Duncan being here, I'd no intention of lingering a moment longer. I crouched down, counting to one hundred. After that, I'd check if the coast was clear and get out of this place as fast as I could.

To be on the safe side, I made the count one hundred and fifty and as I'd almost finished, I heard a door slam, though whether it was the same one as before or a different one, I wasn't going to wait to find out.

I twisted the door handle slowly and peeped out into the corridor, sighing with relief as I saw it was empty.

This was my chance and with as much speed as I could muster without making too much noise, I hurried along back to the kitchen. Thankfully that door was ajar: Duncan must have neglected to close it when he came in.

Scarcely drawing breath until I was outside again, I ran across the car park, taking the stairs two at a time, desperate to reach the road leading back to Brydeshill. There was no sign of Duncan's car but in the far corner almost concealed by the bushes, I caught a glimpse of a motorbike.

It hadn't been my imagination after all, no matter how Gemma had tried to persuade me otherwise. There had been someone in the yard that night…and it may well have been Duncan.

I could feel my heart thudding as I quickened my pace. It wasn't far to Brydeshill, no more than a mile, but it was uphill all the way and I didn't dare to stop until I was well clear of the school buildings. Thank goodness my time on Bute, helping out at the livery yard, had increased my level of fitness, even if only by a little.

As I made my way back to the safety of the farmhouse I couldn't help but look over my shoulder from time to time in case I was being followed. I'd no worries about Gemma catching me up as she was on foot, but Duncan was a different matter. What if he decided to give her a lift back, to drop her back near the yard and they spied me on the road?

Thankfully, the only sound was the owl I could hear hooting in the trees on the far side of the fields as he started his nightly hunt and I arrived at the side road to Brydeshill exhausted. By the light from the stable block I squinted at my watch. One a.m. Everyone would be tucked up in bed by now.

I tiptoed in and went straight to my room. But not to sleep. All kinds of thoughts jumbled in my head. If Gemma and Duncan had decided to meet up for some reason, why choose the old school at that time of night. It couldn't be a romantic assignation, could it? I tried to think of the times I'd seen them together, if their behaviour had shown they were in a relationship.

Eventually, worn out by my night-time adventure and unable to think of an answer to this puzzle, I began to drift off to sleep, promising myself I'd consider this problem rationally in the morning. I might even make some excuse to go back to the school in daylight. There might be something I'd missed.

But at the last minute a thought popped into my head. Whatever Gemma and Duncan were up to, was it anything to do with the death of Fritz?

FORTY-EIGHT

Next morning, groggy from a disturbed night where dreams of being trapped in the old Rothesay Academy kept wakening me, I hauled myself out of bed. The last thing I wanted was anyone questioning me about why I looked so wretched, so I put on make-up, attempting to disguise the worst of my tiredness, though I wasn't convinced it didn't make matters worse.

As I went in to the kitchen, Deborah looked up, a perplexed expression on her face.

'Going somewhere special, Mum? I haven't seen you wear make-up since you arrived here.'

'Oh, I thought it might make me feel I was…I was… a bit nearer getting back to civilization soon.' A feeble excuse, but the best I could muster in the circumstances.

Deborah laughed. 'I'm sure the chickens will appreciate the effort you're making for them.'

I ignored this and concentrated on pouring a cup of coffee.

'You're sure I won't be missed when I leave?' I said. 'That you'll manage without me?'

'I was about to tell you before I was transfixed by your new look. Kath got word last night that the couple she interviewed last week are happy to accept the posts she's offering.'

'Ah, so that's why she was in town all yesterday afternoon?'

'Yes, she didn't want to say in case it didn't work out, but happily all seems to be well. Though I'm sure the chickens will miss you,' she added, a wicked gleam in her eye.

'Funnily enough I think I might miss them,' I said. And it was true. Although I'd a sense of relief that I'd soon be able to return home, I'd become used to this daily routine. Foolish I knew.

Deborah interrupted my train of thought. 'Perhaps you could persuade Dad to have some chickens when you finally settle somewhere permanent.'

'I did consider that, but as quickly dismissed it.' I shook my head. 'Too much responsibility.'

Just then the outside door was flung open and Gemma came in. 'Misty was misbehaving again this morning,' she said. 'That horse needs a firm hand.'

Under cover of drinking my coffee, I had a close look at her, but she didn't seem any different from usual. Whatever she'd been up to last night there was no evidence this morning.

'You should surely be able to handle Misty,' Deborah grinned.

Gemma flung herself down into the chair opposite me. 'You'd think so, wouldn't you?' A moment later she stood up again and went over to the stove. 'Coffee. That's what I need.'

'There's plenty in the pot. Just freshly brewed,' I said, trying to keep my voice light.

I didn't linger. 'Time for my duties,' I said and went into the scullery to get the feed ready.

But as I reached the chickens my mind wasn't on the task as I discovered when the chickens started to peck aggressively round my feet and I realised I'd been standing still, with the bucket full, for several minutes.

There was no help for it. I couldn't let matters rest there. Whatever scenario I came up with, I couldn't think of one that would explain Gemma and Duncan being in the old school the previous night. I couldn't ask Gemma directly and even if I did there was no guarantee she would tell me. I ran through all the possibilities, including my favourite of a clandestine romance. The latter most unlikely – and even if they were in a relationship, the old school was a most unlikely place for a tryst.

No, there had to be some reason, something they were doing that had to be hidden. And as I was leaving the island very soon, I had to find out what it was. Unwise I knew, but I persuaded myself if I went back down to have a look at the Academy in the daylight there could be no danger.

So, later in the afternoon, I checked what everyone was doing before setting off again. Kath was busy in the arena, clearing up, and Gemma was helping her. The sand floor had to be cleaned and topped up regularly, a major undertaking. Deborah was busy mucking out the stables with one of the volunteer helpers and those riders who owned horses at the stables were out on a hack. The stable hands were busy cleaning and sorting the tack and one of them was leading J-Bear out to the field. Perfect. I could slip away without anyone noticing.

FORTY-NINE

The old Rothesay Academy looked more desolate than ever in the daylight. The afternoon sunlight filtered in and, rather than ghostly, the building looked forlorn. Most of the windows were broken, though here and there an attempt had been made to board them up. Shards of glass littered the pathways, the iron railings were rusted, and years of neglect were apparent in the cracked walls.

After a quick look around to make sure there was no one in sight, I walked down the stairs and through the car park to the back of the building.

A quick tug and the door yielded, allowing me to slip inside. Although all was the same as the night before, in the bright light I could see the thick layers of dust everywhere.

Taking a deep breath, I opened the far door and peeped out into the corridor. Silence. Then I thought, how am I going to find out which of the doors Gemma and Duncan slammed last night?

I counted six classrooms in this corridor, three on either side, but a quick glance into each of them convinced me there was nothing suspicious. Most were empty though in the one nearest the entrance a few pupils' desks lay on their side, and a collection of broken wooden chairs was piled up in the corner.

On the left, in the middle of the corridor, a flight of steps led up to the first floor, but I was certain the sound of a door slamming had come from near here rather than upstairs.

At the far end another door led outside but, to my

disappointment it only opened out into a small courtyard. The smell of guano immediately struck me, and I put my hand over my nose. Apart from that there was nothing to see except scraps of litter and piles of soggy leaves that had escaped the winter winds.

I came back inside and stood looking around, wondering what to do next. There was a stout wooden door between two of the classrooms on the right-hand side, but to my frustration it was firmly locked.

It might be worth another try. But no amount of tugging and wrenching the door handle worked. Exasperated by my lack of success, I stood back and stared at the door, as if hoping it might open of its own accord.

'Not having any luck, Alison?'

Intent as I'd been on trying to open the door, I'd failed to hear someone coming up behind me.

I swung round, gasping as I came face to face with Duncan.

'How…how…'I stuttered.

Duncan laughed softly. 'I knew someone had been here last night, I just didn't know who it was.'

'But…' I didn't understand. I'd made no noise, was sure I hadn't been spotted.

'The dust, Alison, the dust. It's everywhere. When I came in last night I noticed there were two sets of footprints on the kitchen floor, leading out into the corridor. One was Gemma's of course, but the other set was clearly someone spying. I reckoned whoever it was would return.' He laughed again. 'I might have realised it would be you.'

He grabbed me roughly by the arm. 'Well since you're so eager to see what we're doing, be my guest.'

Still holding me tightly with one hand, so that there was no possibility of escape, he pulled a key from his pocket with his other hand and leaned forward to open the door.

To my surprise this wasn't a cupboard, but a flight of steps leading down to a basement. Suddenly he let go of my arm and pushed me forward. The flight was steep, but luckily I was able to grab at a handrail to save me from falling.

Urging me on till we reached the bottom, we were faced with another door, but this one wasn't locked, and Duncan forced me through so that I almost tumbled into the room.

At first I couldn't make sense of what I was seeing. It appeared to be a laboratory. In large glass containers liquids bubbled and hissed before going through a series of pipes into a large copper vat. The air was hot, clammy, heavy with the smell of alcohol.

'What is it?'

Duncan made a face. 'It's a small way of supplementing my income, that's what. It's ridiculous that Gin can be made on the island and sold here perfectly legally, but I couldn't get a licence for my product. Ridiculous. Not to mention the tax the government makes you pay. People are happy to get alcohol at a good price.'

'Really? But what is it you're making?' My curiosity overcame my fear.

'Why vodka of course. People are grateful for my help. All quality stuff.'

Now it all made sense. It might explain Duncan's extravagant lifestyle.

'But what do you do with it?' That was still a puzzle. He obviously couldn't sell it on Bute where he was so well known.

‘Why I take it round the other islands of course. I have my contacts and plenty of people are willing to buy it at a decent price, but far less than the supermarkets charge these days.’

Confident I’d be unable to escape, he strode over to a large cardboard box in the corner before pulling out a bottle and holding it aloft. ‘Now you know,’ he said, caressing it. ‘It’s Best Island Vodka. Pure gold,’ he muttered.

So this was what all the boat trips were about – a way of distributing the illegal alcohol.

Suddenly I realised what had happened. ‘Fritz found out. You killed him because he’d discovered your secret.’

Duncan threw back his head and roared with laughter. ‘Of course not. Fritz was in on it. He was the one who obtained some of the supplies we needed and stored them in the cupboard in the arena.’

‘But I had a look in that cupboard – there was no way the boxes there could contain bottles of vodka.’

For a moment he looked baffled. ‘What do you mean? What boxes? I take them directly from here.’

‘Then why was Fritz so angry when he thought I was looking in the cupboard in the arena – the one beside the boot cupboard?’

‘Ah.’ A sly look came over his face. He held up a bottle. ‘Fritz sourced the labels on the mainland. Went over every month and used different printing companies.’

‘Really?’

‘He could hardly use the Print Point, could he? It would have been round the island in no time.’

That explained it, why Fritz was so annoyed when he saw Deborah and me at the cupboards. ‘But you did kill him?’

A look of cunning flitted across Duncan's face. He sniffed. 'He got greedy. Wanted a bigger cut. That stupid notebook of his, listing all the bottles, all the costs, all the profits. Much of it his imagination. Shoved it in my face, said he'd go to the police.'

'Yes, but to kill him. Even had you been caught, your sentence wouldn't have been that long.'

Duncan shook his head. 'I didn't mean to kill him. He threatened me. You must understand that. I only meant to make it clear I wasn't having any of it. I did say I could also tell the police what he'd done.'

A shiver went through me. 'What was that?'

Duncan laughed. 'I may as well let you in on it since you'll not have the opportunity to tell anyone.' He licked his lips. 'That stupid Spaniard. Why was he prowling around in the middle of the night? He could as easily have waited till the morning before coming up to Brydeshill. I can only guess as it was raining so hard he went into the arena for shelter and there was Fritz loading the boxes of labels into the cupboard.'

'But Jose would have no idea what they were.'

'No, but Fritz panicked. He was taken by surprise. He only meant to knock him out, but Jose banged his head on the edge of one of those mounting blocks.' He made a gesture with his hand. 'Dead as the proverbial Dodo. Of course what did Fritz do then but call me for help. It was my idea to put him in Topper's stable, make it look like an accident. Clever, eh? They'll never be able to prove otherwise.'

'But it was an accident. And anyway, forensics now are so good, that I' sure…'

He didn't want to hear this, to hear his plan wouldn't work. 'Don't be stupid. What about my career. I'd never have been able to practise as a vet again.'

This seemed to be a crazy train of thought, but I didn't want to provoke him further. Yet I couldn't resist asking, 'How did Fritz come to be in the woods?'

Duncan laughed. 'I could hardly leave him at the yard, could I. Though it was a lot more difficult to get him to the woods than I thought.'

Suddenly he seemed to recollect that I was now a problem. 'And now I'll have to think of what to do with you, Alison.'

I certainly wasn't going to make a suggestion. Or at least the only one I could make was to let me go and I didn't think that was likely.

He was quiet for a moment, no doubt turning over the possibilities in his mind. Then he said, 'I could leave you here – there are plenty of places in these old school buildings where you wouldn't be discovered.'

'I don't think so. If you kill me and leave me to be found here, the police are surely able to find out the truth this time.'

He appeared to consider this. 'Mmm, leaving a corpse here might create other problems.'

His face brightened. 'Now I do have an idea.' Grabbing me tightly by the arm, he said, 'We're going for a little ride, you and I.'

He pushed me up the steps in front of him and along the corridor to the kitchen, not pausing to lock any of the doors behind him.

Out in the sunlight I blinked hard at the sudden light after the gloom of the basement.

'Where are you taking me?' I gasped, though the answer was soon clear as we rounded the corner, and I spotted his jeep sitting almost hidden by the bushes in the far corner of the car park. Still grasping me tightly he popped open the boot and pulled out a coil of rope. 'This should keep you secure for a while,' he said, proceeding to tie my hands in front of me before pushing me roughly into the passenger seat.

He clicked the seatbelt on, saying, 'We wouldn't want to be stopped by the police because you weren't wearing a seatbelt, would we?'

He ran round to the driver's side and started the engine, crunching the gears in his hurry to be off.

I tried stealthily to loosen the ropes binding my hands but to no avail. And even if I could, it would be madness trying to jump out of a car going at this speed.

Through the town we drove, Duncan making no response to my repeated, 'Where are we going?'

All I could do was gaze out of the window, trying to think of a way to attract attention. But it was no use. People thronged the streets around the ferry, but everyone was intent on their own affairs and tightly tied up as I was, I couldn't rap on the window to attract attention.

Eyes fixed on the road ahead, hands grasping the steering wheel tightly, he drove like a man possessed. My only hope was that there might be a police car somewhere in the vicinity that would flag him down for speeding. But I was out of luck and as we drove through Ardbeg to reach the outskirts of Port Bannatyne the realisation of what he intended to do with me struck me forcibly. Of course. His plan was to set sail in his yacht and dump me somewhere out in the Kyles of Bute.

This wouldn't be an easy task, I thought grimly. Once we reached the boatyard, I'd make so much fuss someone was bound to hear and come to my rescue. Slightly heartened by this thought I sat back as we drove through the village to the boatyard at the far end.

But my hope was in vain. At this time of day the village was quiet and there was no one in the streets, no one at the bus stop and the schoolchildren were safely inside their classrooms.

As we approached the boatyard to my horror it was also deserted, and any thoughts of finding help here vanished.

Duncan's large yacht was moored at the marina and he drew the car to a juddering halt before leaping out and coming round to pull me from my seat. The thought occurred to me he wanted to get this over as soon as possible before he lost his nerve.

He frogmarched me down the pontoon and on to the yacht gangplank, urging me forward on to the deck before pushing me down roughly onto a wooden bench beside the mast, saying, 'Just sit there.'

I was wrong. He hadn't decided what to do with me. Fritz's death, if Duncan was to be believed, had been the result of a dispute because of Fritz's greed. Mine would be premeditated murder. As though that made any difference to my current situation.

As Duncan prepared to set sail, I scanned the deck to see if there was anything to help me loosen the ropes binding my wrists, but the only thing I could see was a grappling hook in the corner. And even if I managed to reach it without Duncan noticing, what would I do then?

I wriggled my wrists. Was it my imagination, or did the ropes feel slightly looser? Then I realised that one of the knots was not as tight as it should have been. In his haste to get away, Duncan had neglected to finish the knot properly. Not particularly good for someone who claimed to be a sailor.

If only I could work this knot to slacken it, but this depended on Duncan being too absorbed in piloting the boat to notice.

I worked on, moving my wrists till I felt the strain almost impossible to bear. There was a slight give in the rope. Only the merest easing, but enough to give me hope.

Suddenly Duncan turned round, 'Don't move, Alison. Don't try anything stupid.'

Had he noticed what I was trying to do? My heart pounding, I stilled my hands in my lap, trying to make it appear the ropes were still tight. But he turned back once more to steering the boat.

As the yacht made its way from the safe harbour of the marina to sail up the Kyles, I could only think that time was running out and didn't dare consider what my fate might be. Killed somewhere out in the Kyles and then dumped overboard?

Refusing to give into these thoughts, I concentrated on the rope, flexing my wrists and all the time watching Duncan as the yacht gathered speed. I was running out of time. Soon we'd been in deep water well away from land and as we passed the deserted fish farm at Ardmeleish I thought, This is the last remnant of human contact I'm likely to see.

Quite suddenly the knot gave way, and my hands were free. I had to bite back a whoop of joy, gazing fearfully over at Duncan in case he'd noticed, but he was too intent on getting as far out into the water as soon as he could. Probably he'd already sussed out a spot where he could safely throw me overboard, but we hadn't reached it yet.

Now I was free, I had to make a quick decision. I could lunge for the grappling hook and hope to take Duncan by surprise. But would I have the strength to land a blow hard enough to knock him out? And then what would I do? I'd no idea how to steer the boat. I expected there was a wireless system on a yacht like this, but even S.O.S. might be beyond my capabilities, trembling as I was with the effort of escaping from my bonds.

No, there was only one thing I could do. The shore was still visible, and I knew there was a farmhouse not far from the old fish farm. If I could reach the shore and make a run for it before Duncan had time to realise what was happening, I might yet be saved. I screwed up my courage, stood up and climbing on to the wooden bench so I could get over the rail, I took a deep breath and jumped into the water.

EPILOGUE

'What I don't understand,' Simon said as we sat sipping a glass of wine and gazing out at the ocean from the balcony of our hotel in Valencia, 'is why you became involved.'

The scent of bougainvillea drifted up on the warm air of the summer evening and I breathed deeply before replying. 'I didn't mean to,' I said, thinking what a lame excuse that was. 'I went over because Deborah was there. It was a good opportunity to see her, to find a way of overcoming my writer's block about that article on Bute as a Victorian holiday destination. Then Kath asked me to find out what had happened to the man found dead in the stable. Not that I was much use.' I sighed. 'To be truthful I was no help at all.'

Simon raised his eyebrows. 'I wish I'd taken time off to come with you. Perhaps then you might have avoided the worst of the trouble. Your desire to help will be the death of you one day.'

Realising what he'd said, Simon chuckled. 'Oops. Wrong thing to say.'

'I couldn't refuse Kath's request. I was the only person there who could investigate without anyone suspecting what I was doing. Anyway, what would you have done on Bute, at Brydeshill.'

'True,' he admitted, 'though I might have helped you with the chickens.'

'The chickens and I got on fine, thanks,' I said primly and then we both burst out laughing.

All was well. Luckily for me someone had been at

home in the cottage near the fish farm when I turned up soaking wet and distressed and the police were quickly summoned. Duncan was picked up in Tighnabruich and what's more, his yacht was found to contain cases of the illegal vodka. Never one to waste an opportunity, he probably intended to take the cases on to his buyers once he'd disposed of me.

I didn't have to explain much. Tara was right – the police were watching Fritz, but it appeared Duncan was also under surveillance.

Gemma confessed all, pleaded she'd been taken in by Duncan. It would remain to be seen how much of her story a jury believed. She'd seemed willingly involved to me.

Kath was understandably upset by this turn of events, but the young couple she'd engaged to help with the livery yard turned out to be a wise choice and a great support to her.

And although Jose was buried in Spain, Diego asked Kath over to attend the funeral.

Deborah stayed on for a couple of weeks, but the lure of the job in the city gallery was too much in the end, as I'd guessed it would be. Country life was fine for a little while, but not for ever. Besides one of her former boyfriends had returned from two years working in Australia and I'd hopes that might come to something, though when I said as much to Simon, he merely shook his head.

We sat in silence, watching the sun dip behind the horizon in a blaze of pink and purple and suddenly it was dark.

'I can never get used to how quickly night descends in this part of the world,' I said, as the lights of the town far below sparkled into life.

'Not as lovely as Bute, then,' Simon said with a

sideways glance at me.

'Different,' I said. 'And warmer. And no midges.'

Simon stood up. 'Another drink before we go into town for dinner? I spotted a little restaurant where the garden looks a pleasant place to eat.'

'Sounds perfect,' I sighed. This week away had been Simon's idea and at first I'd been reluctant. But he was right. I needed a complete change of scene after the events at Brydeshill and with my article finally completed and off to the editor his suggestion was exactly what I needed.

Perhaps we should have decided on a holiday like this some time ago. We'd been working far too hard and the tensions between us had been hard to resolve. But now we were back together, and our relationship was much better than it had been for a long time.

Simon came out to the balcony carrying the glasses of wine. He grinned as he handed one to me. 'On the other hand we could stay here and make do with room service later… much later.'

Acknowledgements

Thanks to Bill Daly for reading the manuscript and making many helpful comments and to Joan Weeple and to Judith Vallely for proof-reading and comments.

Special thanks to Joan Fleming for all her support and encouragement with this novel – Alison has good reason to be grateful!

In matters geographical and historical and for technical support thanks to

Brandanii Archaeology and Heritage
www.discoverbutearchaeology.co.uk

Alison's main research material is from 'One Island, Many Voices,' edited by P.R.J. Duffy.

Printed in Great Britain
by Amazon

62579122R00163